Bottom-Tier

Tier

CHARACTER

TOMOZAKI

Lv.5

YUKI YAKU

Illustration by

Fly

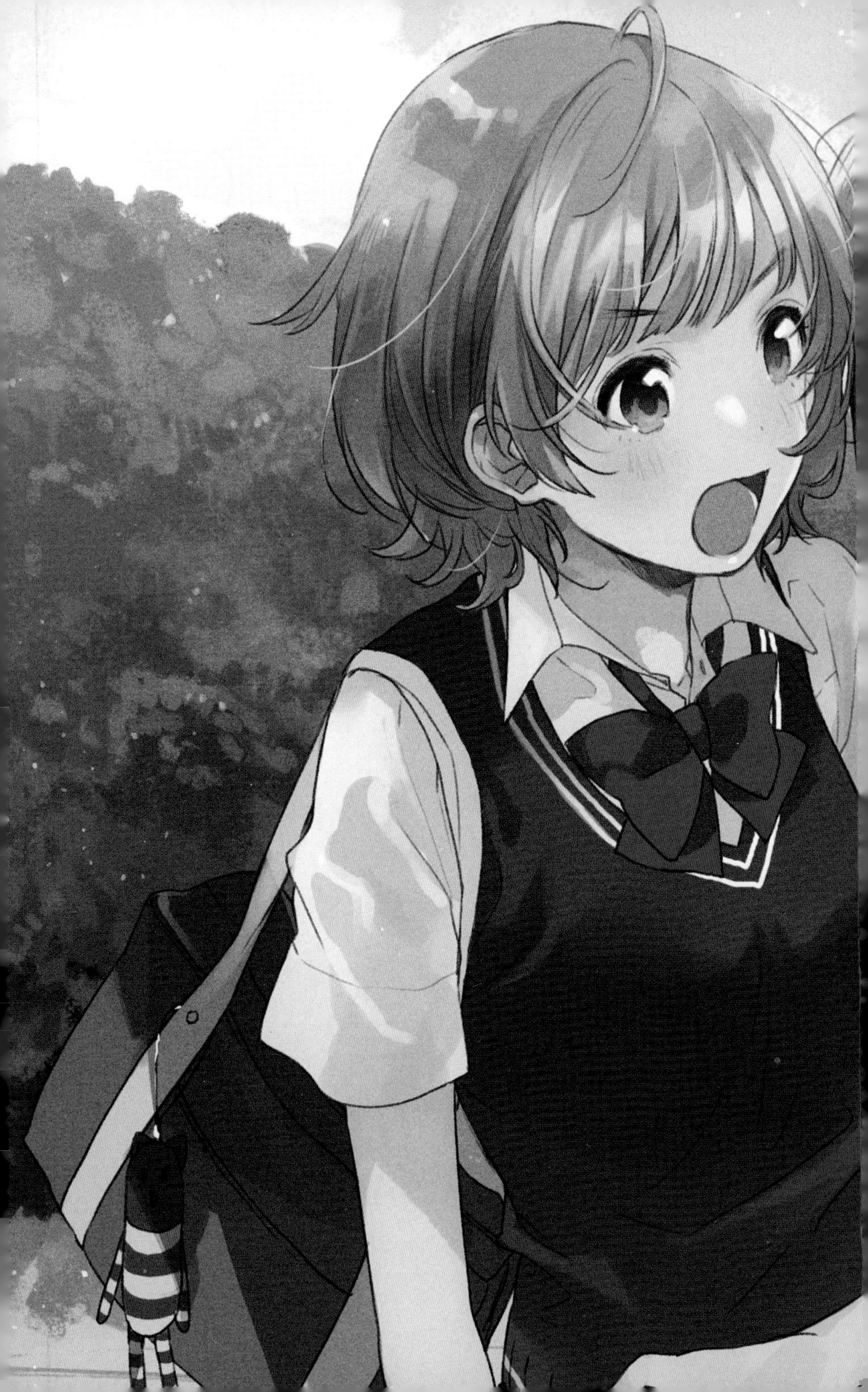

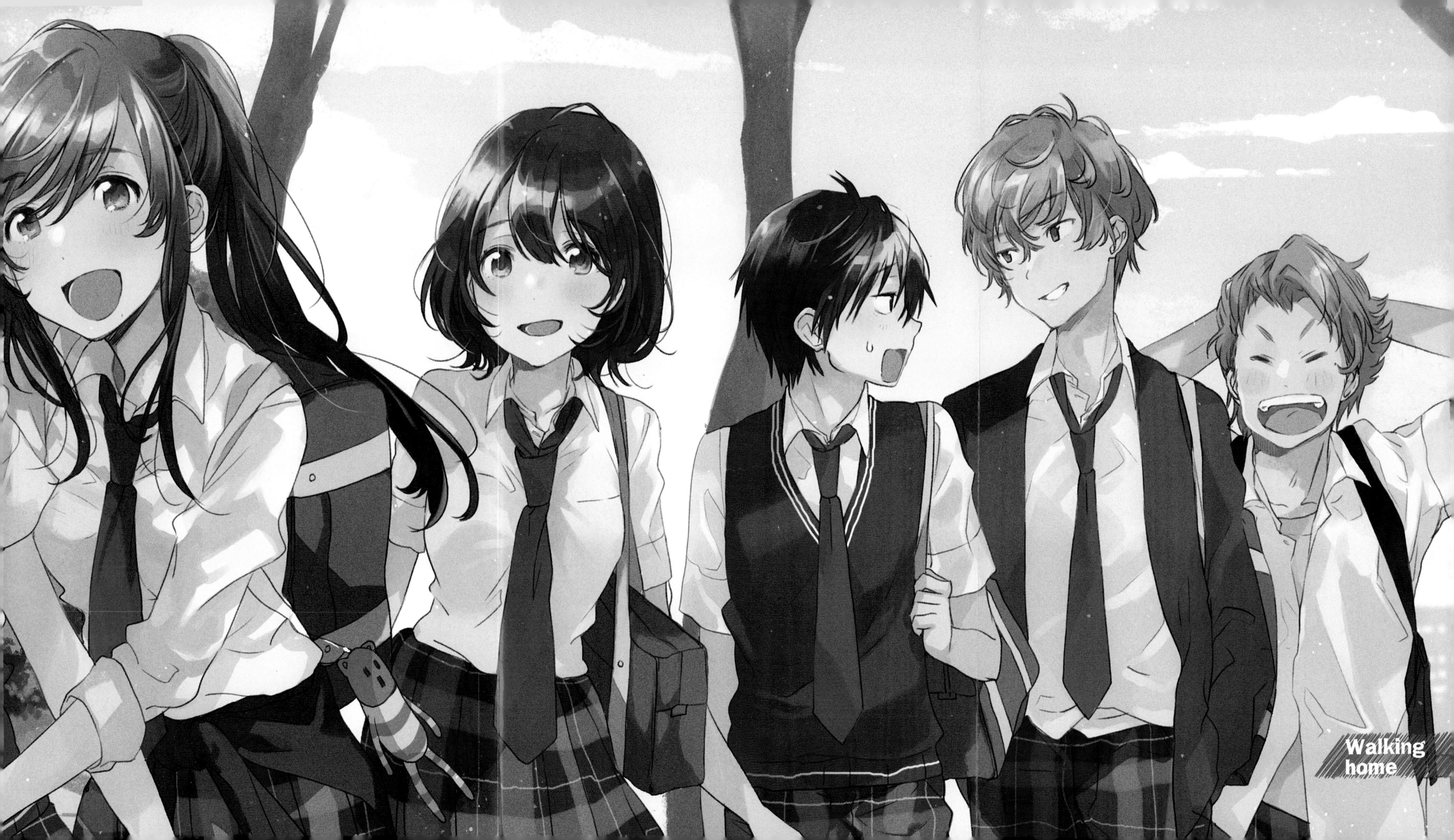
Walking
home

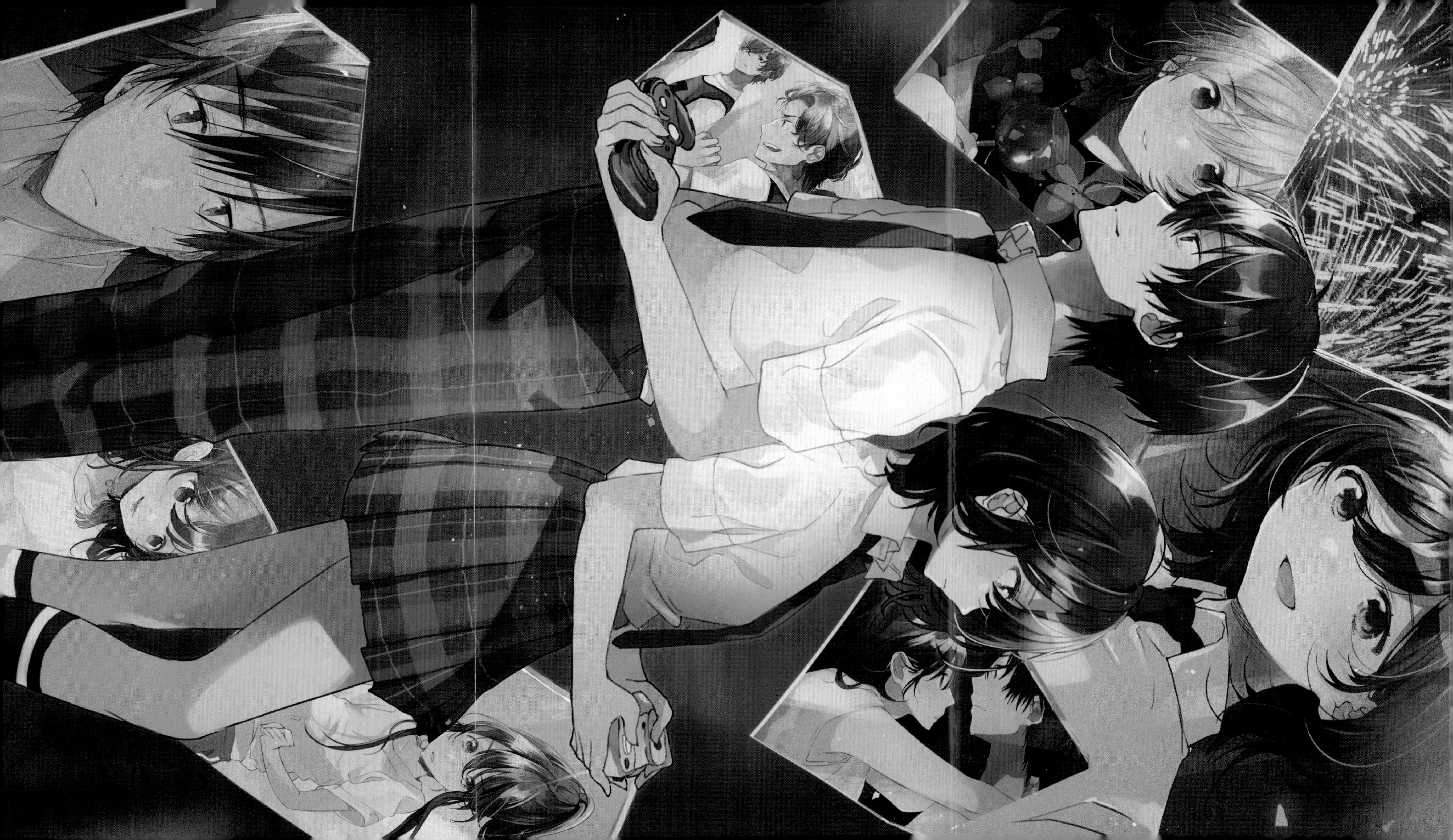

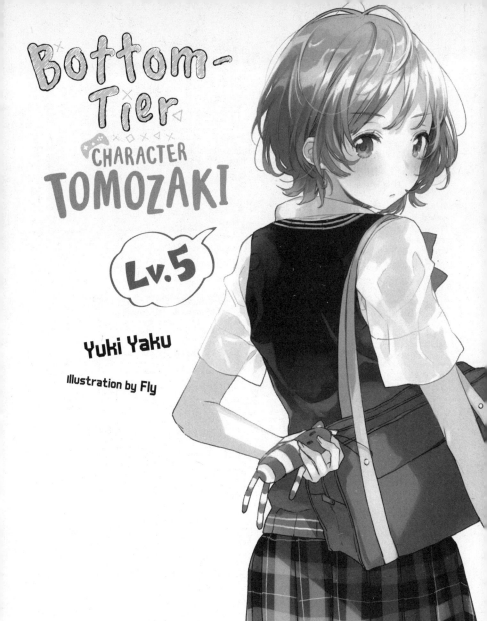

Bottom-Tier Character TOMOZAKI Lv.5

Yuki Yaku

Illustration by Fly

YEN ON

New York

Bottom-Tier CHARACTER TOMOZAKI Lv.5

YUKI YAKU

Cover art by Fly
Translation by Winifred Bird

JAKU CHARA TOMOZAKI-KUN Lv.5
by Yuki YAKU
© 2016 Yuki YAKU
Illustration by FLY
All rights reserved.
Original Japanese edition published by SHOGAKUKAN.
English translation rights in the United States of America, Canada, the United Kingdom, Ireland, Australia, and New Zealand arranged with SHOGAKUKAN through Tuttle-Mori Agency, Inc.

English translation © 2020 by Yen Press, LLC

Yen On
150 West 30th Street, 19th Floor
New York, NY 10001

Visit us at yenpress.com
facebook.com/yenpress
twitter.com/yenpress
yenpress.tumblr.com
instagram.com/yenpress

First Yen On Edition: November 2020

Yen On is an imprint of Yen Press, LLC.
The Yen On name and logo are trademarks of Yen Press, LLC.

The publisher is not responsible for websites (or their content) that are not owned by the publisher.

Library of Congress Cataloging-in-Publication Data
Names: Yaku, Yuki, author. | Fly, 1963- illustrator. | Bird, Winifred, translator.
Title: Bottom-tier character Tomozaki / Yuki Yaku ; illustration by Fly ; translation by Winifred Bird.
Other titles: Jyakukyara Tomozaki-kun. English
Description: First Yen On edition. | New York : Yen On, 2019-
Identifiers: LCCN 2019017466 | ISBN 9781975358259 (v. 1 : pbk.) | ISBN 9781975384586 (v. 2 : pbk.) |
    ISBN 9781975384593 (v. 3 : pbk.) | ISBN 9781975384609 (v. 4 : pbk.) |
    ISBN 9781975384616 (v. 5 : pbk.)
Subjects: LCSH: Video games—Fiction. | Video gamers—Fiction.
Classification: LCC PL877.5.A35 J9313 2019 | DDC 895.63/6—dc23
LC record available at https://lccn.loc.gov/2019017466

ISBNs: 978-1-9753-8461-6 (paperback)
       978-1-9753-8644-3 (ebook)

10 9 8 7 6 5 4 3 2 1

LSC-C

Printed in the United States of America

Bottom-Tier CHARACTER TOMOZAKI

Lv.5

Characters

Fumiya Tomozaki

Second-year high school student. Bottom-tier.

Aoi Hinami

Second-year high school student. Perfect heroine of the school.

Minami Nanami

Second-year high school student. Class clown.

Hanabi Natsubayashi

Second-year high school student. Small.

Yuzu Izumi

Second-year high school student. Hot.

Fuka Kikuchi

Second-year high school student. Bookworm.

Takahiro Mizusawa

Second-year high school student. Wants to be a beautician.

Shuji Nakamura

Second-year high school student. Class boss.

Takei

Second-year high school student. Built.

Tsugumi Narita

First-year high school student. Easygoing.

Erika Konno

Second-year high school student. Queen of the class.

Common Honorifics

In order to preserve the authenticity of the Japanese setting of this book, we have chosen to retain the honorifics used in the original language to express the relationships between characters.

No honorific: Indicates familiarity or closeness; if used without permission or reason, addressing someone in this manner would constitute an insult.

-san: The Japanese equivalent of Mr./Mrs./Miss. If a situation calls for politeness, this is the fail-safe honorific.

-kun: Used most often when referring to boys, this indicates affection or familiarity. Occasionally used by older men among their peers, but it may also be used by anyone referring to a person of lower standing.

-chan: An affectionate honorific indicating familiarity used mostly in reference to girls; also used in reference to cute persons or animals of either gender.

-senpai: An honorific indicating respect for a senior member of an organization. Often used by younger students with their upperclassmen at school.

-sensei: An honorific indicating respect for a master of some field of study. Perhaps most commonly known as the form of address for teachers in school.

Bottom-Tier
Character Tomozaki, Level 5
CONTENTS

Takahiro
Mizusawa

Design Yuko Mucadeya + Caiko Monma
(musicagographics)

The Story So Far

It's the second semester, and as the day of the sports tournament approaches, Tomozaki is hard at work on a new assignment from Hinami: Get Erika Konno, queen of the cool girls, to decide the event is worth caring about. By using Konno's feelings toward Nakamura as part of his strategy, Tomozaki manages to complete the assignment. There's just one problem. When the tournament provides the spark for Nakamura and Izumi to finally start dating, Konno reacts to the news by harassing one of her classmates. Eventually, she turns her attacks on honest, no-nonsense Hanabi Natsubayashi. To protect her closest friend from worrying about her, Natsubayashi decides she'll do whatever it takes to make this stop. She asks Tomozaki to help her fight back by finding a way to change herself...

1

Even with good stats, quests can be tough without armor

School was out for the day. The sun slanted low in the west, casting shadows from the two of us in the classroom. I was there with Tama-chan, who'd just asked me how to fight.

"What do you think I should do, Tomozaki?"

"Well...first..."

For the past few weeks, Erika Konno had been harassing Tama-chan, but now the whole class was subtly victimizing her. This chain reaction had spiraled out of proportion like a multicar pileup, and she was the innocent casualty. That's why I was there this afternoon, promising to fight back alongside her.

"Yeah?"

She waited solemnly for my next words. Tama-chan was confident that she'd handled the situation correctly up to this point, but she'd made up her mind to change so that she wouldn't cause Mimimi any more heartache. I wanted to support her with everything I had.

"I think you need...to learn how to dodge."

"Dodge...?" Tama-chan echoed thoughtfully. Our voices were the only sound in the classroom. The whole school was practically abandoned.

"Yeah. You tend to counterattack every time instead, so everyone else is getting caught in the cross fire..."

Tama-chan listened, staring intently into my eyes.

"Konno was the one who started it all, so you're not actually in the wrong. But when you two fight, everyone feels..."

I wasn't sure how to put it delicately. Tama-chan finished my sentence without hesitating.

"...Uncomfortable around me?"

"Um, yeah."

She had no problem saying the hard stuff. I still wasn't used to how perceptive she could be, and I couldn't help the slight grin that found its way to my face. Despite the situation, I was enjoying myself. Seeing her strong, unshakable core was reassuring; no matter what, Tama-chan would always be Tama-chan. Wanting to respond in kind, I continued talking as directly as I could.

"You're not doing anything wrong, but your response makes people uncomfortable and lowers their opinion of you. If you want to resolve this, I think you need to be a little savvier about how you handle stuff."

I looked Tama-chan in the eye. She nodded.

"I think you're right."

She bit her lip with a hint of disappointment, but an instant later, she shook it off. She focused her eyes and filled her voice with fighting spirit.

"You're definitely right," she said resolutely. After all, she'd made up her mind before we even started talking. I smiled at her, hoping to boost her mood even more.

"That's what you meant when you asked me to teach you how to fight, right?"

She opened her eyes as wide and round as acorns, peered into my face, and smiled warmly.

"Yup. I'm counting on you!"

* * *

A proper gaming-strategy meeting always begins with an assessment of the status quo. Tama-chan and I sat next to each other at some desks by the window and got to work.

"To sum up the situation…first, Erika Konno has been harassing you for a while. Each thing she does isn't much on its own—she's just kicking your desk or saying something mean where you can hear her. It's all stuff she can pass off as a coincidence. She doesn't leave behind any evidence like mean graffiti or something along those lines, right?"

Tama-chan nodded. "Yeah, that's pretty much what's happening. My pencil leads keep getting broken, but she just says I must have dropped them myself. I've got nothing I can pin on her."

I nodded. "But you know it's Konno who's doing it, so you push back."

"Right."

"And then she plays innocent, and nothing gets resolved. She says it's a coincidence and denies there's any harassment going on to start with. And…" I hesitated for a moment.

"Everyone in class has started to think I'm overreacting."

"…Yeah." Once again, I was letting Tama-chan say the hard stuff.

I thought over the situation for a bit.

"And you want to do something to change all this, right?"

"Yeah. It's upsetting everyone," she said softly, looking down at the field far below the windows. I followed her gaze. The track team was having practice. Among the several dozen students, I found myself looking at Mimimi. She was easy to pick out of a crowd, but I think my gaze went to her because I could tell even from a distance that she was giving her all to the practice. I watched as she waved at Hinami, who had finished her lap, and started to chat after taking a drink from her water bottle.

That's when I noticed something else. For some reason, Hinami seemed to be laying low today.

"What should I change first?"

Tama-chan's voice brought me back to my immediate surroundings. I looked at her, and our eyes met. Something in her gaze struck me as unsure. Maybe she was anxious about changing herself because it was new to her.

"Hmmm…"

I ran through the realistic options in my mind, but nothing jumped out at me. Still, I started with what I knew so far.

"I think the first thing you should work on…is the way you speak to people, maybe?"

"You don't sound very confident!"

Tama-chan instantly called me out on my wishy-washy answer. She was definitely quick on the draw.

"Well, I'm a work in progress myself, you know…"

Tama-chan grinned at my excuse. "That's why I thought you'd be a good model."

"…You did say we were similar."

She nodded. "I'm not great at getting along with everyone…and

I thought someone in the same boat would understand me better than someone who's naturally good at making friends," Tama-chan mumbled introspectively. She looked kind of lonely.

I made a silly expression, hoping to cheer her up. "Well, that's good, because I can confidently say I used to be a lost cause. Leave it to me."

"Ah-ha-ha. What are you talking about?"

She laughed a little. Okay, good! The overall situation was so hard on her; at the very least, I wanted her to have fun during this time. Being able to make her laugh if I wanted to was huge, even if I had to use skills that didn't come easily to me.

"Just be aware that your lifeboat is made of mud!"

"Hey! That sounds more like a sinking ship!"

I smiled, relieved to hear Tama-chan's sharp comeback. But she was right—you can't do better than me when it comes to understanding how it feels to fail. I'm a one-in-a-million genius on that front.

But if that was the case, then what about Hinami? Was she born a star? When I first met her, I remember she said something about not being very successful at life to start with, but I'd never asked her about it. As I was lost in thought, Tama-chan started giggling and pointed at me.

"That's what I'm talking about!" she said.

"What?"

"You couldn't make those jokes in the past, could you? Like saying you're confident that you were a failure?"

"…No, not really."

I got her point. Before, I never could have joked around with a girl from my class, even in a self-deprecating way. Making other people laugh wasn't an option for me then. Whenever I tried to crack a joke, I could practically see all the *Fs in the chat* afterwards, so this was a big step forward.

"What did you do to get to where you are now?"

"Well, I…"

I thought back over everything I'd done, believing the most effective way to help her would be found there. Of course, it was embarrassing that Tama-chan had to throw me a life preserver when it came to teaching strategies.

Let's see. The first thing I did, back when I didn't have any friends in class, was make an excuse to talk with Izumi by asking her for a tissue. That led to a conversation with Kikuchi-san. Then I fixed my posture and expression, and then...

"Oh."

I remembered something that would be perfect for what's happening now. Strategy meetings always begin by assessing the current situation—and that should go for this one with Tama-chan, too.

Master, I'm about to steal one of your tricks!

"...Wait a second."

I dug through the bag at my feet. After a minute, I looked back up at Tama-chan without taking anything out.

"What's wrong?" she said suspiciously, eyeing my empty hands.

"Oh, nothing."

"What's that supposed to mean?"

She looked at me blankly, but I brushed it off, and she let it go. I had to keep my plan secret for the moment, or else it wouldn't work. I coughed and continued with the conversation.

"So you were asking me about what I did, right?"

"Yeah."

"I put a lot of practice into controlling my face, my posture, and the way I talk."

"Really?"

I nodded.

"I didn't use to be one for facial expressions. I was pretty much dead-pan all the time. I tended to slouch, too, and I mumbled a lot. It was like I had a sign saying 'socially awkward' attached to my forehead."

"Oh yeah, you did use to be like that."

"Hey, you could at least pretend to disagree!" I feigned chagrin using my well-honed skills, and Tama-chan giggled. Okay! A bottom-tier character has to work so hard just for a light chuckle. It's tough, but I'll do anything to cheer her up. Tama-chan pressed her hand lightly over her mouth like she was trying to hold her laughter in and smiled at me.

"But you sound a lot more cheerful now. You've got a totally different aura."

"Oh, um, you think so...?"

I shifted my gaze around, embarrassed by the sudden compliment. I made a weird semilaugh. Damn, looks like I'm still low-level for endgame.

Of course, Tama-chan picked up on that right away and pointed at me. "You still get embarrassed and awkward, though!"

"Gimme a break! I knew you'd say something like that as soon as I laughed!"

I used the comeback tone I'd been practicing lately. Tama-chan giggled a little again. I'd gotten good at delivering these comebacks; I'd analyzed and broken them down, using a basic combination of contradicting whomever I was talking to and speaking in an emotional tone. Basically, I'd be dramatic and complain about something they said. I'd mastered both of these skills through repeated practice, and now I was able to use them together. Slow and steady wins the race.

I'd been doing a good job of creating a relaxing atmosphere for Tama-chan. I brightened up even more, continuing on.

"Anyway, that's how I came to be the cheerful guy you know today!"

Tama-chan giggled at my theatrical tone. Don't let up the pressure. In *Atafami*, I always get good results by riding the wave when I hit my stride.

"True. But should you be the one to say that?"

"Well, I worked hard to get where I am, so I've gotta have confidence in that! And you said yourself that I've changed a lot," I said a little anxiously.

Tama-chan looked me over from head to toe, then turned suddenly serious. "But you're also obviously still in training."

"Oof."

I felt that one; she wasn't pulling her punches. *Whoops, she put me in my place.* Her words carried that weight because she never lied.

"I'm working on it, I'm working on it," I said, mostly to myself. Tama-chan nodded solemnly in agreement. She wasn't fawning over me or teasing me—she was just accepting me as I was. Pure Tama-chan.

"Uh, um, so…we were talking about what you should do, right?"

"Yeah."

The wind had left my sails a bit, but I managed to steer the conversation back on track. "I think the first step is to take a good look at where you are so you can decide where you want to go."

"Where I am?" she asked, tilting her head.

"Heh-heh, that's what I said…"

"Yikes, why's your laugh so creepy?!"

I ended up getting a little bold, and Tama-chan cut me right down to size. I dug into my bag again, and this time, I pulled out a small device.

"…What's that?"

"This…," I said, holding it up next to my face, "…is a voice recorder!"

"A voice recorder?"

Tama-chan gave me a dubious look, unimpressed by my proud revelation. Our energy levels were totally different.

I was holding the recorder that Hinami had lent me so I could record my voice and listen to what I sounded like when I talked. I still used it every night before bed to make sure the way I actually spoke was consistent with how I wanted to come across. I carried it around with me even now, too.

"What do you use it for?"

"Heh-heh-heh. Let me tell you…"

"I told you that laugh was creepy!"

As Tama-chan shot me down once again, I pressed the STOP button on the recorder. After checking to make sure our conversation had been properly recorded, I put the device on the table and pressed the REPLAY button.

"Just listen."

Tama-chan looked down at the recorder as we listened.

"I put a lot of practice into controlling my face, my posture, and the way I talk."

"Really?"

"I didn't use to be one for facial expressions. I was pretty much deadpan all the time. I tended to slouch, too, and I mumbled a lot. It was like I had a sign saying 'socially awkward' attached to my forehead."

"Oh yeah, you did use to be like that."

"Hey, you could at least pretend to disagree!"

Tama-chan listened, blinking in surprise.

Yup, you guessed it. When I reached into my bag the first time, I secretly pressed the RECORD button. The idea was to capture a natural conversation. I'd stolen the technique straight from Hinami, who'd done the exact same thing to me. Like teacher, like student.

Eventually, Tama-chan shifted her gaze sharply to me, pointing at the same time.

"Eavesdropper!" she cried, eyeing me critically.

"I know, I know...but just listen."

She made a skeptical noise at my concession, but she listened all the same. The two of us fell quiet, and gradual surprise colored her expression. I'd reacted the same way when Hinami did it to me. Of course Tama-chan was behaving like this; after all, this was what she was hearing:

"You still get embarrassed and awkward, though!"
"But you're also obviously still in training."
"Yikes, why's your laugh so creepy?!"
"I told you that laugh was creepy!"

The recording came to an end. I looked at Tama-chan, not saying a word. Then I put the recorder away.

"What did you think?"

She answered very simply.

"I'm kinda harsh, huh?"

I burst out laughing at her objective and completely honest response. She sounded like she was talking about someone else. That's Tama-chan for you—a woman of no lies. But I'd achieved my goal.

"Right?! That's what I wanted to say!"

"That I'm harsh?"

There was no sarcasm in her tone.

"Well, that's a very simple way of putting it, yeah," I said, losing my stride a little. I'm the type to say what I think, but I'm still fairly careful about how I say it. Totally direct conversation tends to catch me off guard. It's not uncomfortable, though. I'd really like to get more used to it, actually. Yup, Tama-chan and I are fundamentally similar.

"I wanted to show you that while you can intend to talk one way or think you're simply saying what's on your mind, it doesn't actually sound that way if you listen to yourself objectively."

I thought back to how I felt when Hinami did the same thing to me. That was the first time I'd listened to my own voice for an extended period of time. And just like Tama-chan, I'd been surprised by how different it was from what I'd imagined.

"If you genuinely understand how you sound from an outside perspective, you'll start to get a sense of how you should change, right?"

I recalled what Hinami had told me and parroted it to the best of my ability. Like teacher, like student, for real. But just a little while ago, I couldn't control my tone at all; who would have guessed that I would be the one giving this lesson today? Life sure is unpredictable.

"Right," Tama-chan mused. "Is that what you meant by seeing where I am?"

"Exactly!" I said, pointing sharply at her. As I said, a proper game-strategy meeting always begins with an assessment of the current situation. In this case, the current situation did include everything happening to Tama-chan, but even more importantly, it included Tama-chan herself. After all, she wasn't planning to change other people's behavior—she was planning to change herself.

"Okay, so Hinami, Mimimi, and I know that's just what you're like, but when you consider the basic principles that govern our class, people thinking you're harsh is a disadvantage."

"Huh. I can see that."

She sounded convinced, but she still looked down with some consternation. In the classroom arena, you've got two options: Read the mood or manipulate it by winning power struggles or a battle of wits. Essentially, bow to the mood or conquer it. If you just rebel because you can't do either, it'll devour you.

Tama-chan fell into the third category, and she'd suffered the consequences according to the rules of our class. That was one way of wording her current predicament.

Of course, not adjusting to the mood isn't necessarily a bad thing in itself. If anything, I think it's beautiful how strongly Tama-chan refuses to change who she is at her core. I'd go so far as to say it's a better way to live as opposed to the majority of people, who fit themselves into a mold because they don't have any values of their own.

But in the context of the class rules, that virtue flips into a vice. Virtue inevitably changes relative to the rules of a given time and place, which meant our only option was to fight on those terms. That is, assuming we'd made our minds up to change the course of this situation.

Tama-chan continued speaking very quietly, her lips trembling. "I have to change, don't I?"

I heard both determination and doubt in her voice. Her expression still looked faintly disappointed, or maybe frustrated.

"Yeah." I looked directly at her and nodded confidently. Of course, it was frustrating for me to watch a person on the moral high ground falling victim to ugly rules. A more beautiful story would have seen her never giving in and sticking with her own vision of justice to the end. Part of me even wished she would. But now wasn't the time.

I spoke my next words slowly, intending to solidify our decision to become accomplices.

"Let's use those rules to achieve our main goal, which is to protect Mimimi."

Tama-chan looked up at me in surprise, her mouth slightly open. Finally, she smiled and pointed sharply at me.

"Right! I have my own reservations about trusting you, but let's do this together!"

"Starting off honest, I see."

With that, Tama-chan and I began our strategy on a slightly unsteady step.

* * *

"Yeah, like that!"

After affirming our decision, we started her initial training. Based on what Hinami had taught me, I checked her tone, posture, and expression and told her how to polish them. At the moment, we were working on an assignment Hinami had given me in the past.

"Are you getting the hang of it?"

Tama-chan nodded energetically, like a little kid. "Ey!" Her voice was quite a bit more cheerful than usual.

"You're a quick learner, Tama-chan."

"Oooh!"

She pumped her fist, grinning. Looking good. Since she was so petite, the gesture suited her really well. *Yikes, I'd better watch what I think.*

"Think you can practice on your own?"

"Aye!" she chirped, giving me a perky thumbs-up. Her eyebrows were arched, and her eyes were fearless. Wow. She didn't seem like her usual self at all. I was impressed by how silly she could be.

Which is to say, we were doing the assignment Hinami gave me when she took me to the café where Kikuchi-san worked—the exercise where you're only allowed to use vowels when you talk. The idea was to concentrate on your tone, expression, gestures, and other nonverbal communication skills by limiting the variety of words you used. I was trying it out on Tama-chan. I wasn't sure how it would go, but as it turned out, I felt like I was playing with a small animal.

"…Okay. You can speak normally now."

"Oh, okay."

She reverted to her usual way of talking. We'd finished stage one of training. I propped my chin on my fingers and thought for a minute.

"Um…" I realized something. "…You're really good at all this."

Before the vowel exercise, I'd checked to see whether she used the expressive muscles around her mouth effectively when she spoke and if she brought her chest forward for a more imposing posture. This final exercise was my way of testing how well she could control the tone of her voice. The results—as far as I could tell, Tama-chan was at or beyond the standard level for all three of those skills.

"Really? I am?"

"Yeah…I mean…"

I looked her in the eye and gave it to her straight. "You're better than me at all of it."

"What?!" Predictably, my confession surprised Tama-chan. "I thought you were supposed to teach me a bunch of stuff!"

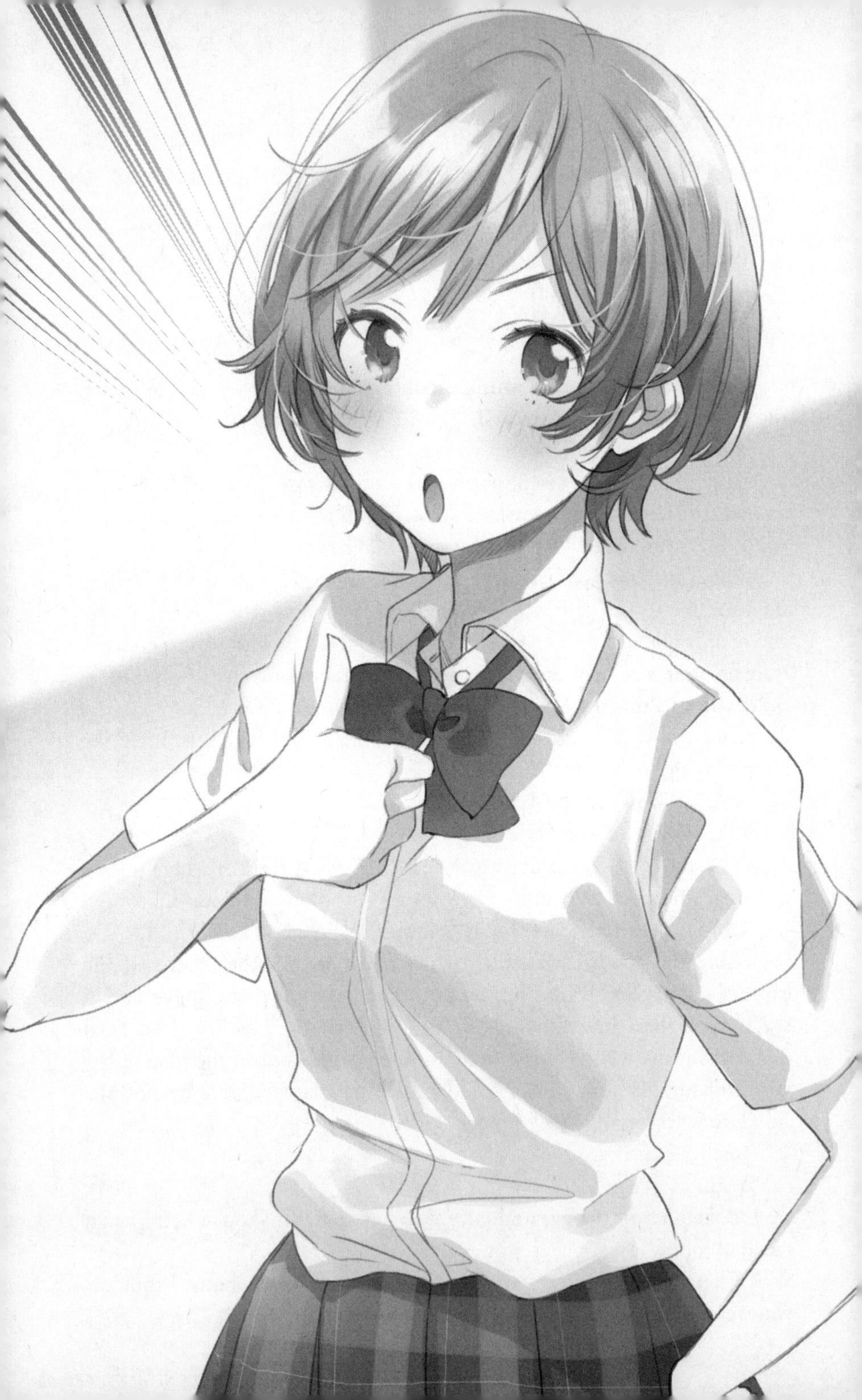

"Patience, young grasshopper. There is yet much I can teach you."

"Well, you haven't taught me anything so far!" she scolded, her emotions clear in her face and voice. Yeah, she was a master of expression. That was more of a comeback than scolding, really—which made me realize something else.

"Um…so the way you tore into me just now…"

"Yeah, what about it?"

She waited blankly for me to go on.

"If you want to get along with everyone—I mean, if you want to be a normie—then it's important to have the skills to mess with people or disagree with them, and to put emotion into your words. Comebacks are a combination of those two things, right?"

"They are?" She sounded a little confused.

"As far as I can tell, you do it perfectly."

"I do?"

"Yeah." I paused for a second, then went on slowly. "I've only learned to do that very recently."

I let out a breath and waited for her reply. I knew the barb that was coming, like *I knew it; you* are *useless!* Maybe I'd even learn something from it.

But instead, she hung her head with disappointment. "I knew I couldn't count on you…"

"H-huh, you've got range…"

Apparently, Tama-chan's repertoire of comebacks included not only sharp retorts but also slower responses like this one. Another variation on emotional content, essentially. *Interesting… Hey, wait a second! Something's wrong with this picture…*

* * *

After that, I had Tama-chan do several more exercises, but she was above average at all of them. Of course, I should have expected that.

For example, take the vowel training. Tama-chan already gets her emotions across using dynamic, nonverbal nuances instead of a broad vocabulary. She speaks loudly and uses big gestures, and her face is very expressive. She specializes in all that stuff, unlike me.

Hinami gave me the vowel assignment because I leaned too heavily on words to express myself at the expense of my nonverbal skills. It was specifically targeted at me in that it got results by shutting me up for a while.

Obviously, applying it directly to Tama-chan would be pointless. What I needed right now was an exercise that focused on the areas she was having trouble with. I needed to think about the type of assignment that would help her—right? So here were my ideas:

"I got nothin'..."

This teacher-student relationship was already on the rocks within half an hour of its formation. *Guess it's still a bit early for me to be teaching other people how to live.*

Still, the situation was what it was, and if we didn't do something, things would keep getting worse. Even if I couldn't do much, I had to keep trying.

"Your training has had results, though, right?"

"...Yeah."

I nodded. It's possible that I misjudged Tama-chan's skills, but I didn't think that was likely. I'd examined my own skill level over and over, and Hinami had done the same, so my perspective shouldn't be that out of whack.

"You're better at most of these skills than I am even now."

"Huh..." Tama-chan sank into thought. "But then why am I having so many problems?"

"...That's the question, isn't it?"

That was the issue, wasn't it?

I'll sound full of myself for saying this, but recently, I'd been getting along with Nakamura's group, and I'd been able to have good conversations with Mimimi, Izumi, and Kikuchi-san. I still didn't feel confident calling myself a normie, but I'd been getting by fairly well, without any arguments or anything. On the other hand, Tama-chan was far beyond me when it came to basic social abilities, but she still had trouble fitting into our class.

Every outcome has a cause. If you want to change those results, you first have to figure out what that cause is. Of course, some causes don't originate within the person—they're external. In this case, Tama-chan had become the target of Konno's continued harassment. The domino cascade of events that led to Konno's shitty mood was a big external cause of Tama-chan's situation.

But her subtle victimization by the entire class was another story. My guess was that in this case, Tama-chan's tendency to get into arguments with Nakamura and inability to fit in without Mimimi's help was partly to blame. I'd hypothesized the cause of all those issues was that she lacked basic skills for interacting with other people, so I'd given her the exact same exercises that had helped me overcome the same problem. But that was starting to look like a bust.

In other words, Tama-chan's current problem areas were different from the ones I'd dealt with in the past. Clearly, applying the same assignments Hinami had given me wouldn't get her the results she wanted. I ran through possible solutions in my mind as I hesitantly offered a suggestion.

"For now...I think it would probably be a good idea to stop fighting back against Konno's harassment."

"You might be right."

She nodded. Every time she fought with Konno, she got irritated looks from our classmates. In order to prevent those negative feelings from piling up, the bare minimum she would need to do was to stop resisting.

However, that was a surface-level response. It didn't reach the root of the problem. It might temporarily alleviate the situation, but getting to the deeper cause was ultimately more important. I guess the "assignment" I needed to give myself was figuring out what that cause was.

"Aside from that..."

"Oh!"

As I was thinking, Tama-chan looked down at the field like she'd just noticed something. I followed her gaze and saw the track team was starting to clean up their equipment.

"Looks like they're done."

"Yeah," she said, leaning out the window a little. "Looks like Minmi is going home today."

"What do you mean, 'today'?"

She turned back toward me. "There was that period where she was running herself into the ground, remember? She was trying to keep up with Hinami's extensive practices."

"…Yeah, I remember." I thought back to that rough period for Mimimi.

"Well, she still practices with Hinami after everyone else goes home sometimes."

"Really?"

I was slightly worried, but Tama-chan went on. "But apparently, she's been going home when she feels like it's too much, like today."

I let out a relieved sigh. "…So she's keeping her own pace."

"Yeah." Tama-chan smiled warmly, nodded, and slung her bag over her shoulder. She always lit up a little when we talked about Mimimi. "She's fine."

"…Good to hear."

I picked up my own bag and walked out of the classroom with her. We headed down the empty hallway, side by side. The sound of our slippers squeaking on the floor echoed through the school as evening fell outside. I was considering our next steps.

"…I guess we should talk tomorrow about other practical measures you can take to change. You're probably going to need to complete some special assignments, so I'll think it over tonight."

I imagined someone specific as I spoke. There was only one person I trusted to identify problems, come up with methods for solving them, and efficiently turn those methods into assignments. I couldn't help remembering the times she'd helped me.

Tama-chan nodded, but I couldn't tell what she was feeling from her expression.

"Okay, sounds good."

We changed our shoes and walked outside to the field. The last of the summer heat was gone now, and the cool, mid-October wind felt pleasant on my cheeks. The breeze brought the faint scent of sweet olive blossoms to us and played with Tama-chan's fluffy, chestnut hair.

"…Listen, Tomozaki," she said, turning toward me like she was about to tell me a secret.

"What?"

She brought her finger to her lips.

"Let's not tell Minmi I'm doing all this for her, okay?" Her smile was pure and full of warm thoughtfulness.

"A secret, huh?" She was so earnestly trying to protect her friend, wasn't she? "Okay, got it," I said, and left it at that. Tama-chan looked across the field at Mimimi.

Her eyes were so clear that I could almost see into her soul. "She never told me what she did for me, right? So..."

She smiled kindly, and a little playfully.

"...I want to do the same for her."

* * *

When we got to the field, we walked over to Mimimi, who was glistening with sweat and smiling as she stood surrounded by her teammates. Apparently, Hinami was somewhere else.

Tama-chan waved dramatically with her petite arms. "Minmi!"

When she heard Tama-chan's voice, Mimimi swiveled her head toward us like a dog perking up its ears and waved back energetically.

"Hi! You waited for me again today? Aww, you're so sweet! I guess you just care about me thiiis much!"

She opened both arms wide, apparently to demonstrate the scale of Tama-chan's love. Still as silly as ever. Her teammates watched with smiles that said they were used to her.

"And Tomozaki, too? This is a rare event!"

"Hey. I was just..."

"What? Falling for me?"

"Yeah, yeah."

I pretended to nonchalantly shake off her words, even though my heart was pounding. Her teammates all looked at me and then back at Mimimi as if to say, *Who's he?*

"Let me introduce you to my Brain!" she said, flapping her hands dramatically. Her teammates looked even more bewildered. *Don't mind me; I'm just a random NPC!*

But Mimimi smiled her usual joking smile. I'm fairly certain she was trying to smooth out any awkwardness, and Tama-chan knew it, too. That's probably why she returned Mimimi's cheerful greeting with her own typical smile and a roll of the eyes.

"Anyway, let's get going!" Tama-chan said brightly.

"You don't have to tell me twice!"

"Hey, get back! You're gonna get your sweat all over me!"

"Soak it up! Can't you feel the love in it?!"

"Love?! It's just sweat!"

Mimimi jumped over to Tama-chan and pressed up against her, and the three of us started off the field. I didn't think my overactive imagination was to blame for the hint of sadness I saw in Tama-chan's smile compared with her smile; it was different from how she used to act before all this drama began.

We really do have to solve this.

As we headed home, I silently made up my mind to do just that.

* * *

The next day was Friday. Despite everything that was going on, Hinami and I were still having our morning meetings. Today's started with her questioning me in an accusing tone.

"You and Hanabi are up to something, aren't you?"

She threw me a sharp look. Instead of surveying everything from a distance like usual, she seemed to be anxious and under a lot of pressure. This wasn't the Hinami I knew.

"…What can I say?"

Hinami snapped back testily to my vague answer. "You said before that Hanabi should change, didn't you?"

"…I did, but…"

"You were waiting for Mimimi with Hanabi yesterday, weren't you? What were you up to?" she asked with a hint of warning in her voice. She must have seen me when we went to meet up with Mimimi after track practice. "You didn't give her any ideas, did you?"

Her tone was quiet but powerful, like she was intent on methodically crushing me. I was a little intimidated, but I met her eyes, determined to stick to my guns. After all, Tama-chan had made up her mind to fight. I couldn't give in now.

"I did give her some ideas, and they probably aren't ones you would approve of."

I was taking her challenge head-on, and she looked a little surprised by that.

"...So you are trying to change her." She glared at me—but was I imagining that flicker of uncertainty deep in her eyes?

"...You're still against it, huh? You really don't want her to change?"

"Obviously. Hanabi is in the right. She shouldn't have to change."

She'd said the same thing when we talked about this a little while earlier. Her argument wasn't fully logical; it wasn't like her. For some reason, she was very obstinate on this one point. And obstinately opposed to me.

But there was something I wanted to run past her. If Tama-chan was going to stick to the path she had chosen—if she was going to fight to the end—then there was no way around the fact that Aoi Hinami was her strongest ally. I tried to choose the right words to draw out the truth of her feelings.

"...What if Tama-chan wants to, though?"

Hinami froze for a few seconds, then looked at me questioningly.

"She wants to change? Hanabi?"

Her voice wavered. That definitely wasn't like her. Even if she had internal doubts, she never let them show this much. This situation was affecting her differently from usual. I didn't know why, but it might be a way to get through to her. If I could use her vulnerability to convince her to help us, then that's the path I wanted to take.

I considered my next words. The root cause was a mystery, but Hinami respected Tama-chan's principles. In which case...

"Yes, she does. She said she wants to change because all this is making Mimimi unhappy. She was clear about that, without any prompting from me."

I emphasized the fact that this was Tama-chan's own wish.

"Huh..."

Hinami put her finger to her lip and sank into thought. She looked very serious, but I didn't have the slightest idea what she was trying to decide or what she wanted out of this.

"If you can, I want you to help her."

At long last, I got to the meat of my request. She stared at me blankly for a few moments. Finally, she pressed her lips together and nodded, as if she'd privately worked through something in her mind. Her eyes were a bottomless, impenetrable black; I felt like I would drown in them.

"...If Hanabi changes, everything is meaningless."

For some reason, her face was filled with unwavering determination. "Hinami..."

Normally, she didn't mind adapting herself to any rules she felt were wrong if it meant she would achieve her goals. But in this fight, she had set aside that principle. Why would she do that? Was she panicking because one of her closest friends was in danger? Or was it something else? I felt like I knew her, but I really didn't. I had nothing even close to an answer.

Still, I'd managed to confirm one thing. My trusted teacher wouldn't be helping me with this one.

* * *

It was the second-period break on the same day.

Bang! Tama-chan's desk jolted to the side. Konno had kicked the leg on purpose, as usual. She still hadn't gotten bored of harassing Tama-chan. I bit my lip and waited to see what would happen. This was the start of the battle.

The class fell silent, and then that annoyed, despairing mood fell over the whole classroom. *Stop it already.* Unfair as it was, their target was Tama-chan.

Konno brazenly ignored it all and sauntered over to her groupies, as she always did.

Up till the previous day, this was when an argument between Tama-chan and Konno would break out. Then the class's frustration would turn toward Tama-chan, and Mimimi would get upset. That was the usual pattern.

I glanced at Tama-chan. She glanced back and nodded slightly.

"..."

She held her tongue. She didn't accuse Konno of anything or scold her. Instead, she completely ignored her.

Konno shot her a slightly surprised look, but right away, she feigned disinterest and turned back to her groupies. The other students let out a collective sigh, watching the scene unfold.

Okay.

This was the first tactic Tama-chan had at her disposal—it was quiet but meaningful. She'd put up with the harassment, even compromise her sense of fairness, in order to soften the attack from the class in general—in order to make Mimimi worry about her a little bit less. From the outside, it probably looked like a tiny step forward. But for Tama-chan, who hated bending to anyone, it was not only a huge step but a hard one to take.

Mimimi watched in stunned surprise but quickly regained her balance and called out cheerfully.

"Tama! Let's go get something to drink!"

That was the signal for the class to relax. *Good. No drama today.* The unspoken relief was visible on their faces. Tama-chan had done a good job of avoiding the usual negativity, and for now, that was enough.

From this one scene alone, you'd probably think she was a helpless, weak victim who deserved pity. But I'm fairly sure it was a necessary step toward solving the root problem.

I looked around me, trying to observe my fellow students and get a sense of the current mood. That's when I saw Hinami staring blankly into space like a mannequin. Her gaze was turned toward Tama-chan and Mimimi.

"Aoi, come with us!"

At the sound of Mimimi's voice, she came to with a start and made herself smile. The three of them walked side by side out of the room and toward the stairwell with the vending machine. To me, Hinami's figure receding down the hall looked dark and gloomy.

At lunch, I felt distinctly uneasy. Hinami was chatting with Nakamura and Izumi. Nothing special about that. Business as usual.

It was hard to put into words, but…something was happening with suspicious frequency.

Hinami and I have this relationship where we talk honestly about our feelings and thoughts in private, so when it comes to the version of herself that she shares with everyone else, I play the role of the casual observer.

That's given me a general understanding of how she acts—and she was talking to Izumi and Nakamura a lot. I'd noticed it gradually starting this week, but today especially stood out.

She was probably working on some sort of strategy.

Unlike me, she was pulling strings behind the scenes. What was her goal, and was it on a collision course with mine? I had mountains of unanswered questions.

All the same, my only option was to keep moving ahead with my own strategy.

* * *

After school, I killed some time at the library and then headed to the classroom to meet up with Tama-chan so we could talk about the day's events.

"Good work staying calm when she kicked your desk. Let's start with that."

Tama-chan nodded decisively. "It was really frustrating...but that's what it's gonna take, right?"

"Yeah," I agreed. That was important for our goal. "But that'll only keep things from getting worse. I don't think there'll be any dramatic improvements."

Tama-chan looked at me uncertainly. "You're probably right...but what should I do?"

I didn't have a clear answer, so I tried to put together the information I did have.

"...I think we need a strategy to actually make this situation better."

Tama-chan tilted her head quizzically. "Sure. Like what?"

"Good question..."

I looked down, thinking. We had to improve two main points. One was Konno's harassment. The other was the general negativity directed at Tama-chan. Right now, we were prioritizing the latter.

At the moment, Konno's harassment didn't leave behind any evidence—which meant there were limits on how much she could do. If Tama-chan could put up with the situation, she'd be able to buy some time while avoiding permanent damage to her image.

The class was a different story.

"The problem is, we don't know what everyone in class is going to do."

"…What do you mean?"

"Right now, everyone is just watching, but eventually, they may start joining in on Konno's harassment."

That's just it. Honestly speaking, I had almost no outlook on what the class would do from here on out. At the moment, the mood had stalled just short of a crisis, but I had no idea what might push it over the edge or what kind of cruelty might occur as a result.

During the sports tournament, it hadn't taken much to bring the class together. In the same way, a small event could push them to come together for evil instead of good.

"Huh, that could happen," Tama-chan said, her eyes full of realization. "Yikes."

"I know. But…it's possible."

There was already one person harassing Tama-chan, so it stood to reason that others might follow suit. The mood was tilted in that direction, too. Everything could change simply because people let other people determine what their values should be. That was the nature of the class.

To prevent that, I'd asked Tama-chan to stop fighting back against Konno. It was an emergency measure, but the antipathy from those daily arguments before could become a major factor in moving the class.

"I think what we have to do now is focus on keeping everyone from avoiding you and, if possible, turn them into your allies."

"Everyone, huh?" Tama-chan looked down with uncertainty. *Everyone.* That was probably the opponent she hated most. She couldn't openly express her thoughts to a bunch of people in the same way that she could one-on-one. "It's so hard to know what the class as a whole is thinking…"

"…Yeah…"

I nodded sympathetically. Essentially, she was talking about reading the mood. You had to think of the group abstractly as a single animal and analyze the rules and values that motivated it—or what Hinami called the standard for right and wrong—in order to understand its thought process and actions. None of that was easy.

"I can get what specific people are thinking, but when it comes to the whole group, I have no idea."

Tama-chan looked around the class gloomily. So many desks and chairs. The square space was so lifeless and confining. Just over thirty people coexisted here over the course of a year, filling it either with their excitement or with a sense of claustrophobia. And through it all, the mood was roaming around like a monster on the prowl.

"But…sometimes, everyone makes a move all at once, you know?"

"Yeah…"

When the mood of the group changes, it can be like a muddy river carrying along helpless individuals. The process isn't always fair, and it doesn't always make sense—that was one reason I used to think life was a shitty game. But you could also think of it as one of life's most important rules. It's too powerful to ignore.

"Tomozaki, do *you* know what everyone is thinking?" Tama-chan looked up at me uncertainly.

"Um…"

I paused for a minute, unsure what to say. I was thinking about the monster tamers like Hinami, Mizusawa, Nakamura, and Konno. I was also considering all the experiences I'd amassed during my training and where they'd led my mind in the recent months, as well as the skills and new perspectives I'd gained. I ruminated over all of it, reviewing the conclusions I'd reached, and realized something.

"Well, recently, I've started to figure it out."

"Really?"

"Yeah."

I nodded with a bit of confidence. For example, I'd taken one step toward boosting my self-esteem when I'd completed the exercise on standing up for my opinions. When I helped Mimimi with her speech for the student council election, I'd gotten a sense of how to read the mood. And when I successfully motivated Erika Konno's group to participate in the sports tournament, I'd gotten a sense for how to direct it. By filtering all these experiences through nanashi's particular gamer perspective on battles, I'd developed a fairly practical image on how to read the mood.

"I used to be bad at figuring out how people thought, but I'm getting better at it after some experience."

"You are?"

I realized something else: the reality—and also, I think, the hope—that I was steadily improving.

"And if I was able to figure it out with some assignments and training…you should be able to, too."

Tama-chan's eyes brightened. "You think so?"

"I'm sure of it." But then another realization hit me. "But, uh…," I mumbled.

Tama-chan tilted her head. "What?"

It was a very simple but very basic problem.

"It took me about five months…"

"Oh. Right."

The excitement level quickly dropped. Hinami's training was completely orthodox and straight as an arrow. It involved slow and steady effort. That was the most correct, most certain, and most powerful approach, but it took time. As a gamer, I knew that real improvement always required putting in effort for the long haul.

"Five months like this…is impossible."

"…I know. It's too slow."

The mood could turn at any moment. If Tama-chan spent five months steadily training, something irreversible might happen in the meantime and destroy the whole plan. The chances of that happening were fairly high. She couldn't take on this fight at a leisurely pace.

"We need something that will turn everything around in a short period of time…," I muttered, but I knew that wasn't how growth worked. Okay, technically speaking, there might be a miracle solution that flipped the entire situation around—if we could think outside the box, reverse our perception, and outfox the enemy. After all, that was how nanashi approached every game. I was confident I could do that under the right conditions. But I had to fully understand the subtler rules of the game first. And when it came to this one, I wasn't there yet.

"…Hmmm."

"Not looking good, huh?" Tama-chan said, peering into my face.

"Yeah…"

Based on the leads I had at the moment, I couldn't come up with a strategy I felt confident about.

"It's hard when time is so limited…," I said.

"Hey, you two!"

Suddenly, I heard someone calling theatrically to us from the door of the classroom. I turned around in surprise and saw a figure standing there with one hand raised nonchalantly, a sardonic smile on his face. Mizusawa.

My surprise didn't take any of the wind from his sails as he strolled over to us and placed one hand on my shoulder. Then he raised one eyebrow and looked me in the eye with an infuriatingly cocky expression.

"You seem troubled, my friend," he said with a smug, overly confident smile.

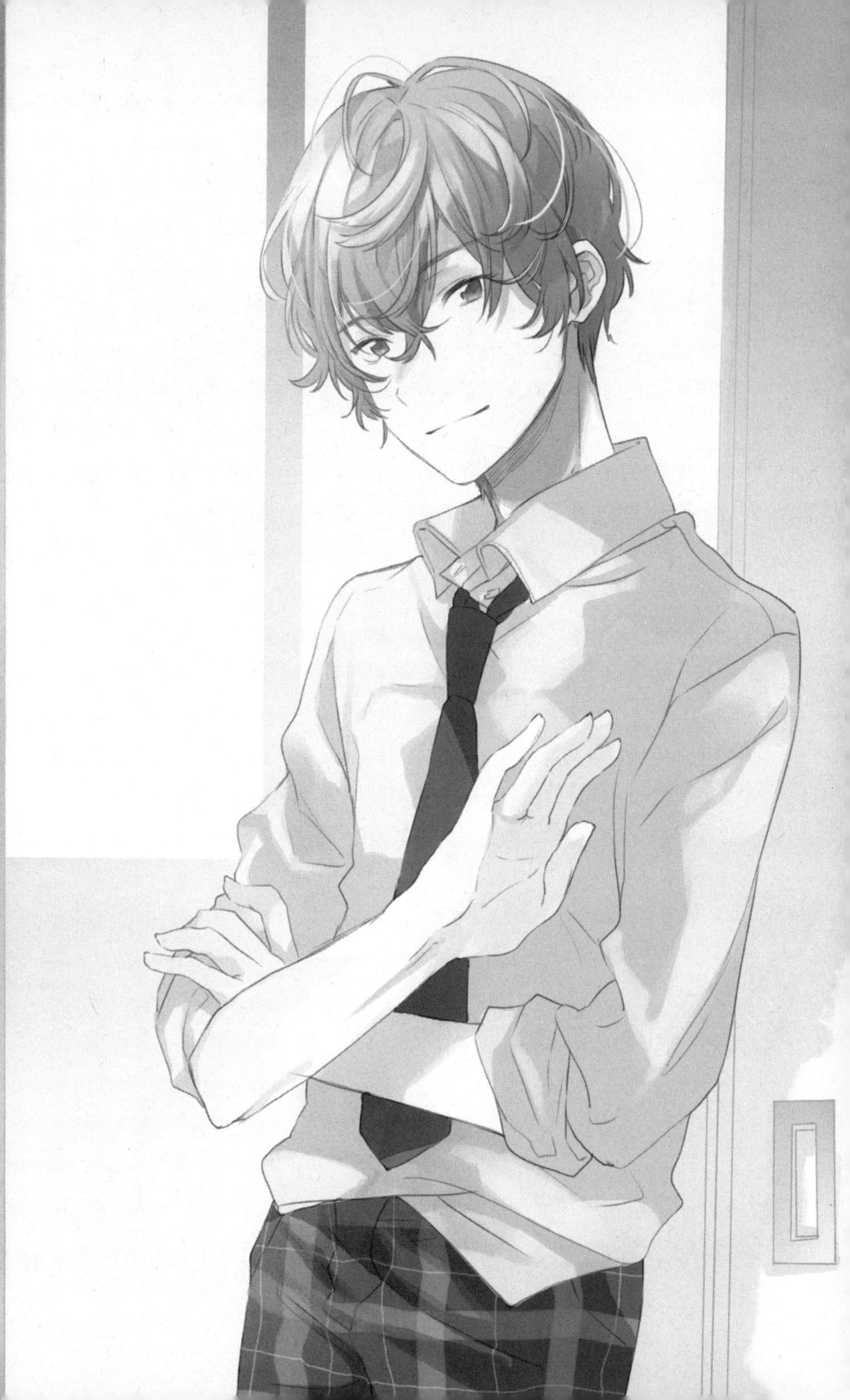

2

Battles go better when you're fighting alongside someone whose signature move is the opposite of yours

"…Mizusawa?" I said, still startled by our unexpected guest.

He settled into the desk on my right, so I was sandwiched between him and Tama-chan.

"Okay, Fumiya, fess up. You're up to something, aren't you?"

"Wh-what are you talking about?" I sputtered at the cryptic accusation. Tama-chan stared at him suspiciously.

"Come on, you were scheming with Mimimi, too, and during the sports tournament. I bet you and Tama-chan are coming up with a strategy against Erika right now, aren't you? You keep pretty busy when no one's looking, huh?"

"Uh…"

I felt his words were carrying me toward an unknown destination.

"And Tama, you ignored Erika when she kicked your desk today, didn't you? That got my attention, and I figured something was up when I saw you two look at each other. Then just now, right as I happen to stop by class after practice, here you guys are by the window. So what's going on? A secret conference?"

All I could do was listen as Mizusawa smoothly exhibited how perceptive he was. When did he take over my private meeting between Tama-chan and me? Leadership slipped from my hands before I had even noticed.

"Well? Am I right?" he asked, peering at me with a teasing smile. I gave in and smiled back. He was as sharp as ever. No lying to him. The guy should become a detective or something.

"On the nose."

He laughed as I lifted up both hands in surrender.

"Okay then, since I've done such a good job," he said as he looked at Tama-chan, "let me ask: Have you been okay lately?"

"…Yeah, I'm fine."

Even though Tama-chan seemed flustered, she answered right away. But she shifted her gaze from him to me and then down at the ground uncomfortably.

"Ha-ha… Would you two prefer if I wasn't here?" he asked wryly.

"No, it's just…why *are* you here?" I changed the subject to what I really wanted to know.

"Huh? I mean, you two are trying to figure out what to do about Erika, right?"

"Yeah, we are."

"Well, I just thought a sketchy guy like me could smooth out the process…"

He smirked again and looked at Tama-chan.

"But maybe it's not that important?"

Tama-chan was staring at her hands, which were folded on her lap.

"…Tama-chan?" I said softly. She glanced at me but then looked back down again right away. I remembered something. I'd seen her like this before. It was during the first semester, when she'd been pulled into a conversation with Nakamura and his buddies during home ec. She'd acted exactly like this.

"…Um, Mizusawa?"

"Yeah?"

He looked straight at me.

"Your group doesn't really get along with Tama-chan, does it?" I asked point-blank. That was my guess anyway, based on her reaction in home ec and the context Hinami had given me later on. There seemed to be some deep-rooted enmity going on.

Mizusawa widened his eyes like I'd caught him off guard, then looked at me and finally burst out laughing.

"There you go again, Fumiya!"

"What?"

He then narrowed his eyes and cackled.

"She's right here, y'know. Or is this not weird to you?"

"Oh…that's what you mean."

Made sense. Tama-chan and I were used to each other after our honest conversation here two days earlier, but from Mizusawa's perspective, my question must have come from left field. He didn't know this was our natural state.

"Get used to it," I said casually and fairly naturally. I was getting more comfortable talking with him these days. I was even able to use two different skills at the same time!

"Ha-ha-ha. And here I thought you were the conscientious type!" His smile was genuine.

"What can I say?"

"It works for you."

I smiled in return. "Anyway, back to my question…"

He scratched his neck and made a pensive noise. "I wouldn't say we don't get along…but we're not very compatible."

"…Compatible?" I echoed, not sure what he meant. I glanced at Tama-chan, but she was still avoiding looking at him.

"I mean, Tama-chan sticks to her guns, right? That's why she's been fighting with Erika so much lately. And since Erika is the boss type, she won't give an inch, either. They're like oil and water."

"I'd agree."

"Right? And…," he said, pausing imperiously before continuing in a more humorous way. "A certain someone in our group can be just as pushy as Erika, am I right?"

As soon as he said it, a light bulb flickered to life in my mind.

"Oh…Nakamura."

"Correct!" He frowned and then gave me an exasperated smile. "Shuji and Tama are like oil and water, too."

He glanced at Tama-chan. I did, too. She didn't make any attempt to speak. I knew she didn't get along with Nakamura, and I guess the same went for Mizusawa. I looked back at him.

"So she doesn't get along with Nakamura's whole group?"

"Basically," he said, nodding. "Now and then, they snap at each other, or he'll make some stupid joke. You even got dragged into it once, didn't you?"

"Um, yeah, just that one time."

He must mean the incident in home ec.

"Thought so. Happens to Takei and me almost every day. Once, they had a huge fight, and things got awkward. They still are."

"Ha-ha...got it."

I gave a little huff of a laugh. But things made sense now. Nakamura and Tama-chan were incompatible, so she often got into little conflicts that involved his whole group. Those conflicts made their relationship awkward. The situation was a little complicated, but thankfully not as serious as I'd feared.

"I wouldn't say the two of you are completely incompatible...but cliques are cliques, I guess."

"Yeah. We don't argue directly, but if I'm involved, I'll take Shuji's side, and I'll tease her sometimes. I'm not surprised she doesn't like me much."

He smiled sheepishly. Mizusawa was essentially a kind person, but he did tend to poke fun at people a lot. Not long ago, he'd piled on when Nakamura was imitating how I spoke. The explanation made sense.

I turned to Tama-chan again. She was still looking down. She might not want to talk about this stuff, but I wanted to hear her side.

"Tama-chan... Do you feel awkward around Mizusawa because you've argued before?"

She raised her head and glanced back and forth between the two of us, gauging us. But she stayed silent, and her gaze gradually fell back onto the desk. An indecisive silence fell over the group. Mizusawa grew serious for a minute, then smiled again without any hint of resentment.

"Anyway, I'm here if you need to talk. Lemme know if I can help. Later, guys," he said cheerfully, trying to ease the awkwardness. Then he slid off the desk and walked toward the classroom door. He acted like nothing important had happened, but even I could tell that wasn't the case. He was trying to slip away because he could tell that his presence was making Tama-chan uncomfortable. He'd even announced he was on our side and promised to help us.

"Gotcha. Thanks—"

Right then, a jolt of inspiration flashed through me.

I thought of Mizusawa's thoughtful behavior toward Tama-chan.

I thought of Tama-chan staring down at the desk.

I thought of all the assignments Hinami had given me so far.

All the pieces came together, and an idea took shape in my head.

I had a feeling that one of the assignments Hinami had given me might have a big impact on helping us solve Tama-chan's problem.

"—Mizusawa, wait a second."

I put one finger to my lip and looked down as I spoke. Mizusawa's footsteps stopped in the middle of the classroom.

"What's up?"

When I looked at him, I saw he was looking at me with a mixture of anticipation and bewilderment.

"Um...I was wondering if you could help us with something."

"Help you?"

"Yeah," I said, nodding and then looking at Tama-chan. "—Tama-chan."

"What?"

She looked at me, surprised to suddenly hear her name.

"I was saying the other day that you'd need to complete some training to solve this problem, right?"

"Yeah...," she replied awkwardly; I was acting a little too excited about this. I gave her a serious look as Mizusawa watched us with interest.

"I figured out what assignment to give you first."

Maybe she guessed what I was thinking from my expression, because she turned serious, too.

"...What is it?" she said, then waited quietly for my answer.

"Well..."

I thought back to *that* assignment from the barbecue trip.

"Starting today...I want you to become friends with Mizusawa."

She looked at me blankly. Mizusawa looked back and forth between us. There was a brief silence, and then Mizusawa spoke.

"Uh, what's the idea behind that?"

"Um, well..."

Better explain—of course they wouldn't get it right away.

"Tama-chan and I have been talking since yesterday, and the first thing she needs to do is get everyone in class to stop avoiding her."

"Makes sense," Mizusawa said, leaning against a desk. Tama-chan listened silently.

"And if she wants to do that, she needs some training to build up the skills that'll help her fit in better with everyone."

"Huh. So she can start practicing by becoming friends with me?"

"Right!"

Mizusawa caught on quick, as usual. I looked over at Tama-chan.

"Watching you, it occurred to me that one of the reasons you have trouble fitting in is that once you've closed yourself off to people, there's no going back. Like what just happened with Mizusawa."

Tama-chan turned her gaze from me to Mizusawa. Predictably, she seemed vaguely uncomfortable. But she didn't look down.

"I'm guessing you assume you won't be able to get along with anyone in Nakamura's group. I think breaking through that shell is the first step toward getting along better with the rest of the class."

"Shell...?" she murmured, looking down. This time, though, she seemed to be examining herself rather than escaping eye contact with us.

"Yeah."

"Wow," Mizusawa said. "You've grown up, haven't you, Fumiya?"

What's with the sudden role shift? You sound like my dad or something.

"What you're saying is surprisingly logical, too."

"Y-yeah?"

Probably had something to do with all my close-up observations of a certain hyperlogical someone. After all, I'd stolen her assignment outright. Never expected this would be the one I'd choose for Tama-chan, though. Mizusawa gave a few small nods.

"Okay. I'll help out since you asked, but it's up to Tama-chan to take the initiative from here on out."

He turned to Tama-chan. She was still looking down at herself.

"I..."

She slowly raised her head and pursed her lips. She'd always stayed true to her own wishes. That time in home ec, right now with Mizusawa, and probably for a very long time, she'd refused to talk to people she didn't like, with Nakamura first and foremost among them. She probably had some powerful reason for not wanting to interact with them. But right now, she wasn't sure. Which path would she choose? It was a question of priorities; there was no right answer. I waited silently for her decision.

She waited another moment, and then she directed a determined look at me.

"Okay. I'll try."

Mizusawa and I turned to each other, smiled, and nodded. Tama-chan had just made another crack in her shell.

* * *

Mizusawa and Tama-chan faced each other across a desk.

"I think this might be the first time we've really talked."

"Maybe so."

I was standing a few steps away, my back to the window. In contrast to Mizusawa, who was talking in his usual soft tone, Tama-chan sounded indifferent. More than nerves, though, I think it was just that she wasn't used to talking to him, and she wasn't trying to hide it.

"So what do you think now?"

"Now?"

"I mean, I can understand why you don't like talking to Shuji, but what about me?"

Mizusawa wasn't beating around the bush. He wasn't being unkind, but this level of directness was slightly unusual for him. He was probably adapting to Tama-chan's blunt honesty. If so, props to him. The power of the socially adept.

"I'm not sure. My image of you is that you always say mean things."

She sounded flat and a bit stiff.

"Ha-ha-ha. I'm mean, huh?"

"Yeah. You always go along with the mean things Nakamura says."

"Ha-ha, really?"

"I'm not a fan of that, so I avoid you."

"Huh. Oh…"

Even Mizusawa was starting to flinch from Tama-chan's one-two punches.

"Hey, Fumiya, I found someone even blunter than you."

"She's just getting started, dude."

"Seriously?" Mizusawa smiled goofily. He seemed to actually be enjoying her bluntness. Figures. "Well, I'm guessing you don't like me much. Seeing how you've been avoiding me."

Tama-chan's expression didn't change.

"I don't know. I won't know what kind of person you are without talking to you."

Her round eyes met Mizusawa's.

"...Hmm," he murmured, with a hint of surprise. After all, it was an odd answer. She avoided him because he was mean to her, but she wouldn't know if she disliked him or not until she talked to him. There wasn't anything wrong with that, but it was definitely unusual. It also fit her perfectly. She couldn't hide those genuine feelings of hers.

"Well, is there anything you want to ask me, then? In the interest of getting to know me better."

"Um...no?"

"Ha-ha-ha! Thought so!"

He opened his mouth wide and laughed. It was nice that he seemed to be enjoying himself. Right now, Tama-chan was telling him exactly what she thought, and he was accepting it, with a laugh, even. They were actually getting along great. Seemed like they'd be friends in no time.

"Oh, actually, there was one thing!" Tama-chan said a little more excitedly.

"What?" Mizusawa asked, grinning. He looked as relaxed as ever, but he also didn't know what was coming.

"Do you like Aoi?"

"Urk!"

That was me, not Mizusawa, sputtering in shock at her candid question. For his part, Mizusawa looked amused even though he didn't know how to answer.

"Well that came from left field," he said very calmly, throwing my own lack of stoicism into sharp relief.

"I heard some rumors, so I was wondering what the story was. I'm curious, since Aoi keeps a lot of secrets."

"Huh…"

Mizusawa stared at Tama-chan, trying to figure out exactly what she meant. Her expression didn't change. Mizusawa was making full use of his natural shrewdness, but I think she may have been so honest, she didn't even realize he was trying to pry into her motivations. This was definitely a mixed martial arts showdown.

I'd already seen Mizusawa declare his true feelings to Hinami, so for me, it was a nerve-racking situation. I held my breath as I watched, but Mizusawa didn't show any signs of panic.

"Yeah, I like her."

"Mizusawa?!"

"Wow! So it's true!"

I reacted at the same time as Tama-chan.

"Yeah," Mizusawa said, smiling casually. "As a friend."

His tone was joking—so that's how he planned to brush it over. He had me there for a second. But wow. He sure had guts to stay so cool and admit it after Tama-chan sussed out his real feelings, only to turn it on its head and surprise us. He was so relaxed, you'd never think he was lying. Hinami had done the same thing before. Must be a special normie skill. No way I can copy that one.

"…Oh, okay." Tama-chan nodded, apparently convinced, and Mizusawa smiled teasingly.

"So you get a kick out of romantic gossip, huh?"

"Th-that's not true!" she protested, a little jolted by his joke.

"Well, I answered your question, so now it's my turn. Do you like anyone right now?"

"No way! And I wouldn't tell you if I did!"

"Oh! So there is someone? Who is it?"

"Hey! Stop assuming I like anyone!"

Tama-chan pointed sharply at Mizusawa. He cackled deviously.

"You say that, but these little after-school, one-on-one strategy meetings with Fumiya look awfully suspicious to me…"

"What?" I sputtered at this surprise attack, but Tama-chan stood firm.

"No way!"

"Really now?"

"That's completely ridiculous!"

"Ha-ha-ha! She says it's completely ridiculous, Fumiya."

"I'm not sure I can handle that level of rejection…"

"What?! Oh, s-sorry?"

Swept up in the wave of conversation, Tama-chan shot me a question-slash-apology. Mizusawa smiled with satisfaction and sighed, while Tama-chan freaked out, and I sank into depression. What was going on?

"Man, you guys are funny."

"How did I get dragged into this…?"

Little by little, Tama-chan was completing her assignment and gaining the ability to converse naturally with Mizusawa. Never mind that I was the one being sacrificed for their amusement…

* * *

"You came again today, my darling Tama! And you're with…Tomozaki… and Takahiro?"

"'Sup."

When we walked down to meet Mimimi after track practice ended, she fixated on Mizusawa.

"I've gotta know! What's going on?"

For some reason, she sidled up to me, her eyes sparkling.

"Um, well, Tama-chan has a new friend?"

"What? I mean, you don't usually see these two together!" she said, surprised.

I kept calm as I replied. "I know… They didn't get along very well before."

"Not beating around the bush, huh?"

Apparently, our little circle of honesty was a bit confusing. Mizusawa cackled as he stood next to her.

"Well, it's true. Things were awkward between Tama and me because we were always involved in those arguments between her and Shuji."

"What, you're in on this, too, Takahiro?!"

Mimimi couldn't keep up with our blunt trio—especially now that Mizusawa was included.

"Anyway, Minmi! We're heading home!"

"What? Oh right…?"

The ever-competent conversationalist Mimimi was suddenly flustered. That was rare, and I liked it. The four of us headed out together.

"Okay, you guys, what's this all about?"

Mimimi held an imaginary microphone in her hand like an aggressive reporter. One of her usual tricks.

"Um…"

What to say? I had to hide the fact that we were all hard at work helping Tama-chan avoid making Mimimi sad. But she had probably already guessed from the timing and situation that it had something to do with Erika Konno. That left me with one option.

"Guess you could say it's an Erika Konno strategy meeting."

Mizusawa nodded. "Yeah, just ignoring her won't solve it. The whole class could end up targeting Tama over that BS."

Mimimi clapped her hands and nodded.

"Gotcha! Wow, Tama, you have two protectors? A beautiful boy on each arm!"

Mizusawa smiled and rolled his eyes at Mimimi's joke, which was unusually romantic for her.

"Ha-ha-ha. 'Beautiful'?"

"Well, what should I call you, then?"

"How about a knight on each arm? Duty bound to protect her!" Mizusawa put his hand on his chest in a chivalrous pose.

"Ha-ha-ha! You're shameless! But okay!"

Mimimi pointed at the sky. Okay. I'd better join this conversational wave, too.

"Wait a second, Mizusawa might work as a knight, but I don't think that describes me, either!"

That was just me putting myself down as usual, but Mimimi pouted.

"There you go again, Tomozaki! You're cooler than people think, so have a little faith! The world is your oyster! You might actually be popular if you didn't say stuff like that!"

"Oh, um, okay."

I was caught off guard being called cool at the same time I was being called unpopular. She switched tactics fast.

"Yeah, you do tend to do that."

"R-really?"

Mizusawa joined in. They were right, though—I do beat myself up a lot.

"If you keep putting yourself down, the damsel in distress will be sad. You gotta tell her she can leave it to you! With confidence!"

I nodded. "O-oh, okay."

I couldn't imagine nanashi delivering that line, let alone me, the bottom-tier character in life. But their advice did strike a chord; I shouldn't put myself down so much. In a way, self-deprecation had provided me an easy out. It took less effort to kick myself than it did to raise the bar by acting confident and playing around in a way I wasn't used to. Huh. Guess they were saying never to give up the fight. Was that the path to acceptance?

Tama-chan was listening in on our conversation with interest.

"I've thought that before myself," she said.

"Well, if you agree, too…I promise to keep learning," I said in a mournful tone. *Guess I won't improve unless I'm constantly attempting something new.*

Tama-chan smiled faintly and nodded. "Yeah, I hope you can say, *Leave it to me!* with real confidence one day, too."

"…Yeah."

The nuance was a little different coming from her. While Mimimi and Mizusawa seemed to be saying I should act confident on the surface, I think Tama-chan was telling me to have genuine confidence that would show in my words. She had her own unique perspective when it came to stuff like this.

"…Well, then." Mizusawa reacted with surprised admiration, while Mimimi energetically tied up this thread of conversation.

"That's what I'm talking about! Minami Nanami has high expectations of you!"

I bet Mizusawa was thinking the same thing as me, but Mimimi didn't seem to pay attention to the subtle meaning behind Tama-chan's words. Even though Mizusawa and Mimimi were both good at communication, they were polar opposites in that sense.

"Y-you're making me nervous!" I said.

"And the self-doubt strikes again!"

"Oof." I staggered at Mimimi's comeback.

"Ha-ha-ha. But you do tend to talk after everyone else, Fumiya," Mizusawa commented. His tone was light, but he was basically backing up what Tama-chan had said a minute earlier, with a slightly different nuance. I thought about those two stances as I answered him.

"Well, I'm not sure which is better, but for now, I'm just trying not to overdo it and make everything weird."

Tama-chan nodded.

"Yeah, you should just act natural. It does get weird when you try too hard."

"Ha-ha-ha! Telling it like it is, Tama!"

The three of us continued talking just like that, complete with our subtle differences in tone. Mimimi watched in a daze, like she couldn't keep up. Eventually, she gave up, laughed, and pounded my back.

"Whew, this conversation is beyond me!"

"Ouch!"

Our chat on the way home from school was much more honest than usual. But was this all really helping Tama-chan?

* * *

The next day was Saturday. When I got to Karaoke Sevens for my shift, Mizusawa and Gumi-chan were already there.

"'Sup, Fumiya."

"Hey. You're on today, too, huh?"

"Good morning, Tomozaki-san."

"Morning, Gumi-chan."

I managed to get through the morning formalities without tripping over my tongue. The manager stuck his head around from the front desk and greeted us. That caught me off guard!

"G-good morning." I stuttered a little as I spoke to my boss.

"Good luck today!"

"Yessir!"

After that, I headed to the changing room, put on my uniform, and came back. Once I'd clocked in with the vein scanner, I started working. The computer screen showed a couple of rooms that hadn't been cleaned yet, so I did those while Mizusawa and Gumi-chan took care of the orders. When I walked up to them after, Gumi-chan was washing some cups, and Mizusawa was rinsing them in the sink next to her.

"Slow day, huh?" I said, trying to make conversation.

"Yup," Gumi-chan said listlessly before seeming to remember something. "Oh, by the way! How did things go with the queen?"

"Um, well…"

What should I say? I had asked her for advice on my assignment with Konno for the tournament…but it felt weird to tell her the ultimate result had thrown the whole class out of whack. While I was trying to decide what to say, Mizusawa jumped in.

"…By 'the queen,' do you mean Erika?"

He gave me a smirk, and I mumbled something noncommittal.

"Oh right! Mizusawa-san, you go to the same school as Tomozaki-san, don't you?"

"Sure do."

"Did you know Tomozaki-san was trying to get your class queen to care about a tournament?"

Having finished washing up, Gumi-chan wiped her hands with a paper towel.

"Yeah, I had an idea," Mizusawa answered, stacking the clean cups in the dish rack. Luckily, he did already know, but what if he hadn't, and she had spilled the beans without asking me first? Still, it was hard to dislike her for some reason.

"Oh, you did? So does everyone know Tomozaki-san is from Planet Effort?"

"Planet Effort? What the heck is that?"

Mizusawa raised his eyebrows. Gumi-chan groaned, like explaining was too much trouble.

"Can't you figure it out yourself?"

"Huh?"

Mizusawa appeared unsatisfied, but Gumi-chan was probably used to that, because she went on efficiently lining up the cups without even trying to clarify. What a pro.

"Anyway, how did it go?"

Gumi-chan looked at me. What to say?

"Um, it went okay..."

I couldn't think of a good answer, so I just gave her something vague. Even a bottom-tier character like me knew I'd score a zero in terms of slick cover-ups. Gumi-chan gave an uninterested snort and changed the subject. Maybe she didn't actually care to start with?

"Speaking of which, didn't the tournament help you both get into relationships? I thought you mentioned something like that before!"

She really did love that kind of gossip. Her question made me nervous, since summer vacation had been full of twists and turns for me.

"Nope," Mizusawa said, smiling casually and glancing at me.

"Me neither."

Gumi-chan snorted again. "I'm surprised you both aren't taken."

"Huh?"

That was a shock to hear. I mean, she wasn't just talking about Mizusawa—she was talking about me, too. If I hadn't misheard her, and she wasn't saying it to be nice, well, that was incredible. And fairly unlikely.

"You two are boring. Don't either of you even like anyone?"

She sulked. Her question did bring a certain someone to mind, but to cover it up, I forced myself to sound calm.

"...Sorry, nope."

Gumi-chan looked at me in surprise.

"What was that pause about?! So there is someone!"

"Ha-ha-ha. He did sound suspicious."

"No way!" I said, trying to hide my panic behind a mask of cheer.

"I see. So Tomozaki-san does have a crush. And what about you, Mizusawa-san? Any prospects?"

"Well, I've been hanging out with someone, but that's it."

He brushed away her question with complete calmness. Huh. He was such an incredible actor that even after witnessing that conversation between him and Hinami, I was almost convinced by his story.

"Hmm. I never know if you're lying or telling the truth…"

"Ha-ha-ha. Too bad. Guess you've got some work to do."

Mizusawa thumped Gumi-chan on the shoulder. Sheesh, that was way too smooth. Gumi-chan just looked at him with a mixture of disappointment and apathy. Guess this is how normies interact. Physical contact? No big deal.

"In that case…," Gumi-chan said, suddenly turning to me with a scheming gleam in her eye. "Tomozaki-san. Is Mizusawa-san telling the truth? Did anything happen over summer break or during the sports tournament?"

Her gaze pierced into mine. *Wait a second, don't ask me!*

"Uh, n-no, nothing happened."

She stared at me for another few seconds before yelling:

"What?! Something definitely happened! So there is someone, Mizusawa-san!"

"Come on, Fumiya…" Mizusawa pressed his temples and slumped over.

"Hee-hee-hee, looks like you got caught! As long as Tomozaki-san is here, you can't hide the truth from me!"

Gumi-chan grinned, her eyes glittering wickedly. *Sorry, Mizusawa…*

* * *

After work, Mizusawa and I headed to a Gusto diner nearby. Gumi-chan had gotten off before us because she only did short shifts.

Huh, I didn't know there was a Gusto here. It was in the building that used to have a Loft in it, and now there was a Saizeria diner next door. Might as well remember them as a pair. That time when I went to Omiya Station with Kikuchi-san, I hadn't known where to find a place like this, so this was good info to have. A Gusto and a Saizeria. Got it.

"Whew. Good work today."

After the waiter showed us to our seats, Mizusawa put his tote bag, which was black with a red logo on it, down on the sofa.

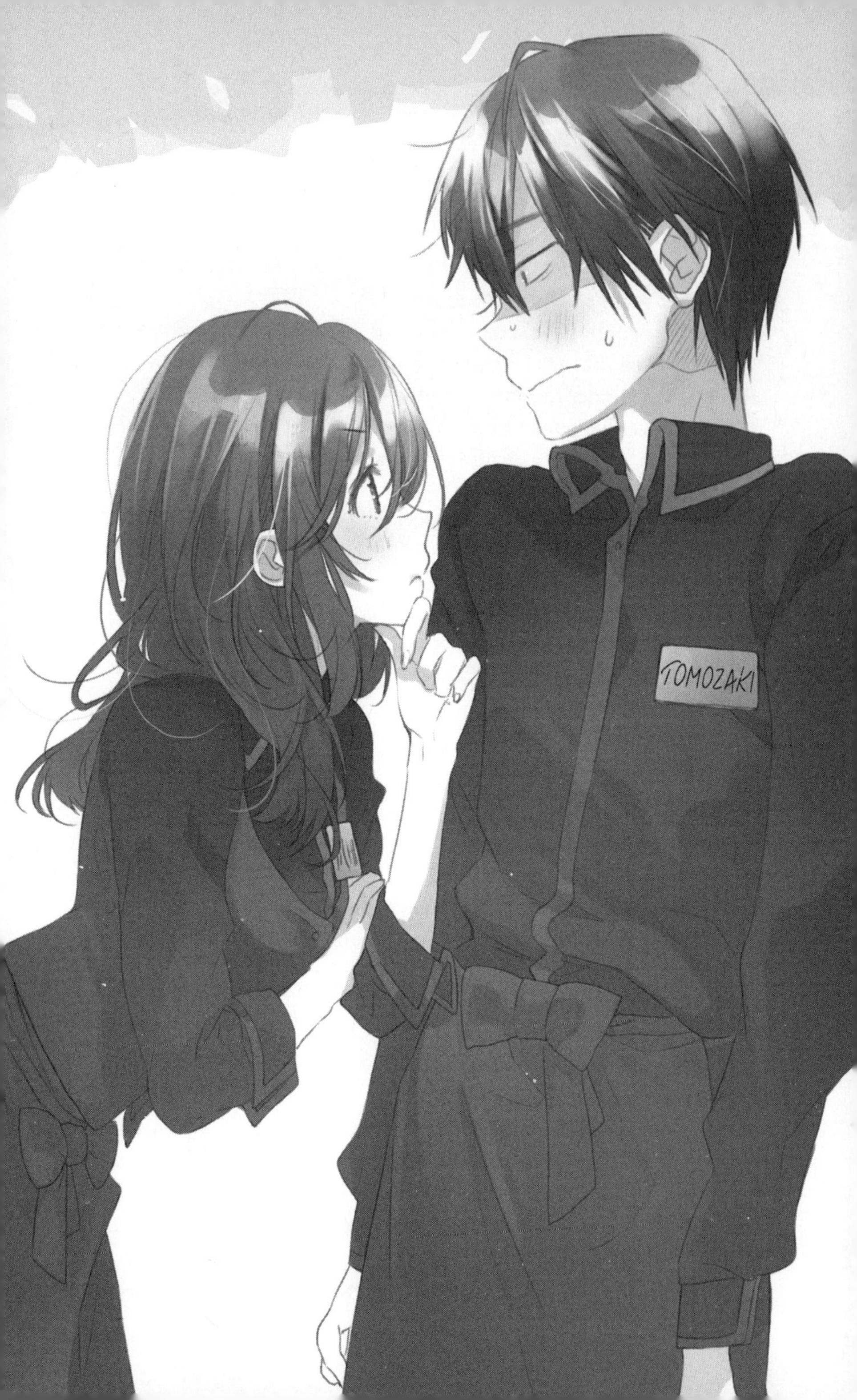
TOMOZAKI

"Yeah, good work."

I put my black backpack down on the seat next to me. Mizusawa glanced over the menu and smiled naturally.

"Figures it got busy as soon as Gumi left. She's got the magic touch."

"Ha-ha, now that you mention it, that's true," I said, chuckling. She really was born under the star of apathy.

"I bet she's either gonna become famous or fall apart completely in the future."

I nodded.

"Yeah, maybe she's suddenly gonna get married to some rich guy. Kind of a scary thought."

"Ha-ha-ha, very true."

I perused the menu as we chatted casually. I was completely used to this kind of conversation by now. When we'd both decided, we called the waiter over and placed our orders. After the waiter left, Mizusawa brought up Tama-chan.

"So what should we do about Tama?"

That's what we'd come here to talk about in the first place.

"Well, you have any ideas?"

"Hmmm…"

He looked down for a second before continuing.

"Right now, I think it's good that she stopped fighting back against Konno. If she'd kept that up, everyone would have felt like they had a get-out-of-jail-free card to attack her."

"A get-out-of-jail-free card?"

He nodded.

"You know how sometimes, people feel like they have the right to beat on someone because that person doesn't know how to act appropriately? Once people have a surface-level excuse for attacking someone, it can deteriorate into bullying overnight."

"A surface-level excuse, huh…?"

I ruminated on that idea and tried to piece together what he was getting at.

"Guess that's pretty much true for everything, right? Like, it's okay to beat up on that person because they did something bad. You can gang up on whoever you want, as long as you use 'justice' as an excuse."

"Even if it barely resembles justice at all," Mizusawa added, laughing cynically.

I mulled over that for a bit and decided it made sense.

"Huh. Can't say that doesn't make sense. It's like cyberbullying, right?"

"Yeah, exactly."

A mob would string someone up in the name of justice for the tiniest infraction. It wasn't even that rare anymore. I should know, since my primary habitat until recently was the Internet. "As long as you have a surface-level excuse, you can pretend attacking someone is 'punishing' them."

Mizusawa smiled wryly at my twist on his interpretation.

"Once that happens, it's impossible to get the situation back under control. If Tama went on fighting back against Konno, they might have started 'punishing' her. So I think it was right for Tama to stop."

"Huh…groups tend to be like that, don't they?"

"So you get what I'm saying?" Mizusawa grinned.

"Basically."

"Like I said, you've grown up lately, Fumiya."

"Who are you, my dad?"

"Ha-ha-ha. Just take the compliment." He laughed jokingly.

He had this kind of softness that made it impossible not to forgive him when he said things in that particular way. *Damn. Special normie techniques.*

I got back to the topic at hand, conscious that in a battle of social skills, he could still kick my ass.

"Anyway, since she stopped resisting, there's no excuse for Konno to attack her now, right?"

"Yeah."

"And if she's able to get along with people better, she should be able to win them over, don't you think?"

"Yeah, but getting along with people is the tough part." Mizusawa deflated a little. He had a point.

"I feel like she broke through her shell a little by starting to become friends with you—but that's not enough, is it?"

Mizusawa shook his head. "Nope. She's not ready to take down the wall between her and everyone else. Hey, wanna go to the bar?"

"What bar?"

"The drink bar?"

"Oh right. Sure."

Of course that's what he meant. Caught me by surprise there for a minute. Mizusawa cackled as I tried to play off my confusion.

"You've changed a lot lately, but you still don't know some really basic stuff."

"Uh…yeah, I guess."

"Anyway, let's go."

Thanks to him, I went to the drink bar with a friend for the first time in my life. I used to go with my family sometimes, but it'd been ages. Talk about a blast from the past.

I filled my glass with soda and dropped in a couple of ice cubes carefully, so they wouldn't splash, before going to my seat. I figured Mizusawa had some smooth method for this kind of thing, too, so I watched him get his drink. He put the ice in before the iced tea. Duh. Obviously. Once again, the difference between us was in the details.

When he got back to our table, he stirred a single flavor packet into his tea and picked up the conversation.

"So we were talking about how Tama can break down the walls between her and other people, right?"

I slurped up some soda with my straw. "Yeah."

"And basically, we just teach her a bunch of ways to do that?" he said calmly, taking a sip of his iced tea. I nodded.

"That's one idea…but I'm not sure."

Mizusawa was caught off guard. "What, you have a better idea?"

He seemed to be expecting something good. Uh-oh. His expectations of me were always high.

"N-no, I'm not really thinking in specific terms…"

"But?"

He looked at me excitedly, increasing the pressure. *Stop it.*

I told him my idea—it wasn't anything special, but it drew on my own past training. "Teaching her like we're in a class is fine, too, but I think it's more important to create a space where she can practice and fail without getting hurt."

Speaking from experience.

"...Huh."

For instance, take the first assignments Hinami gave me, like when I pretended to have a cold so I could talk to Izumi. Even if I screwed it up, Izumi would have blamed it on the cold, so it wouldn't have been a big loss. I'd gained EXP while hedging my bets at the same time.

"So our best option is to create those situations for her."

"Makes sense," Mizusawa murmured in admiration. "Given the stakes, we do need some kind of safety net."

"Right. If she messes up and makes it even worse, we'll just end up further away from her goal."

Since the situation was so delicate, we had to ensure that any mistakes she might make on the assignments we gave her didn't impact the class directly. That was when Mizusawa pitched a suggestion.

"In that case, how about we invite Takei to hang out with us after school on Monday?"

"Takei?"

At first, his suggestion surprised me, but it made sense.

"Oh, so her next assignment would be to make friends with Takei?"

Mizusawa nodded, grinning. "Exactly. With him, she can mess up all she wants."

"Ha-ha...true enough."

The plan was simple and easy to understand. She'd successfully made friends with Mizusawa, so now it was on to Takei. And since Takei was kind of an idiot, failing this would have zero impact on the rest of the class. Yeah, good plan. I wasn't sure if this assignment would be harder or easier than the Mizusawa one, but her risks were mitigated, and she'd be guaranteed a sizable chunk of EXP. Not a bad way to grind.

"Sounds good to me," I said.

"Okay, then I'll get in touch with Takei."

"Thanks."

The conversation was moving right along. Compared with thinking things over by myself, talking about the situation with him produced more ideas, and we could split up the tasks. The outlook was brightening.

As we chatted, our orders arrived. I got the ginger-pork set, and Mizusawa got the mixed-grill set with rice. I took a bite and brought up a new issue.

"I wonder how Takei and Tama-chan will get along."

"Yeah, I dunno..."

Takei started in on his mixed grill. It was huge, with a hamburger patty, a sausage, and some sautéed chicken. Mizusawa had a surprisingly big appetite.

"I mean, the reason I asked for your help is that I assumed you'd accept Tama-chan as she was, but Takei... He's not a bad guy, but he's really oblivious. I'm not sure how things will go with him."

"Ha-ha-ha. I feel ya."

He laughed casually, then rested his cheek on one hand and peered at me with interest. "You thought I'd accept her, huh?"

He smiled, like he was very interested to hear my answer. Uh-oh, he'd homed in on that one point. I wasn't sure how to answer, but he always managed to guess my true thoughts, so I didn't try to hide it.

"No, I mean, what I was thinking was, you seem to get a kick out of people who do what they want."

"You're right." He took a bite of his hamburger and waited for me to go on.

"Plus, well...there's the stuff I overheard that one time."

"Ha-ha. You did hear some juicy stuff."

"You were praising people for being idiots. Or for being sincere."

"In other words, people who are like you," he shot back.

"Uh, yeah."

"I had no idea you were listening in."

"I know. I'm sorry..."

"Ha-ha-ha! You don't have to apologize. Anyway, go on."

I paused, a little flustered, and tried to pull my thoughts together. "Well, I figured Tama-chan is sincere in the same way I am."

Mizusawa seemed satisfied by that explanation.

"Gotcha. So you thought I'd get a kick out of her, too."

"Yeah…basically."

In a sense, the reason I'd chosen Mizusawa for her first assignment was because it was…well, Mizusawa. I figured he would accept the most important part of her personality, so he wouldn't hurt her. She'd been hurt so much already—that was the one thing I wanted to avoid.

Mizusawa sighed, his mouth full of rice. "If that's what you're thinking, Takei should be fine, too."

"You think? How come?"

He raised his eyebrows.

"I mean, Takei's that type, too."

"…Oh."

So that's what he meant.

"He's right up there with you and Tama."

That was true. "He does tend to say what he's thinking and live life how he wants."

"Exactly," Mizusawa said, smiling. "I don't think they can clash too much. They're too similar."

"…Yeah, maybe not."

There was no guarantee, but he was probably right.

"Anyway, it's Takei," I said. Mizusawa laughed.

"Ha-ha-ha. Yeah. No need to overthink Takei."

"Right."

Honestly, Takei being Takei was more convincing than his similarity to Tama-chan. Which, let's face it, was very Takei.

"Okay. So Monday after school, right?"

"Okay!"

I'd just about mastered the Izumi-style *okay*. But Mizusawa's next comment caught me off guard.

"We've gotta be careful Shuji doesn't hear about this," he said with a smirk.

"What do you mean?"

He frowned. "I mean what I said… Wait, you don't get it?"

What was that supposed to mean? I ran through the possible reasons why it would be bad for him to find out.

"Uh…you mean because Tama-chan and Nakamura have argued a lot?"

Mizusawa gave a little nod. "Yup. They don't just argue—it's become this deep-rooted thing. It's not a good idea to let him see us supporting Tama."

"Huh…"

"Part of it is just him being stubborn. Gotta keep up appearances and all."

Hinami had said something similar before. Something about Nakamura being touchy.

"He's part of the reason Tama's status is in such bad shape right now. Most of the guys know her as Shuji's enemy, which makes it hard for them to jump in and help. Now that she's Konno's target, too, she's on the bad side of two class bosses."

That surprised me.

"Really? If that's true, then things are worse than I thought."

"Yeah," Mizusawa said, holding up his drink. "I'm taking a pretty big risk helping her like this."

He smiled and took a gulp of his tea. The ice clinked in his glass.

"Huh, I didn't realize that… Thank you. It means a lot."

So he'd offered his help despite the messy situation. This guy was too good to be true—handsome, good-hearted, and apparently, devoid of any weakness.

"Ha-ha-ha. At your service."

He smiled breezily. Against this perfect specimen of manhood, I was nothing.

"…You're amazing."

"Where'd that come from?"

He smiled wider, looking amused by my honesty.

"I don't know, it's just… You can do anything, but you're never mean about it. I'm kinda blown away by how good of a person you are."

Delivering the compliment so directly was a little embarrassing, but he really was saving our butts this time. He looked at me with a calmer expression than before.

"That's not true."

"…What?"

His expression was surprisingly forceful. He drew back a little, like he was slowly aiming an arrow at the center of his target.

"I don't do everything out of the goodness of my heart." He wore a teasing expression, but there was a sharpness to his eyes. "You'd be surprised by how much of a schemer I can be."

"R-really?"

I was thrown off-balance by the combination of his intimidating aura and friendly grin. He nodded and flicked the edge of his glass with his fingernail. The soft little *ting* rang high and cool.

"I mean, take the reason I stopped by the classroom after school the other day. I thought you and Tama might be there...with Aoi."

"...Oh."

He kept talking as I reacted.

"I'm just another guy who's doing what he wants."

He glanced down standoffishly. His long eyelashes hid his irises.

"Y-you are?" I said, flustered. He slowly raised his eyes to meet mine. His expression had grown cocky. Then, as if he was talking about nothing important at all, he went on.

"After all, a certain someone taught me that it was best to go straight for it."

Now his smile was powerful. He was looking directly at me.

"...Oh right."

I nodded. He was aloof and solemn in a way that was somehow different from usual.

So he'd thought Hinami would be there. Something about the way he said it was hard to connect with the ever-cool-and-collected Mizusawa that I knew.

* * *

The weekend ended, Monday morning rolled around, and my meeting with Hinami was more awkward than ever.

"...This isn't really the time for a new assignment, is it?" Hinami muttered, fiddling restlessly with the ends of her hair.

"No... Before I can even consider one, I want to do something about Tama-chan's situation."

She stared at me. "...Well, what you're doing may go against what I believe, but I don't have the right to stop you."

She sounded resigned and vaguely frustrated.

"You mean about changing Tama-chan?"

She nodded. "If that's what she wants, and you want to help her, I can't say anything. All I can do is work on my own plans. Agreed?"

"Hinami...?"

Her quiet tone was typical Hinami, but rather than reflecting her usual calm, it seemed like an attempt to suppress her emotions. Her words, too, sounded more like they were intended to convince herself than me.

"I'm fine. The most important thing is not to lose the war."

"Hinami, I don't really understand..."

She nodded to herself and looked straight at me.

"Right. Let's suspend our morning meetings for now. You can't very well start a new assignment at this point, and it wouldn't be right to give you one you might fail at while you and Hanabi are involved in something. If we can't do anything productive, we should at least use this time for something else."

"...Okay."

She was kinda bouncing from thought to thought, but I at least understood she wanted to stop meeting every morning, so I nodded.

"We'll pick things up again when the situation with Hanabi has clearly improved. I guess I'll be in touch then?"

"Sure...but..." I looked her in the eye. "Are you sure you're okay?"

She stared at me for a moment before answering.

"...What do you mean?"

She genuinely seemed like she didn't understand—but I couldn't say for sure. It could have been an act, or it could have been real.

"It's just...you've been acting strange lately."

"Wouldn't anyone be upset if their friend was going through a rough patch?"

"...Okay. If that's all it is," I said, unsatisfied.

Hinami quietly stood up. "It is. Well, see you later."

"...Yeah, see you around."

I didn't have any more words or strategies to keep her there, so our morning meeting ended with an awkward silence.

* * *

Konno's harassment continued as usual that day.

During every break, she kicked Tama-chan's desk and said mean things about her. Nevertheless, Tama-chan resisted fighting back. The hateful atmosphere didn't get any better, but she managed to hold the line and prevent it from growing.

More than that, though, the thing that stuck out the most that day was Hinami's strange behavior. Last week, she'd spent all her breaks talking to Izumi and Nakamura, but this week, she switched to talking to one of the girls in Konno's group—I think her name was Akiyama. Hinami was openly talking to her all the time; I'd never seen her act like this before.

I didn't have a grasp on the whole picture, but she was obviously planning something. I wanted to believe she wouldn't do anything to put me at a disadvantage, since we both wanted to help Tama-chan—but she'd made it clear in our morning meeting that our strategies were completely opposed to each other. My guess was that she was working on a plan to keep Tama-chan where she was.

I'd never seen her looking so down before. I felt justified in worrying about her a little, like a student might worry about his teacher. Just a little, of course.

…That's why I decided to do some reconnaissance. She wouldn't have told me her strategy even if I asked, so I took another approach.

"…Izumi?"

As soon as fifth period ended and break began, I turned toward Izumi's desk. I figured Hinami wouldn't notice if I did it now, and I'd be able to talk to Izumi quickly and naturally. I had a massive geographical advantage, so I was on easy mode. Nanashi always uses his advantages shamelessly.

"Huh? What?"

Izumi turned to me with a blank look. As usual, she had all her makeup and accessories on, but her eyes were round and friendly. I'm guessing her tired expression had to do with the recent drama.

"I wanted to ask you something…about Hinami."

"What about Aoi?"

Last week, Hinami had clearly been focusing her attention on Izumi and Nakamura. Even considering she was friends with both of them, the timing and obvious increase in contact suggested she was laying the groundwork for something. Her chats with Akiyama were probably an extension of the same strategy. First, she'd made preparations with Izumi and Nakamura, and now she was reaping the results of some sort with Akiyama. I didn't know the concrete details, but everything seemed connected. We're talking about NO NAME, after all.

"You were talking to Hinami a lot last week, right?"

Izumi widened her eyes even more. *Okay, that was a weird question.*

"Huh? I mean, yeah, I was talking to her..."

She looked a little suspicious. *S-stop looking at me with those eyes. I don't have the defense for this.* I may have gained some skills lately, but my armor is still made of paper.

"It's just...well, things being what they are, I was wondering if she mentioned anything different from usual. Something about Tama-chan or Konno."

"Oh..." Izumi sank into thought. "Things are really rough right now, huh?" she said.

"...Yeah."

"I don't know if this is *different* from usual, but...she asked if I could hang out less with Shuji for a while."

"...Really?"

Izumi nodded. "There's not much else I can do. I asked Aoi for ideas, and she said that was something she wanted me to do."

"Oh, got it."

"She thought that might improve Erika's mood a little."

The logic made sense. Even if Erika already knew the two of them were dating, seeing them together all the time might be adding to her stress.

"I see. She could have a point."

"Yeah. I told her I'd try. I'd been keeping an eye on Erika's mood, and I wanted to help out. Shuji was kind of annoyed about it, but he went along with the plan."

Izumi giggled. I smiled, too, imagining their conversation. So he'd gotten annoyed. I'm sure it was partly because he just doesn't like being told what to do, but it was funny that he'd been grumpy about not getting to spend as much time with Izumi. And typical that he'd agreed to do it instead of telling her directly that he wasn't happy about it.

"I've been knitting something to cheer him up," Izumi announced proudly.

"Y-you think that will cheer Nakamura up?"

"Y-yeah. Maybe I'm being silly...but I've always wanted to knit something for a boyfriend..."

Her voice was getting softer and softer; she sounded super embarrassed to say the word *boyfriend*. *Oh boy. Izumi, you shouldn't leave yourself so open, especially now that I'm familiar with the art of teasing.*

"...Come on, don't say it if you're just gonna get embarrassed!" I said, hoping to ease the tension. Izumi blushed.

"I'm not embarrassed!"

"Oh, really?"

I smiled wryly. Izumi changed the subject.

"Shut up! Anyway, we were talking about Aoi!" she said, contorting her expression. Her facial muscles were well trained.

"Oh right. Did she say anything else?"

Izumi pursed her lips, thinking.

"...That was the only unusual thing she said."

"Okay... So she didn't seem any different from usual to you?"

Huh. So Hinami had been talking to Izumi and Nakamura in order to reduce the stress on Konno. Her goal was probably to prevent the situation from getting any worse. Now that the groundwork had been laid, she was working on something with Akiyama. I still didn't have a clear idea of what she was up to.

"No. I wanted to do something myself, but it's tough because I can't talk to Erika about the situation directly..."

"Yeah...that's true..."

This whole string of events likely started because Konno was upset that Izumi and Nakamura were dating. That made it harder for Izumi to do anything about it than it was for me, Hinami, or Mizusawa, since she was part of the original cause.

"What, are you doing recon again?" Izumi rolled her eyes and smiled. Well, I had started asking some sudden, weird questions when I was trying to motivate Konno, and now I was doing it again.

"Yeah, kind of. Everything's been awkward lately, and Hinami has been acting weird," I said vaguely. Izumi nodded twice.

"I did notice that Aoi has been kinda...tense."

"You did?" I'll admit I was surprised to hear her echoing my own thoughts.

"Yeah. I was thinking all this must even be getting to her..."

"...It could be."

I nodded back, hoping Izumi wouldn't catch my surprise. I knew Hinami's true nature and some of her real feelings, so of course I'd notice her unusual behavior, but this must be the first time someone else had caught a glimpse of her exhaustion. On the other hand, she could be putting on another act—this was an unusual situation, after all, so maybe she was adjusting to match.

"That's why I wanted to ask around about what she's been up to," I explained.

Izumi seemed to be puzzling through something and seriously considered what I said. "Huh. Yeah, I can see your point... Let's see, did she say anything else?"

She was now racking her brain for additional memories. She pressed one hand to her head and squeezed her eyes shut. I could practically hear her mental gears turning. If she kept this up, I wouldn't be surprised to see a spring pop loose.

"Izu—"

"Oh!" she blurted out. "She asked me not to see him on weekends, either, and I remember thinking that was strange."

"Weekends, too?"

She nodded.

"She said it was because we might run into Erika. But that's kinda extreme for her, so I thought she must really be desperate or something..."

"Huh..."

Saitama high schoolers didn't have many places to go out to, so I could understand why she mentioned the weekends. Still, that was toeing the line. Usually, the only person she pushed that hard was me. At the same time, it fit into her scheme to take pressure off Konno. And Hinami was the only one who currently knew what the ultimate aim of that scheme was.

"That is weird now that you mention it."

"Right? She must be running out of options…"

"Could be."

I nodded. I might not know what she was up to, but I definitely sensed her desperation. Izumi peered at me solemnly, then finally seemed to make her mind up about something.

"Well, since there's not much I can do right now…I'll try to keep an eye on Aoi."

"…Ah, okay."

When we were dealing with the Hirabayashi issue, she'd talked to Hirabayashi-san during breaks, providing emotional support. This time, Mimimi and Hinami were filling that role for Tama-chan. Even though Izumi couldn't do much, she'd made up her mind to try to support the usually invincible Hinami from the shadows. That was classic Izumi: flexible but strong.

"Thanks, Izumi. You've been a big help."

"Really? Glad to hear it!"

She waved good-bye cheerfully and headed over to Konno's group.

* * *

That afternoon, Tama-chan, Mizusawa, and I met up first and waited for Takei. Apparently, soccer practice was running long, and he was going to come when it was done.

"So today, we were thinking you could break down some more walls by becoming friends with Takei."

"Takei…," Tama-chan muttered nervously.

Mizusawa smiled gently, probably guessing how she felt.

"Don't worry; he's dumb as a brick. You don't have to get too nervous. Plus, you've got quite a bit in common with him."

"What are you talking about?! I'm not like him!"

She frowned in horror, rejecting Mizusawa's suggestion sharply. Poor Takei. Okay, my turn to jump in.

"Actually, I think you are."

"Not you, too, Tomozaki!"

Mizusawa enlightened the flustered Tama-chan.

"You really are. Both of you always do exactly what you're thinking. You're totally honest, all the time."

"Oh...," Tama-chan said, looking down pensively. "I can see that." She gave Mizusawa a very disgruntled look.

She had to accept what he was saying, but I could tell she didn't want to. I decided to tease her a little. Taking a page from the master himself standing next to me, I tried to sound as jokey as possible.

"Geez, you really hate being compared to Takei, huh?"

"Uh, I mean...it's Takei," she said, like it was self-explanatory. Mizusawa and I looked at each other and laughed.

"What can we say?" Mizusawa said.

"Anyway, that means he's like Tomozaki, too!" Tama-chan said.

"Guilty as charged," I joked.

"Yeah! You're like us! Just like us!" she shot back, like she was clinging to a sliver of hope. Mizusawa laughed.

"Why are you so desperate not to be the only one?"

"Why *wouldn't* I be?"

As we all joked around about Takei, a doubt occurred to me. It had crossed my mind when I talked to Tama-chan, and it had to do with our strategy moving forward. She and I hadn't been able to figure it out on our own.

"Um, Mizusawa?"

"What's up?"

I decided to tell him my concern. Maybe we'd find a new perspective if the three of us talked about it. Over the past couple days, I'd gained a sense of how important it was to deepen my understanding of a problem by talking it through.

"You were saying that Tama-chan and Takei are similar, and that I am, too."

"Yeah," Mizusawa said, nodding.

"Takei has always been a guy everyone knows and likes, and lately, I've been having normal conversations with Nakamura and stuff. But Tama-chan always seems to have a hard time."

"Uh-huh."

"I wonder what the main reason for that is."

Takei, Tama-chan, and I all tended to say exactly what we were thinking. And yet, he was the beloved class moron, she was an outsider who
couldn't read the mood and fit in, and I was a loser who'd only recently
started being less of a loser. Why was that? I couldn't figure out what
brought on that difference.

Even if my sketchy aura was to blame for the fact that I wasn't as popular as Takei, Tama-chan's face, posture, and vocal expression were all those
of a perfect normie. There wasn't much difference between her and Takei
in terms of latent ability. Granted, she had a tendency to put up walls
between herself and other people, but one of the main reasons she'd done
so with Nakamura and his buddies was that Nakamura didn't enjoy her
Takei-like habit of speaking her mind, and they'd argued a lot as a result.

In Takei's case, that trait worked in his favor, but in Tama-chan's case,
it didn't. What was the difference? I couldn't figure it out. But whatever
the underlying cause was, it could become a bridge connecting Tama-chan
to the rest of the class.

Mizusawa sighed in agreement. "I do think that's important. You're
pretty sharp sometimes, Fumiya."

"I—I am?" I stuttered, a little embarrassed by Mizusawa's straightforward compliment. If I were a girl, I'd probably be swooning.

"But there are tons of differences, like how you guys talk. And whether
people are used to you."

"Oh...true."

I thought about what he'd said. The two examples he gave matched
what I'd experienced and observed myself. As far as the first one went, I
paid attention to tone on a daily basis, so Mizusawa's observations fit with
mine. Takei had that strangely cheerful way of speaking without being
mean at all—on that front, he was on Mizusawa's or Hinami's level. But
the part about people being used to him resonated even more.

"That last point really is important."

"So that rings true, huh?"

He gave me that expectant look again. I decided to try explaining my
thoughts. Exchanging opinions is an important skill, after all.

"Okay, take the day we were deciding on what to play in the sports
tournament. I had a thought."

"Oh?"

"Yeah," I said, replaying the scene in my mind. "Takei was one of the class captains, but he was just saying what he wanted. He was like, *Nooo, I wanted soccer!* Everyone knew what he was doing, but they all just rolled with it. Just Takei being ridiculous."

"Ha-ha-ha. That's Takei for you." Mizusawa smiled.

"...But with Tama-chan, it was a little different."

Tama-chan looked at me questioningly. "What do you mean?"

"Remember when you suggested the girls choose volleyball? And when you had to give a reason, you just said...*'Because I want to play volleyball.'*"

"Oh yeah, she did say that! Good memory, Fumiya!"

"Thanks." Back then, I was laser-focused on observing the class.

"Yeah, I remember," Tama-chan said.

"Right. But when you said that..." I paused in thought.

"Yeah?" Mizusawa said, nudging me along. Tama-chan was waiting silently for me to continue. I looked from one to the other, pulled my thoughts together, and went on.

"...you were basically saying the same thing as Takei."

It was like a light bulb had just gone on for Mizusawa. "You're right! Both of them were just giving their opinion, with Takei for soccer and Tama for volleyball."

"Exactly!"

As usual, Mizusawa caught on quick. Actually, I felt like he'd leaped past me and was waiting for me to catch up. He cackled and glanced at Tama-chan.

"Like I said, two peas in a pod."

"Shut up!"

Mizusawa didn't miss a beat in teasing Tama-chan, but she was right there with her comeback. And there I was, just watching their high-speed conversation. Huh. Tama-chan did have major potential. It was hard for me to keep up and get my thoughts out at the same time. I did a mental reset and kept talking.

"So they basically said the same thing…but when Tama-chan said it, the mood got a little weird."

Tama-chan nodded. "Yeah, I remember that. Minmi came to my rescue."

"Oh yeah," Mizusawa said.

Once they'd both agreed, I went on.

"Tone probably had something to do with it…but I think it was more than that. I think it was the fact that everyone accepts Takei's character."

Mizusawa nodded enthusiastically. "You've got a point there, for sure."

"Y-you think so?"

I felt an unexpected wave of relief at getting Mizusawa's stamp of approval.

"Yeah, I had a similar thought myself," he said, as if he just remembered something. Dang, this conversation was going really well.

"Oh yeah?"

"All right, so…" He paused self-importantly, successfully pulling me in. Tama-chan was staring at him intently, too. Conversational theatrics really were his strength, and he could do it so well because of his self-confidence. With both of us watching, he waited a good while before continuing. "What's more important than anything else…is charm."

He looked extremely sure of himself.

"Um, charm?"

I kind of got his point, but not entirely. I waited patiently for him to explain.

"I mean, there's something about Takei that's impossible to hate, right? That just kinda charms you? That's what people expect of his character."

"Yeah, I get that."

"But with Tama, her aura is more sullen. She's not gonna win you over easily. In the end, it's all about charm. And I'm not talking about cuteness or looks."

I nodded.

"Yeah, 'cute' isn't a word I would use for him," I joked.

"Ha-ha-ha. Very true."

We both laughed.

"I'm basically following you…but I'm not good at that stuff," Tama-chan said. She looked anxious, probably because we were pointing out shortcomings she was already aware of. "How am I supposed to get more charm?" she asked.

It was a simple question, but a tough problem. Even though the word *charm* sounds straightforward, it's actually very abstract. You could lose a lot of sleep trying to pin it down in concrete terms. Mizusawa didn't seem disturbed, however.

"That's the question. I've thought about it a lot."

"And?" Tama-chan asked. Mizusawa nodded, cool and collected as always.

"I think charm is all about…consistent vulnerability."

"Vulnerability?" I asked.

"Yup," Mizusawa said casually, nodding. "Look, right in our circle of friends, we've got the world's best actress. She's constantly recreating herself, right?"

"R-right."

It made me nervous when Mizusawa hinted at Hinami's behind-the-scenes self. We couldn't just *tell* Tama-chan about that.

"You mean Aoi?"

"Bingo!"

Guess I was worried for nothing—Tama-chan saw it herself.

"Aoi's who I mean," Mizusawa continued.

"Uh, Mizusawa…"

"She's incredible," Tama-chan added.

"Uh-huh…"

In the end, we didn't delve into what he meant. Guess I overreacted? Just because he said she re-created herself didn't inherently imply she could cut people to ribbons with her words.

"Aoi can do anything. She propels herself forward. Ordinarily, people like that are easy to hate, right? But she's got that charm, so everyone loves her anyway."

"Yeah, that's true."

I regained my calm. Leaving aside the question of who she really was, her onstage self was exactly like Mizusawa said. She was perfect but charming, too, which only added to the sense of perfection she had. Tama-chan nodded.

"That description does fit Aoi well," she said.

Seeing we were both convinced, Mizusawa continued.

"I've thought about why that is, and the conclusion I reached...is that she does a good job of consistently making herself vulnerable."

"Um, does she really?" I asked.

Mizusawa did another one of those dramatic pauses. "For instance, there's her extreme love of cheese."

"Ah."

I was starting to understand.

"She doesn't normally show her desires or weaknesses, but when it comes to cheese, she makes a point of it, just a little. She innocently lets her desire show a bit, and that creates an obvious vulnerability."

As I recalled all the cheese incidents, I realized that she definitely did appear extremely vulnerable on that front.

"Yeah, it's like you can see her heart at those moments."

Mizusawa smiled.

"And since the cheese thing is so consistent, people accept it as part of her character. Now every time she talks about cheese, the people she's with are like, *there she goes again*, right? I think that sense of *there she goes again* is a sign that people accept and like her character."

"...Interesting."

His argument was fairly convincing—especially given that Hinami was putting it into practice in an easy-to-grasp way. It would be like her to analyze how people engender charm and implement her conclusions. When it came to cheese, my guess was that she honestly liked it to start with, but she played it up a little for maximum effect.

As I was silently admiring Mizusawa's insight, Tama-chan asked him a question in a fascinated tone.

"Wow, Mizusawa, do you always think that hard about stuff?"

"Huh? Well, Sometimes, I guess. Not every day. Probably not *tama*rrow."

"Oh, come on, I'm so tired of that!"

"Whoops, you got me."

They shared a laugh. It was good to see them getting along so well.

I had a guess as to why Mizusawa might be so interested in this particular topic. Or maybe I was jumping to conclusions—but had he reflected on this question so deeply because he liked her? I did feel like he was analyzing a kind of battle strategy for her, though. As I was thinking this over, Mizusawa kept talking.

"Getting back to my original point—Takei has tons of weaknesses, right?"

"Huh? Oh yeah, you're right."

He startled me out of my thoughts as they started to veer off in a strange direction, so my answer came across as a little surprised. But his point did make sense. If you wanted to understand this "consistent vulnerability" concept, look no further than Takei. They say 70 percent of the human body is made up of water, and in Takei's case, the remaining 30 percent was vulnerability. And because people saw that as the "typical Takei," it drew them into liking him. Huh, interesting.

"But you think Aoi does that intentionally?" Tama-chan asked, tilting her head.

My heart skipped a beat again. As I was wondering how to cover for her, Mizusawa jumped in.

"I'm not sure. But either way, it's a good lesson to learn from."

He glanced at me and smiled conspiratorially.

"Y-yeah." I nodded with feigned calm. I was fairly sure Mizusawa had not only figured out Hinami's behind-the-scenes character but also knew that I knew, which was why he was helping to keep it hidden from Tama-chan. Wow, he's good. *Let me warn you, man—her real personality is fifty times more extreme than you've ever imagined. Even I haven't seen the full extent of it yet.*

Tama-chan lowered her eyes. "Vulnerability, huh...?" she mumbled, frowning.

"Right. And you, Tama, have almost none of that, no?"

"Yeah...I guess."

She nodded. I agreed with Mizusawa's point. Behind her petite appearance, she was unshakably solid. She was always with Mimimi, but Mimimi was the silly one letting down her guard, while Tama-chan's role was to poke fun when she did.

"What I'm saying is, if you create some easy-to-see vulnerabilities and get everyone used to them, you can win people over. You're already petite, and your nickname is a popular name for cats. You're brimming with potential. It's all a question of how you make use of it."

That did seem like a good strategy for resolving the problem.

"Seems worth trying," I said, turning to Tama-chan. She looked back and forth between the two of us. Her expression was brave, with a hint of fear and a whole lot of will to fight.

"Yeah. I'll give it a try," she replied decisively. She'd taken one more step forward. Little by little, she was making the choices she needed to in order to change. Mizusawa smiled gently at her.

"Great. Now, on to the special training."

"Right," I said with a relieved smile. "So how *do* you create vulnerabilities?"

Mizusawa put his hand to his chin.

"Well...there's lots of ways."

Suddenly, we heard footsteps clattering down the hallway. Mizusawa grinned.

"And if you want specifics..."

"Sorry, guys!! Practice ran late!"

Takei burst into the classroom and immediately banged his leg on the corner of a desk near the door.

"Owwwww!!" he cried out. Mizusawa rolled his eyes, smiled, and thumped Takei on the back as he doubled over in pain.

"And if you want specifics—your teacher has arrived."

"Although, he might be an unwilling one," he added to his cocky announcement.

"Hey, what are you talking about?!"

Takei was left out of the loop, but he made zero attempt to hide that fact. *There he goes again.* Wide-open.

"He *is* perfect for the role."

"What?! What am I perfect for?!"

We all ignored his excited question, and with that, Tama-chan's charm school began.

3

Villagers have their own way of life

"Are you okay, Tama?! Sorry I haven't been able to help you at all!"

"Oh, it's fine. Thanks, though."

"I want to stop her, but I'm not that brave!"

"Ah-ha-ha. Yeah, Konno is pretty scary."

"She sure is!"

A couple of minutes had passed since Takei arrived in the classroom. Mizusawa and I had asked Tama-chan and him to have a one-on-one conversation, hoping to kill two birds with one stone: we wanted her to learn the secrets of charm and practice breaking the ice. We were watching silently from the sidelines.

The situation was totally unnatural, but Takei had unquestioningly accepted Mizusawa's request to encourage Tama-chan with his natural cheer, and things were rolling along smoothly so far. *Nice work, Takei. You're so easy to control.*

By the way, I'd also asked Tama-chan to record the conversation using the recorder I'd lent her so she could listen to it afterward. I wanted her to objectively compare her tone with Takei's to see how they were different.

"Once Erika gets mad, she stays mad forever! I don't think you did anything wrong!"

"You don't? Thanks, Takei."

"No, don't thank me! I should be saying sorry!"

"Ah-ha-ha. Okay."

Maybe it was their similar natures, or maybe it was the power of Takei's sheer obliviousness, but as far as I could tell, the conversation wasn't going too badly. As for what Mizusawa and I were up to, well, we were searching for hints—how Takei left himself vulnerable and how Tama-chan could apply the same techniques.

"What do you think, Fumiya?" Mizusawa said, looking toward me. From this angle, his nose and chin looked flawless, perfectly offsetting his sidelong glance. He was at least 30 percent more handsome than usual. On top of that, his hair looked like he could be a model in one of those magazines at the hair salon. Damn, his stats were off the charts. I tried not to compare myself as I answered him. Stay positive! Self-confidence is key!

"To me, it seems like his charm is coming from how he doesn't hide his true feelings."

"That jumped out at me, too."

"But Tama-chan does the same thing…"

"Yeah. Maybe the difference is how goofy he is about it?"

By talking about what we noticed, we were hoping to tackle the problem by finding a new angle that we wouldn't be able to see alone. Mizusawa was smart, and he had a normie perspective, which made him an incredible asset to this project. As for me, I felt fairly confident in my analytical ability. Together, we should be able to come up with a strategy to break the current stalemate. I was doing my best to clearly convey each step in my thought process.

"They do talk in totally different ways… I guess the simplest idea would be for Tama-chan to copy the way Takei speaks so she can create some vulnerability. I bet she could mimic him just fine if she put her mind to it."

I thought back to the tone exercise we'd done on the first day of training, where I'd had her talk only using vowels. I had no doubts that she could produce a tone that was just as cheerful as his, based on what I'd observed of him.

"True, stealing directly from him could work, as long as she can make it natural. If she suddenly started speaking like Takei, everyone would wonder if something was wrong with her. She'd have to keep it within reasonable limits."

"Very true."

I almost burst out laughing as I imagined her dialing the silliness all the way up, but I managed to tell Mizusawa I agreed with him. People would definitely worry if she started pointing at the ceiling and yelling *Yeah, dude!* Mizusawa smiled and looked back at Tama-chan and Takei.

"So we'll ask her to do that...and what else?"

"Hmm..."

We sank into silence and went back to observing their conversation.

"You've got people on your side!"

"I know. And now I know you're one of them. That's a relief."

"Right?! Mika was saying the other day that she thought Erika was going too far!"

"Um, Mika?"

"You know, Mika! Erika's friend, Mika Akiyama?"

"Oh, Akiyama-san. The one with the short hair?"

"Yeah, her! So it's not like everyone is against you!"

While I was still analyzing the exchange, I was a little surprised by what Takei had said. One of Erika's friends had started saying she was going too far? I glanced at Mizusawa.

"Akiyama... She's one of Konno's groupies, right?"

I was sure she was the girl Hinami had been talking to this week.

"Yeah," Mizusawa said with a grin. "But 'groupie' is a pretty direct way of describing her."

"Oh...yeah, guess it is."

That's how I'd always thought of Konno's crew when it came to this issue—Hinami's, too—so it kind of slipped out. *Groupie* was my perspective; from within the clique, she was just another member. Guess I was a little sloppy in my characterization.

"So anyway, she's one of her groupies. You could also consider her a friend," I said.

"Right. And?" Mizusawa cackled. I felt embarrassed, but I soldiered on.

"Does this Akiyama girl dislike Konno?"

Mizusawa thought for a second.

"It's not exactly dislike...but Erika is harder on Mika than she is on anyone else in the group."

"How so?"

"You've seen it before, right? How hierarchies form? In that group, Erika's at the top, and everyone else watches her reactions."

"It does seem like that."

I could tell that much, even from the outside.

"Erika always dumps the annoying stuff on Mika...so sometimes, Mika complains behind her back."

"Gotcha..."

"My guess is that she's the one who actually has to go and break the pencil leads and pens."

"Really?"

"Yeah. So the friendship is a little complicated."

I could see his point. Konno was the obvious autocrat in her group, so it would be natural for the other members to obey her in public but complain about her in private. And it was easy to imagine the weakest member of the group being assigned the dirty work and going along with it, not having much of a choice. It was a little suspicious that Hinami was making contact with this particular member of the group. But if what Mizusawa said was true, I saw a possible opportunity for a breakthrough.

"Doesn't that mean the longer Konno keeps harassing Tama-chan, the more isolated she'll become in her own group, and the shakier her position in class will be? I mean, she's the one creating all the tension, and no one really liked her to start with."

Mizusawa frowned.

"I don't think that would happen without intervention."

"Really?"

Considering how arrogant she was, a fall from grace seemed entirely possible. I must be missing something here.

"How do I put it...? She has an amazing sense of balance for that kind of stuff. I mean, she's kept her position for this long. She makes sure people don't rebel even if they're tired of her BS. Like with Akiyama. She's usually hard on her, but when they're in a small group together, she's really nice. Stuff like that."

"A sense of balance, huh...?"

"Yeah. Like with Tama, she hasn't done anything really dramatic, right?"

"...Uh-huh."

I'd had the same thought myself.

"You're right. She only does little things that could be seen as a coincidence," I said. "She just does it a lot." Mizusawa nodded.

"My guess is she's purposely stopping short of anything that would make people feel really bad for Tama. And I hate to say it, but Tama didn't exactly fit in to start with. Put the two together, and people's general reaction tends to be *Ugh, she overreacts to everything.*"

I bit my lip, thinking about our class.

"That sounds about right..."

"What I'm saying is, she's a master of class politics."

Politics, huh?

"You mean she's good at knowing the effects she causes?"

"Yeah. It's not like she doesn't think about all this stuff. I mean, part of it is probably instinct, of course."

"Interesting..."

Konno appeared to be acting based on emotion, but Mizusawa didn't think so. To maintain a position at the top of the class, you really would need some sort of ability that the other members of the class lacked. In her case, that was political skill and a sense of balance.

"Which is why you think things won't get better if we leave them alone?"

I could still just say *It's a crappy situation* and call it a day, but it was important for me to get a better grasp on the rules governing that situation. Mizusawa was watching Tama-chan and Takei with narrowed eyes.

"So what do you think about those two?"

"The question is, what's different aside from their way of talking?"

"Exactly."

I started watching them again, too.

"And Yuko was worried about you, too!"

"Who's Yuko?"

"Ueda, Yuko Ueda! She said you didn't do anything wrong!"

"...Huh. Thanks."

Takei was still trying to cheer Tama-chan up. Takei's vulnerability was really obvious in the way he was talking.

Mizusawa and I continued our discussion.

"I think Tama needs to volunteer more of her own thoughts, and she also needs to express more emotion," he commented.

"...Could be," I answered, nodding. But I'd noticed something else about their current conversation, and maybe about their entire exchange so far. There was something else she needed to look out for.

"You know, Mizusawa..."

"What?" He glanced at me.

"I think I figured out another reason Tama doesn't get along with people very well."

"Really?" His eyes were glittering.

"Yeah."

I nodded quietly but confidently. This was more than a hunch—it was intuition. No, it was practically a certainty—because I'd been the exact same way.

I stood up and looked at Tama-chan. "Hey, Tama-chan, can I talk to you for a second?"

She looked at me and walked a couple of steps in my direction.

"Did you figure something out?"

"Yeah," said Mizusawa, "Fumiya seems to have a reason why you're having such a hard time."

"Really?!" Takei yelped. "Ooooh, tell us!"

I ignored his shouting and went on with my explanation. *Sorry, Takei. Hope you can understand why this is important.*

"Well...the reason I know this is because I used to be the same way myself."

I've spent so many years looking out at a world without color.

"So...what?"

And I'm fairly sure this is way more important than skills or techniques when it comes to interacting with other people.

"Tama-chan..."

I recalled my old frame of mind.

"You're not very interested in the other kids in our class, are you?"

She shut her mouth and stared up at me in surprise. Mizusawa stared at me, too, blinking.

"Fumiya, what's that me—?"

"You're right. Honestly, I'm not," she said, interrupting Mizusawa's question. He looked even more confused. But I was right.

"…Thought so."

I let out a breath. The same thing had happened several times in this conversation with Takei. He'd brought up someone's first name, and Tama-chan hadn't known whom he was talking about.

"And that's what you think is key?" Mizusawa stared at me searchingly, like he guessed what I was thinking. I kept talking, partly so he could decide if he agreed, and partly to get new ideas from him.

"Well, speaking from experience, yeah."

"Huh."

I thought back to what happened during summer vacation.

"As Tama-chan and Mizusawa already know, I've been doing a bunch of stuff to change myself lately. Practicing how I talk and being more expressive and things like that."

"Uh-huh."

Tama-chan was looking me straight in the eye as she listened. Takei was just staring with his mouth open; we'd left him in the dust a while ago.

"But before I started, I wasn't interested in any of that. I thought life was like a broken game, so trying to get better at it was pointless. I assumed the normies who were super into it were all stupid, even though I didn't have a good reason to believe that."

"Ha-ha-ha. Really?"

Mizusawa laughed with a mixture of surprise and amusement.

"Yeah. I was super cynical back then."

"Huh. You know, at first, I wouldn't have even noticed if you were absent."

"Oof…"

It was a painful jab, but I kept talking.

"Anyway, since I thought everyone was stupid, I obviously wasn't interested in them. I had no reason to care about what they were doing, so I didn't pay attention to gossip or anything… But something happened that made me want to change, so I decided to start practicing how I spoke and all that."

"And what happened?"

Tama-chan was watching my mouth, like she wanted to catch every word I said.

"Well, I slowly became better at talking to people. And the results from gaining that experience encouraged me to do more."

"Ha-ha-ha. Gotcha. You sound like a gamer."

Mizusawa spoke in a casual tone, but he'd actually hit the nail on the head. What I'd described was exactly what I'd call gamer effort. In other words, trial and error with the intention of advancing toward a goal. Effort made with the controller in your own hands. I was impressed that Mizusawa could understand my mindset and not just his own perspective as a normie. He was something else.

"As my motivation increased, I improved more and became able to talk to more people. I could give my own opinions and ask other people for theirs—and then I realized something."

I thought about all the normies I'd interacted with and all the nameless students I'd watched from the classroom window as they practiced sports.

"All those normies I'd brushed off weren't stupid. They had their own thoughts and worries and goals." I smiled wryly. "...I mean, of course they did."

"True," Tama-chan said. Her eyes wandered uncomfortably for a second.

"Up to that point, I'd been talking to others just to level up, but once I got to know a bunch of different people, well..."

I met Tama-chan's gaze.

"...I started talking to them because I wanted to know what they were thinking."

She stared back at me.

"Once I got interested in other people, I wanted to know specific things about them, and when I asked the questions to find out, it led to a conversation. I started thinking about what I wanted them to know about me, and what else I wanted to talk to them about, and then I'd have something to say."

"...Huh."

Mizusawa crossed his arms and pursed his lips in thought.

"Of course, it's not always easy. Sometimes, I do use topics I've thought up beforehand or other stuff I've practiced," I said in a slightly joking tone.

Mizusawa chuckled. "Ah-ha, I see. And?"

"Well, if Tama-chan wants more people to accept her and wants to make more friends, it's definitely worthwhile to practice surface-level skills like having a more cheerful tone, but that's not the biggest thing."

I thought about how my own state of mind had changed, how color had come into my world.

"I think it's important to take an interest in everyone else and work on accepting them."

When I finished talking, Tama-chan looked down at her hands. After a moment, she clenched them into fists and nodded slightly.

"…Yeah, you could be right. I won't really get along with people I don't care about, will I?"

She looked up at me again, and this time, her face was full of positive determination. Tama-chan was back to her usual self, with her old strength.

Mizusawa unfolded his arms and gave us a calm, gentle look. "You're full of surprises, aren't you, Fumiya?" He was back to normal, too, with his smirks and teasing.

"What's that mean?"

"It's a compliment, so don't worry about it."

"Okay, if you say so…," I said, mystified. Yeah, Mizusawa was always in control.

Suddenly, I glanced at Takei. For some reason, he was looking at me with moist eyes.

"Uh, Takei…?"

"…Dude!! That was some good shit!!"

"Huh?"

He rushed over to me and shook my shoulders. Wait a second! I thought I'd lost him a while back. Or maybe he'd picked up a general sense of what I meant? Either way, it was amazing he'd get teary-eyed over that.

"Oh look, everyone's getting ready to go home."

"Oh yeah, you're right. Should we go?"

"Amazing, Tomozaki!!"

"S-stop it…"

I didn't quite know how to handle Takei's inexplicably emotional reaction. Meanwhile, Hinami and Mimimi finished up their late practice down on the field, and our meeting came to an end. I guess this was just the usual Takei—maybe overenthusiastic, maybe a simple guy, but oddly charming either way.

* * *

"There's even more of you today!"

When Tama-chan, Mizusawa, Takei, and I appeared on the field, Mimimi's surprise was extremely evident. Glad to see she's putting those high-jump skills to good use. Hinami was sitting on the step leading to the team office, smiling sardonically.

Takei jumped on the bandwagon and approached Mimimi, palm raised. "Cheers!"

"Cheers!" she said, giving him a high five. What the heck? When these two get together, it's double the craziness. Hinami and Mimimi were the only ones left on the field because they'd been practicing late, but you'd never have guessed it from the level of excitement.

"Cheers, Aoi!" Takei said.

Hinami's eyes sparkled. "What? Cheese?" she cried theatrically.

Takei burst out laughing. "No, no! You are way too into cheese, Aoi!"

"Ah-ha-ha, whoops. *Cheers,*" she parried with a grown-up smile. A second ago, she'd been wearing a totally different, beguiling persona. What was with the quick-change act? "Anyway, what are you four up to? You came last week, too, right?"

Her tone was soft, but the slower delivery helped draw our eyes to her and give her control of the group. I had a better sense of all this now that I'd been working on tone myself. It was surprisingly hard to speak in that slow, imposing voice when you were the only one talking in a group. You had to have confidence, but Hinami was also able to soften that confidence. The higher my own level got, the more I understood just how much better Hinami was at all this.

I was a little uncomfortable giving my reply.

"We were just talking about what we could do about Tama's situation."

"Oh, you were?"

She nodded solemnly, like she took the situation very seriously—but for a second, she glanced at me. *Uh-oh.* After all, she was totally opposed to us trying to change Tama-chan. Wonder how this would turn out...

Mimimi laughed, maybe trying to cover up the slightly dark mood coming from Hinami. Then she looked back at us.

"Okay, but why is there one more person every time you come?!" she asked intently, her eyes sparkling.

"I guess Team Tomozaki is growing," Mizusawa said, thumping my shoulder. *Team Tomozaki, huh?*

"Wait a second—I didn't know this was my team."

"Of course it is. It was your idea, right?"

"N-no...I mean, I guess."

"Right? We're counting on you, boss."

"U-uh, boss...?"

As I was floundering under this bewildering pressure from Mizusawa, Mimimi gave an impressed sigh next to me.

"That's Tomozaki for ya! Half brain, half boss!"

"Hey, stop giving me extra titles..."

"Yeah, that's Tomozaki for you."

"...Uh..."

As we headed off school grounds, I felt like I was being crushed by Mimimi's weighty title and Hinami's ironic jab. My stomach was starting to hurt...

The six of us, including Hinami and Mimimi, were walking toward the station. As the buzzing of insects filled the air on the country road, Mizusawa sighed and fiddled with his phone.

"Seems like Erika's never gonna get tired of her game."

Once again, that was the topic of conversation. I was on edge trying to figure out how to act with Hinami around.

Mimimi smiled wryly in response to Mizusawa's comment. "Yeah, where does she get the energy for all that?"

"Good question. Maybe she just hates to lose. Or she's insanely stubborn." Mizusawa frowned and stuck his phone in his pocket.

"Yeah… We really have to do something," Hinami said, joining the general flow of the conversation. She bit her lip.

"…Yeah!"

Mimimi's cheerful tone sounded like she was trying to hide her anxiety. Up till now, Mimimi and Tama-chan had avoided talking about Konno when they were together and pretended they were just messing around like usual. But now, probably because Mizusawa and Takei were there, we were all talking about her.

Takei peered at Tama-chan with concern. "Are you okay after all that?! I mean, they broke your pencils and stuff, right?"

"Yeah, they did…"

Tama-chan looked away, as if she was searching for the right words.

"Oh, Tama, I just remembered!" Mimimi yelled loudly. "I wanted to give this to you!"

She opened her backpack and pulled out a plastic bag.

"What's that?" Tama-chan asked. Mimimi opened the bag dramatically and showed it to us. There were about ten packs of mechanical pencil lead inside. Puffing her chest out jokingly, she pulled one out to display it.

"I got these for really cheap in my neighborhood! She can break all the leads she wants, and you'll keep pulling out more! Like you've got a little factory!" She passed the whole bag to Tama-chan.

"But I should pay you back…"

"Don't worry about it! Anyway, you always let me nibble your cheeks. Consider it payment for my snacks!"

"…Really? Thanks, Minmi."

"Uh, payment for your snacks…?" I retorted softly, but my heart was actually warmed by this little scene. These two really do have a one-in-a-million friendship.

"And now…for the main attraction!"

With that, Mimimi pulled out a small, rectangular box. It was a case for pencil lead that was covered in cute decorations. I'm guessing she put the decorations on herself.

"This thing looks cheap, so she won't suspect a thing. If you put the leads in here, you'll be in good shape!"

She stuck the box into Tama-chan's chest pocket. Tama-chan ran her finger over it and sighed appreciatively.

"...Thanks, Minmi. I'll take good care of it."

She smiled softly for a brief moment. Hinami watched the two of them, apparently moved, and then put her hand to her chin.

"You know, if you keep your leads in your pocket, you don't need to fool her, right?"

Mimimi froze for a second, then laughed awkwardly.

"True!" she said. Yup, same old Mimimi.

* * *

We kept walking toward the station.

"What do you think, Aoi?" Tama-chan asked solemnly.

"...Well...," Hinami said, matching her serious expression.

"..."

I watched them nervously. There were six of us in the group. I didn't know this when I was a loner, but when this many people do something together, they don't always talk as one, big group. A lot of times, the group seems to break up into smaller conversations. Currently, those subgroups consisted of Mizusawa, Takei, and Mimimi, then Hinami, Tama-chan, and me. The most nerve-racking breakdown possible.

I was trying to solve the problem by changing Tama-chan, Hinami was trying to solve the problem without changing Tama-chan, and Tama-chan herself was between us now. I had no idea what we were going to talk about. Since this was Hinami, she'd manage to create a conversation that was appropriately serious but not provocative enough to ruffle any feathers.

At least, that was what I was expecting.

Hinami's shoes made a rough, almost shaky sound as they hit the ground.

"Hanabi, do you want to change?"

*   *   *

I gulped and glanced involuntarily at Hinami. She was being so direct. It was like she'd plunged an ice pick into the center of whatever the source of the tension between us was. Her eyes were hesitant and somehow sad.

"...Aoi?" Tama-chan seemed surprised

"Oh, sorry. I've just been wondering!" she said, dialing up the cheer and softening everything.

Tama-chan seemed convinced by the act and responded after a pause.

"Oh, okay... Well..." At first, her words were halting. "Yes, I do want to change."

Then they were suddenly decisive.

Hinami's expression didn't change much, but her eyebrows twitched upward. To me, it was an undeniable sign that Tama-chan's words had pierced her like an arrow.

"Oh..."

She looked down, her eyes so sad that she could hardly hide it any longer. Tama-chan gazed up at her, worried.

"Do you think I shouldn't?"

"...I..."

Hinami hesitated, her voice quavering uncharacteristically and her gaze shifting. There was an uncomfortable pause as she frantically searched for the words to get the conversation back under control. Was it another act? Or was it real? I couldn't tell.

After a few seconds, she continued. "I don't want you to change."

Tama-chan blinked twice in thought. Then she looked deep into Hinami's eyes without a hint of pretense. When she spoke next, she was trying to make sure of something—or at least, get a general sense of something.

"You don't *want* me to change?" Her tone was careful and penetrating. "Not 'you don't think I *should* change'?"

She waited for Hinami's response. I was startled. Tama-chan was right—the phrase wasn't something Hinami would normally say.

"I don't want you to change."

Those weren't the words of someone thinking about the best strategy one should take to solve the problem. In a sense, they disregarded problem-solving altogether for the sake of her personal wish.

"Right," Hinami said. "I don't want to think you made a mistake by facing her head-on."

Her gaze was distant, but her tone was full of definite emotion. She was being harsher than usual and strangely earnest, almost like she was atoning for a time when she wasn't.

"Hinami...?" I whispered. She took a breath, startled. For an instant, her expression was unguarded, but the next moment, her usual mask returned.

"...You're not in the wrong, so I don't want you to change. Of course, I don't have the right to decide that for you. That's just what I want!"

Those were the words of the perfect heroine. Her voice was strong and cheerful, like a single, strong line traced over the shaky one she had drawn a moment ago.

"...I understand. Thanks for worrying about me, Aoi."

Tama-chan smiled gently, accepting Hinami's words at face value.

The final boss had slid her mask back on before I knew it, as if it had never slipped at all. The change was so complete that even I wasn't sure how far the mask went.

"...I know this is tough for you...so try not to overdo it, okay?"

"Okay. But Tomozaki and the others are backing me up, and I do want to see if I can change a little." She turned to me and smiled brightly.

I sensed a gray storm cloud over Hinami, but I tried to take heart in Tama-chan's words and answer her cheerfully.

"Right, let's do this!"

"Yeah. I'm counting on you! Not for much, but still!"

"Remember what we said before about being too honest...?"

Tama-chan laughed.

Hinami widened her eyes and nodded, apparently satisfied. "Huh."

She smiled. Was I imagining things? I felt like a very small but sharp point of sadness lay behind that smile.

Hinami went on talking.

"You really are two of a kind."

There wasn't anything strange about her words—in fact, they were just another part of her perfect-heroine persona. Still, I couldn't help but

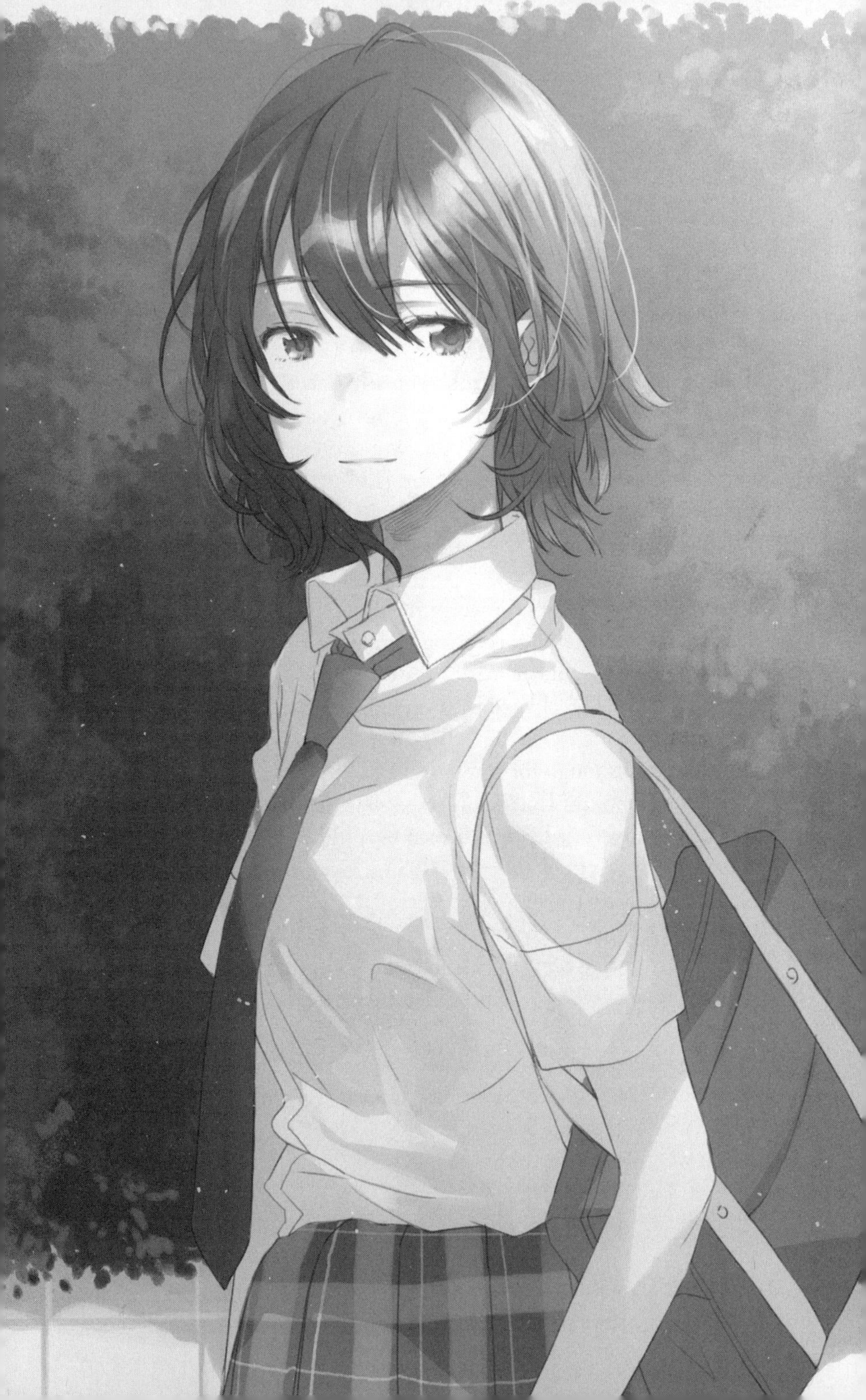

sense such a lack of commitment behind them that it almost felt like despair.

"Anyway, if that's the case, I'm behind you!"

But in no time at all, that vibe vanished so completely that I wondered if it had been nothing more than the product of my own preconceptions. A soft, gentle aura once again surrounded Hinami.

"Oh right! Aoi?"

Mizusawa was calling to her from behind. She dropped back to join his group, and our conversation ended. The prickly discomfort receded, and the sun came out again around us. Still, I felt like what she'd said to Tama-chan and me revealed something inside her. I wondered if she would ever let me near it—if that was even possible.

Maybe even that expression beneath her mask was just another mask, too.

* * *

That night, I was sitting on my bed, my body stiff with nerves, having a staring contest with my phone. The LINE chat app was on the screen. Mizusawa had created a three-person strategy chat group, and we were talking about our plans moving forward. The members were Tama-chan, Mizusawa, and me. As usual, Takei wasn't included because he wouldn't be much use. Sorry, Takei.

I'd advanced enough that this by itself wouldn't have made me nervous. I'd vacillated for less than a minute after the sudden invitation arrived, and a few deep breaths had been enough to calm me down. That wasn't the problem. The problem was the message Mizusawa had sent.

[*Wanna do a conference call around nine?*]

That was a shock to the system.

I was used to in-person conversations, but for some reason, phone calls still made me nervous. A conference call might as well be a one-hit KO. Maybe I would have survived if I had no warning, but since he'd told me the time in advance, there I was, waiting with my heart pounding.

It was currently 9:02 PM. He'd said *around nine,* which meant it shouldn't matter if he was a couple minutes late, but the ambiguity just made my nerves worse. *Hurry up and put me out of my misery.*

And the phone rang.

"Whoa," I said with such good English pronunciation that you'd never guess I was Japanese. Once I'd calmed down a bit, I tapped the JOIN button on the screen. I was already wearing headphones, and a voice reached my ears.

"Hey."

Cool and calm, like the ideal older brother. Mizusawa. Through the headphones, he sounded smug and casual, but also smooth. His voice had a mysterious tone to it that I could never reproduce. Geez. And all he'd said so far was *hey.*

"Hello? Can you hear me?"

That was Tama-chan. Her voice sounded young and cute, but her pronunciation was crystal clear and easy to understand. From the moment she started talking, her words were crisp and distinct. The modulation really reflected her personality.

"Yeah, I can hear you," I said. I didn't know how the two of them felt about hearing my voice through the phone, but based on the many times I'd recorded myself and worked on improving my voice, my guess was that I was cheerful but nothing special. That was my own self-evaluation at this point.

Now that we were all connected, the meeting began.

"What should we talk about first?" Mizusawa said, taking on the leadership role. I decided to bring up something that was on my mind.

"Well, I was wondering…"

"Yeah?"

"Tama-chan, have you tried listening to those voice recordings yet?"

She waited a beat before answering. "Yeah, I did."

"And?" Mizusawa asked.

"Well…I did sound different than I'd imagined. I really noticed the gap between me and Takei," she said pensively.

Mizusawa responded encouragingly. "Oh, that's great. So do you think you can open yourself up like he does?"

"I'm not sure. Wouldn't it be weird if I took it that far?" She sounded a little nervous.

"Yeah, probably," he replied.

"Okay, so that was a bad idea!"

"Ha-ha-ha. All you have to do is keep it subtle enough so that it doesn't sound weird."

"Oh, yeah. I guess that could work."

"Think you can do it?"

"...I'll try."

"Okay."

"Okay," I finally said.

I didn't really know where to jump in on the phone, so I hadn't said anything between my initial question to Tama-chan and that last *okay*. I was psyching myself up to try harder next time, when Mizusawa said my name.

"Fumiya, do you have any advice as a veteran?"

"Uh, a veteran?"

"Yeah. As I recall, you took inspiration from someone else," he teased.

"Oh right."

I heard him cackling on the other end of the line. *Ergh, shit.* That "someone" would be Mizusawa himself. Sometimes, the model you were copying found out what you were up to, so you had to be careful.

"You did, Tomozaki?"

"Uh, kinda. Anyway, you wanted some advice."

I hustled the conversation forward before she could ask who I'd copied. That was too embarrassing to talk about with Mizusawa on the line.

"Yeah. I wanna know if there's anything to watch out for when I'm copying him."

"Ah, gotcha."

"You can't really know until you've done it yourself with this stuff, huh?"

"Yeah, true."

Now that she mentioned it, I realized not many people were familiar with the art of copying someone else's way of talking. In that sense, I guess

I'm a highly valuable resource. Finally, my status as a bottom-tier character had a purpose. Glad to be of service.

I thought back again on that experience—about what I'd been thinking about when I copied Mizusawa's conversation style, and what I'd watched out for.

"Let's see... One thing is, it's fine to go in pretty hard from the get-go. In my case, even when I thought I was doing a great job, I'd listen to the recordings of myself later and realize I was still way too monotonous—stuff like that."

"Huh, really?" Mizusawa said. It was emotionally confusing to have my model responding to my comments, but I went on talking.

"Well, basically. Anyway, start off bold and then see how you did later by listening to the recording. Just do it over and over and you'll be good."

"Got it. Over and over. I'll practice tonight."

Tama-chan was a very earnest student.

"Okay, so today at home, she'll work on fixing her tone. The question is...how to put it into practice starting tomorrow."

"Um, yeah."

I tried to keep up as Mizusawa efficiently moved the conversation forward.

"...After you practice tonight, it might be a good idea for me or Mizusawa to tag along with you tomorrow and watch while you practice some more. If you record yourself practicing during breaks and we give you feedback on what to fix, you should be able to get a lot done in one day."

"Huh. Good idea," Mizusawa commented.

"Yeah, I don't have much time. I'll give it a try."

"Okay then, are we good?"

Just as the plan was coming together, I started to worry about something. "Uh...," I mused.

"Fumiya, what's wrong?"

"Nothing, it's just..." I thought about what Mizusawa had said. "It's just, I'm wondering how much changing your tone will actually create that sense of consistent vulnerability."

"...Yeah, you do have a point there."

It was true she might open herself up a bit by copying Takei's tone and general aura, but it wouldn't be so straightforward or easy-to-understand.

"It might be better to have something really obvious, like the thing Mizusawa pointed out with Hinami and cheese."

"True. If you want people to get used to your character, a classic routine will probably help the most."

"A routine..."

Essentially, it means an immediately recognizable item or characteristic has become iconic for that person. If there's a certain pattern of actions that goes along with that trait, it becomes especially recognizable, and that creates charm. In Tama-chan's case, it would probably have to relate to her nickname or appearance, but it was hard to think of something specific.

"Hmm...I wonder what would work."

I thought about it for a minute, but I had no idea where to even start.

"Well, it's not the kind of thing you can create overnight," Mizusawa said. "I'll give it some thought. You two should do the same."

"Okay, got it," I replied.

"Okay!"

"Well..." Mizusawa started wrapping up the meeting. "Are we good for today? Do either of you want to add anything?"

"...Um..."

I thought it would be a good idea to touch on the problem of her being disinterested in the people around her. But that issue was deeply rooted in her underlying mental stance. A few words on the phone right now wouldn't do much to solve it.

"Never mind, I'm good. For now, let's just agree to meet up tomorrow during breaks, okay?" I said.

"Sounds good. But I usually hang out with Shuji during breaks, so I might not be able to go every time. Is it okay with you two if I just sneak away when I can?"

After all, Nakamura and Tama-chan had their ongoing feud, so Mizusawa wasn't entirely free to act.

"Of course. I'll be the main one shadowing her. I'm just thankful you're helping us out at all. Don't worry about the rest."

"Okay… I appreciate it," Mizusawa said a little timidly.

"Anyway," I said as casually as possible, "I think this plan's got potential!"

"Yeah. If you practice that much, it shouldn't be too hard to improve."

"So everyone on board?"

"One hundred percent."

As Mizusawa and I psyched each other up, Tama-chan chimed in softly.

"…Thanks, guys."

She was thanking us, but something about the way she said it was apologetic or even helpless.

"Of course! No worries!" I said, as dramatic and silly as how I talked during the vowel exercise. It was oddly entertaining to talk that way because it felt so weird. It was perfect for making a fool of myself.

"Ah-ha-ha. Thanks," Tama-chan said with a giggle.

"Yeah, Tama!! You better cheer up!!"

Mizusawa followed my lead with an unmistakably Takei-like form of encouragement.

"Ah-ha-ha. I'm on it!"

"That was a little sample of how to copy Takei."

"Yeah, yeah, thank you."

After we joked around like that for a minute, we wrapped up the meeting.

"All right, guys…if anything changes, get in touch," Mizusawa said.

"Okay, will do."

"Gotcha."

"Okay, later," Mizusawa said.

"Later," Tama-chan echoed.

"L-later," I stuttered.

With that, the group call ended, and there I was, alone again on top of my bed with that loneliness that came after ending a fun phone call.

"But…yeah."

We were moving gradually forward, and a path toward our larger goal had come into sight. This time, I wasn't fighting alone like I always had with *Atafami*—I was heading down that road with friends I could count on. I set my phone down softly next to my pillow, oddly tickled by the idea that I was part of the group.

* * *

The next morning, with no meeting to go to, I got to class earlier than usual and sat at my desk, grappling with the Tama-chan issue.

There were two main questions I was struggling with. One was what specific vulnerability she might be able to create. The other was how to deal with her lack of interest in other people.

Hoping to find some new hint in the actions or conversations of our classmates, I shifted my gaze, observing them carefully. Mostly, they were talking about TV shows and online videos or casually teasing each other according to established conversational etiquette. If there was a solution here, it must lie in how they were each creating their own vulnerabilities and familiarizing the group with their character. *Hmmm.*

As I was processing everything, Mimimi walked in. That's when I had another idea. If observation wasn't helping…it was time to gather some intel. Past experience led straight to that conclusion. Mimimi in particular seemed like a prime source. She was equally good at messing with people and being messed with, so she could probably provide lots of new ideas. She'd also helped Tama-chan become more integrated into the class when they first started high school, which meant she likely held the key to getting us out of this dilemma.

I left my bag on my desk and walked over to Mimimi, who was looking around the classroom.

"Mimimi?"

"Huh?" she said, turning toward me with a blank look. "Oh, Tomozaki! You're here early! What's up?"

She giggled and punched my shoulder. She sounded happy, but I could tell from the strength of her hit that she was actually a little bit down. It might be a dumb way to judge someone's mood, but as the Brain, I could tell.

"Um…," I said, pulling my thoughts together. I wanted to figure out how Tama-chan could create a specific vulnerability and get everyone familiarized with it. Like Mizusawa said, it would be best if she had a classic pattern, so it'd be ideal if I could find some ideas on that front. Which meant the first thing I should ask was...

"You like to mess with Tama-chan a lot, right?"

"Wait a second, Tomozaki, I can't let that slide. I'm not messing with her; I'm just expressing my love!"

"Oh."

"That was weak. I need a stronger comeback! Don't kill the joke!"

"Now, now, Mimimi, everyone needs variation in their comebacks."

That was a lesson I'd learned from Tama-chan. Mimimi seemed at a loss for words.

"...Indeed. Count on the Brain to be a little different!"

"R-really?"

"Of course! I've only got one partner, and that's the Brain!"

"Next thing I know, you'll be making me do comedy routines."

Mimimi pounded my shoulder again, still a little more weakly than usual.

"Um, but anyway, when you teas—I mean, *express your love* for Tama-chan, what parts of her do you, uh...express love for?"

Mimimi smiled with satisfaction at my self-corrections.

"Hmm...how cute she is, and how small she is?"

"Huh. That's what I thought."

I reflected on what I'd just learned, hoping to find some new angle, but even Tama-chan's best friend, Mimimi, teased her about easy-to-understand, surface-level things. Mizusawa had said her success would depend on how she used those same qualities. Hmm.

Maybe surface-level qualities made for better vulnerabilities. But it was still important to figure out the right angle to make them funny.

At times like this, I needed to use...a real pro as my model. You have to start by copying the experts. And so...

"Oh right. Sorry to change the subject, but have you seen any good comedies or stand-up routines lately? I could use a couple of recommendations."

"Huh? What's that all about?"

Mimimi stared up at me with her big, bold eyes. Whoa. I didn't notice it when she was fooling around, but when she gave me a look like that, I was suddenly struck by how beautiful she was. That face was invincible.

"Oh, I'm just working on some different ideas for helping Tama-chan."

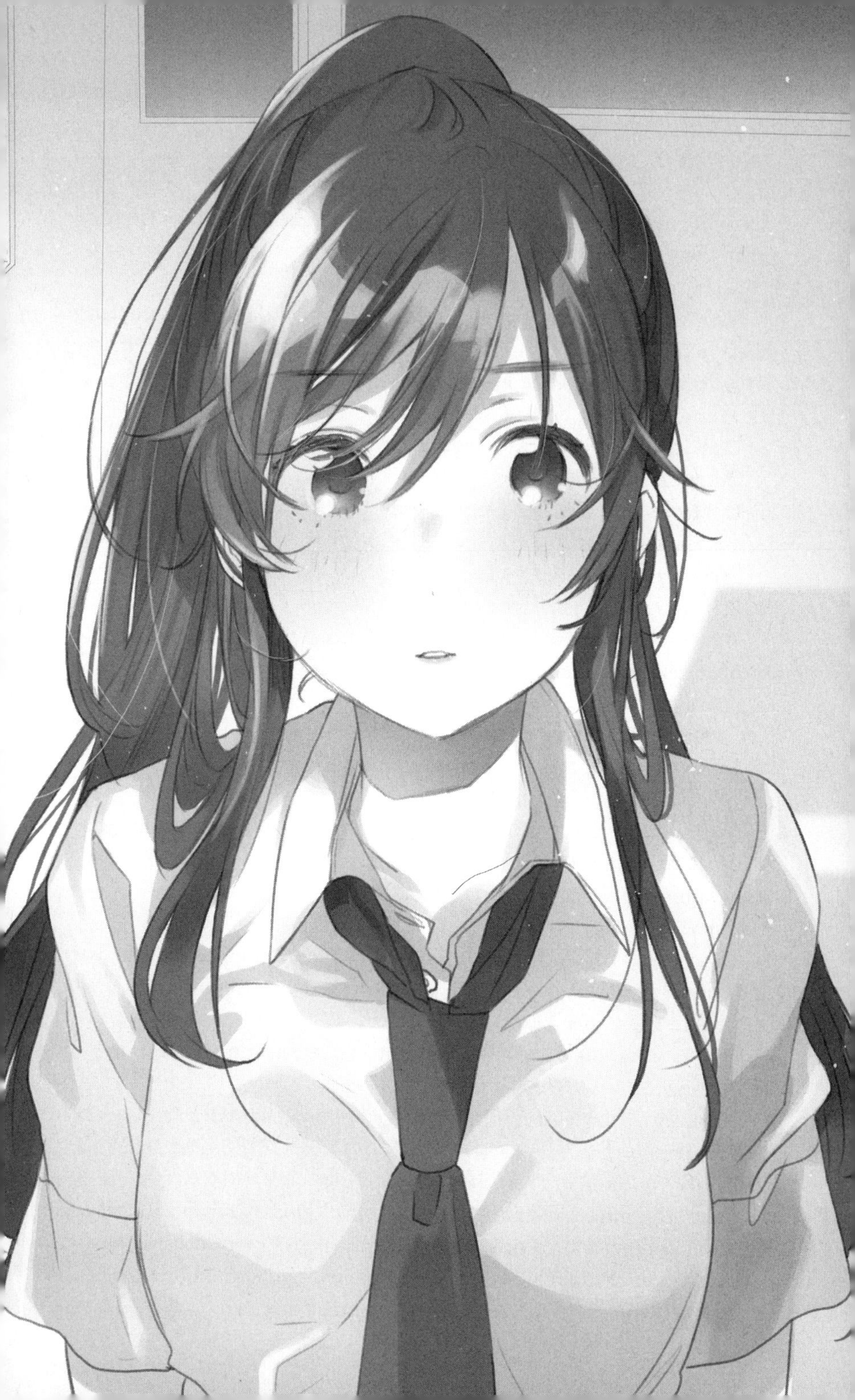

To create our classic routine, I wanted to take some hints from the pros—that is, comedians.

"...Huh."

Now she was studying me. The fact that she didn't seem completely aware of her own beauty made it all the more overwhelming.

"Uh, yeah. It's not the kind of problem that's gonna solve itself..." I felt my face growing hot and glanced away.

"...You sure are sneaky, Tomozaki," Mimimi muttered.

"Huh?"

I was still blushing, but I looked back at Mimimi, confused. For some reason, she was pouting.

"You act all shy, but you really turn up the heat when it counts... Well?"

"Ouch! What are you doing?!"

She was shoving my nose up, making it look like a pig's snout. What was the sudden attack for?

"Your messiah complex has granted you a pig's nose for your sins."

"What the heck is that supposed to mean?!"

"Ah-ha-ha! You don't need to know!"

She laughed innocently. Shit. It was impossible to be mad at her when she smiled so beautifully.

"Damn, that's really ugly on you!"

"Hey!"

I was about to say that I was always ugly, but I stopped myself. After all, I'd just gotten that lecture about how it was bad to put myself down too much. Okay then.

"Sometimes, ugly people are, um, beautiful on the inside! Or something!"

I almost chickened out, but I managed to say it confidently.

"I know that!"

"...?!"

Mimimi grinned and peered into my face. *Wait, what?* She was hitting me with another totally unexpected attack. Why? I was completely at a loss for words. Suddenly, she released my nose and started fiddling with her phone.

"You wanted some recommendations for funny videos, right? Um…"

"Oh right…"

The detour in our conversation left me feeling the aftershocks more strongly than I normally would have, but Mimimi recommended a bunch of videos, and I saved them in a video player app on my phone. Man, my heart was still pounding.

* * *

During lunch break, Mizusawa, Tama-chan, and I met in a stairwell in an abandoned part of the school.

"Sorry I couldn't stop by before, guys," Mizusawa said, smiling attractively at us. Tama-chan and I had been meeting in this stairwell during every break for tone training, but Mizusawa hadn't been able to slip away from Nakamura. Finally, at lunch, the three of us managed to get together.

"Well, you are a regular in Nakamura's group," I said. He apologized again, bringing his hands together in a plea for forgiveness.

"So how's today's training going?" he asked with a serious expression. Tama-chan looked at me questioningly.

"Um…what do you think, professor?"

"Th-that's me, right…?" I smiled awkwardly.

"Of course," Tama-chan teased.

"Oh, okay… Well, I think you're making good progress."

"For real?" She sounded unsure.

"Yeah, I promise."

"Really?" Mizusawa broke in.

I nodded and made a conscious effort to sound casual.

"Although, the professor would like some instruction from his professor at this point."

"Ha-ha-ha. The professor's professor is me, I take it?"

"Of course."

I looked from one of them to the other and grinned. For some reason, Mizusawa smiled happily.

"Fumiya, you're sounding pretty slick these days," he said, maybe reflecting with some nostalgia for the old me, and leaned against the wall.

"What can I say?" I said cockily. Now that I was in a position to teach Tama-chan, I was motivated to get my own act together, and I think I was succeeding these days.

Mizusawa heaved himself off the wall and clapped his hands once like he was ready to get down to business.

"Okay, Tama, show me your Takei act."

"Sure!"

She let out a long breath and assumed a super-cheerful expression.

"Bring it on!" she said, raising one fist near her face.

Mizusawa nodded, looking impressed. "Wow, you already sound way brighter."

"Right? I've been training hard!" she said, puffing out her cheeks proudly. Her eyes were round and playful.

"Ooh, nice. So what kind of training have you been doing?"

"Well," she chirped, "I've just been recording myself talking and then comparing myself with Takei and other people and fixing things!"

"So basically what we talked about before."

"Right! But then I thought of some other people to model myself on!"

"Now that you mention it, we didn't say anything about that, did we?"

The closest person to Tama-chan had an inborn sanguinity that was impossible to dislike. Considering they were the same gender, too, there couldn't be a better person for Tama-chan to learn from when it came to conversation style. Even when Mimimi wasn't there in person, she was able to help Tama-chan.

"Yeah, it wasn't Tomozaki's idea; it was mine! Star pupil, right?"

"Ha-ha-ha. Yeah, very good, very good," Mizusawa said in a joking singsong, smiling kindly.

"Hey! That wasn't very genuine!"

"Oh, you're right, so sorry."

"That wasn't, either!"

In a sense, Tama-chan was still as sharp as ever, but because of her expression and slightly brighter tone, along with the flow of conversation that had led us here, she came off as friendlier than usual. She was progressing nicely.

"Okay, okay, I'll try to be more sincere."

"I'm not convinced!"

"Ha-ha-ha."

Their conversation was bouncing along so smoothly, it was hard to believe that until recently, the two of them had an awkward relationship. The mood was really upbeat, too.

Tama-chan was quiet for a moment, then she peered at Mizusawa again.

"...So what do you think? I'm trying to sound more cheerful..."

Mizusawa nodded right away. "Yeah, it's way easier to talk to you now, and I think you've got a little more charm than you did before."

"R-really?"

Tama-chan looked very pleased to hear that. I pumped my fist into the air, too.

"Now if you could just come up with a routine for everyone, that would be ideal... I haven't been able to think of anything yet," Mizusawa said.

"Speaking of which...," I broke in calmly.

"Oh, you thought of something?" Mizusawa said, looking at me with an expectant smile. *Stop already.*

"More like stole it, but..."

It had to do with creating an easy-to-understand character, and the standard routines you could implement to get other people used to it—although, this was easier said than done.

I winked at Tama-chan. During our earlier breaks, we'd been studying the comedy videos Mimimi had recommended and had taken some lessons from them. Now it was time to try them out on Mizusawa.

"Um, wanna do it now?" I said.

"Uh, okay... I'll try," she mumbled with a mixture of nervousness and embarrassment. I was super nervous, too, because I was about to do something I wasn't used to. I took a deep breath, going over what we'd already practiced a bunch of times this morning.

"...Uh, Tama-chan, why are you so far away?" I asked. Tama-chan jabbed a finger my way and gave a sassy answer.

"I'm just short! I'm not far away; it's the law of perspective!"

"Oh, really?"

"Really! It's an optical illusion!"

Mizusawa stared, blinking, at this odd exchange between Tama-chan and me. I could feel his gaze burning into me. But I wasn't giving up. I played the fool again.

"Oh, huh… Hey, did you notice how big this stairway landing is?"

"I told you, it's because I'm short! It just feels big because *I'm* so small! It's actually tiny!"

Mizusawa snickered, apparently having figured out our schtick. I looked at Tama-chan's drawstring bag, which she was holding in her right hand and which had her lunch inside.

"Weird…your bento box sure is huge."

"It's because I'm short! My bento box just looks big! It's completely normal!"

"Really?"

"Really! I told you, optical illusions."

Mizusawa smiled and gave a small, impressed hum. He pulled out his phone casually and glanced at Tama-chan.

"Wow, fifteen minutes of lunch break have already passed," he said.

Tama-chan answered immediately.

"It hasn't actually been that long!" she snapped. "It just feels long because I'm short!"

"Ha-ha-ha! What the hell?"

He put his phone back in his pocket. Since he'd gotten in on the joke and we'd basically shown him what we wanted to show him, I wrapped up our little skit.

"…Easy to understand, and specific. If we do that, I was thinking it would help people get used to Tama-chan's weak spot."

I'd based the routine on a similar one; there was a comedian who was popular for a little while when I was in elementary school, but his running gag focused on how big his face was. It was among the videos Mimimi had recommended that morning. When I saw it, three things linked together in my mind.

First was the fact that a surface-level feature could work as a vulnerability.

Second was the fact that Tama-chan's size was one of her most noticeable surface-level features.

And third was that Tama-chan was great at sharp comebacks.

All we had to do was fit Tama-chan's shortness into a classic pattern and turn the comedian's joke on its head, and we'd be able to reproduce the same, general routine.

"Wh-what do you think?" Tama-chan asked Mizusawa nervously. It was typical Tama-chan to be really nervous but still fire off those quick comebacks during the actual performance. Mizusawa nodded twice, looking a little world-weary as he smiled, but still like he was having fun.

"Not bad, not bad. I even wanted to get in on the joke myself. With this kind of thing, it's key for other people to want to be a part of it."

"...Which means...?" I asked.

Mizusawa raised one eyebrow and smiled cockily. "Looks like we've nailed down our strategy."

"Yes!" Tama-chan and I both yelled.

Mizusawa slapped my shoulder. "Not surprising with such a good teacher, eh?"

"Uh...guess so!"

Suppressing my instinct to act humble, I answered with a joking, cocky tone. Self-confidence, right? Plus, it seemed rude to the student for the teacher to demean himself in front of her.

Mizusawa was quiet for a second, like he hadn't expected me to answer like that, then sighed.

"Looks like you're advancing as fast as your student, huh, Fumiya?"

"A-am I...? You could be right."

I'd vaguely realized if I was going to teach someone else what I'd learned myself so far, I had to take responsibility for it. That's why I'd tried hard to put my experiences in perspective and express them in words. If I didn't try to understand my own knowledge more and break things down, it would be hard to communicate them to someone else. That process was a sort of training in itself.

Mizusawa was looking at Tama-chan and me with a satisfied expression.

"Yeah, you've both grown a lot. As I'd expect from such a talented teacher and student."

Tama-chan and I responded at the same time to his compliment.

* * *

"Heh-heh…I am talented, aren't I?!"

"Uh…thanks."

Mizusawa burst out laughing. He looked at me and grinned.

"One thing is a little sad, though… The teacher is being totally out-done by his student."

I'd been vaguely aware of that fact, but he was making it crystal clear. I slumped my shoulders.

"I—I was worried about that…"

"Too bad for you, Tomozaki!"

Tama-chan gave me a smile bursting with charm and cheerfulness. It seemed to express all her guileless honesty, like a sunflower shining in the summer sun.

And so, as I silently admitted to myself that Tama-chan had outpaced me with her overwhelming potential, stage one of her charm school came to an end. Yeah, we bottom-tier characters need to take things slow.

* * *

After that, we talked about what to do next as we ate our *bento* and sand-wiches. Mizusawa crammed a big bite of his fried yakisoba bun into his mouth.

"It might be okay for you to start mingling with other kids in class tomorrow, but it could come off as a little weird. As Fumiya said, we've gotta think about risk management."

"Yeah, true."

I nodded, chewing on my croquette sandwich. He had a point. The other day, I'd talked about the importance of practicing in a safe environment. From that perspective, it was slightly dangerous for Tama-chan to jump straight from training with us to conversing with the rest of the class. She was fine with Mizusawa and me, but that might be because she was used to us.

Once she was out in the real world interacting with different people, she couldn't afford to get nervous, mess up, and be stuck spinning her wheels. It would be especially painful to see her mess up the *because I'm short* joke.

I tried to think of how to create a safe space, but all that came to me was a headache.

"...That's a hard one right now."

Mizusawa nodded coolly.

"It is?" Tama-chan asked, tilting her head as she took a big bite of *tama-goyaki*. Maybe the effects of our routine earlier were lingering, because the gesture felt slightly vulnerable—charming. This was a good sign. Mizusawa gulped down the bread in his mouth and turned to Tama-chan to explain.

"I'd like to invite someone to meet up with us after class to do a dry run, but right now, they're all avoiding you."

It was true. The whole class was treating her like an inflamed wound they shouldn't touch. It seemed unlikely anyone would help us out.

"Oh...," Tama-chan said glumly.

"This is tough."

"It is. Aoi and Mimimi are on your side, but you're too close to them, so it wouldn't be real practice. Who else could we ask? Who'd help us out?"

I considered it for a second.

"Um...how about Izumi?"

I remembered our conversation from the previous week. She seemed like a promising candidate. But Mizusawa didn't look hopeful.

"I think she'd help, but...if Konno happened to catch her with us, her position would be at risk."

"...Oh."

On the one hand was Konno's obvious enemy, Tama-chan. On the other was her closest friend, Izumi. If Konno caught the two of them colluding, she'd be pissed. Hinami had already warned me about something similar in a different situation. Thanks to the Nakamura incident, Izumi had found her identity in helping other people, so she'd probably say yes if I asked. But I wanted to avoid all the potential problems that could cause her.

"Yeah, makes sense. That's probably not a good plan," I said. We were all silent for a moment.

"...So who else is there? Someone who's neutral and low-risk even if she messes up, and who's not close with either Konno or Tama."

Mizusawa sighed, apparently running through the qualifications in his mind as he searched for a candidate. But who could tick all those boxes? Someone who wasn't influenced by the anti-Tama-chan mood in class, who wouldn't make a big deal out of flubs, who didn't have much to do with Konno, and who didn't know Tama-chan well, either. I was thinking how unlikely we were to find someone when suddenly, a face popped into my head.

"Ah-ha!" I blurted out.

"What, you thought of someone that might be a good fit, Fumiya?"

"Well, it's not that they 'might' be a good fit…"

She was right in the center of the Venn diagram. She met all the conditions to a T. She was the perfect candidate.

"Oh?"

"Um…"

Yes.

Kikuchi-san.

For some reason, my heart was pounding, but I focused on speaking slowly.

"…Let me see if they're interested."

"So you do have someone in mind?" Mizusawa looked at me expectantly.

"Um, yeah…but I'm not sure."

Tama-chan seemed very interested. "Ooh, who is it?"

Her eyes were sparkling with curiosity. She definitely came off as friendlier than before. I almost gave in to the pressure but managed not to.

"Uh, I don't want to tell you until I'm sure they'll help us out."

I put off a real answer. I wasn't sure how I felt about throwing Kikuchi-san's name out there, since she had that divine aura that set her aside from worldly concerns. I didn't want to tear open the sacred boundary around her, so I concealed her identity—and I'd feel bad if this started any rumors about us.

"I'm going to check with them first."

"Gotcha. We'll let you handle it, Fumiya," Mizusawa said nonchalantly.

"Thanks."

Something about the phrase *we'll let you handle it* made me strangely happy.

"If you say so, Tomozaki!"

Tama-chan went along with Mizusawa and didn't ask me any more questions. Why'd they trust me so much? Now I was all warm and fuzzy.

As I was basking in that glow, Mizusawa started to wrap things up as usual.

"So for now, we should just keep in touch if anything changes, right?"

"Right."

"Okay!"

Even when it came to those formulaic ending words, Tama-chan outdid me in every respect. With that, our lunch meeting disbanded.

* * *

After school, I went to the library to wait for Tama-chan and Mizusawa to finish with their club activities. Lately, I'd been coming to the library every day after school, so I was getting used to this new schedule—or I should have been.

Today, though, one thing was different from usual.

A voice like the trumpets of angels heralding the birth of new life rang out, blessing my eardrums.

"I-I'm nervous…"

The intelligence in her voice resonated with the pages of the books in the library, but it also carried a warmth like an embrace from the Holy Mother. It swirled through my very cells, permeating my entire body.

Yes, you guessed it. Today, Kikuchi-san was sitting in the chair next to mine.

"Um, yeah. That makes sense."

After our last homeroom, when everyone was hurrying off to their clubs and team practices or going home, I'd walked over to speak with her. Specifically, I'd asked if she would help with Tama-chan's training after school.

"All I have to do is talk to her like I normally would?"

"Yeah, just like normal."

I'd simply said I wanted her to have a conversation with Tama-chan. This would be Tama-chan's dress rehearsal before applying her tonal practice and *because I'm short* strategy to the whole class. And Kikuchi-san was going to play the role of her conversation partner.

"A-all right."

I told her Mizusawa would be there, too. Her voice was unsteady and nervous, probably because she was imagining herself leaping into such an unfamiliar situation.

All the same, she'd agreed to my request in order to help Tama-chan out. As I suspected, it wasn't just her looks and surface-level actions that were angelic. Even her heart was made from holy material.

Incidentally, I didn't mention that Tama-chan was changing her way of talking or anything else like that. I thought it would be best for her to make her own judgment without any preconceptions.

"You haven't talked much with Tama-chan, have you?"

Kikuchi-san shook her head slowly. "No. When I see her in class, she strikes me as a really powerful person…but I've never really talked to her."

"Huh."

Our conversation petered out. We'd already gone over the key points for the rehearsal, and I didn't have anything left to explain. All the same, I stayed calm and thought about what I wanted to say to her, searching inside myself for my genuine feelings. Keeping it natural, no big-guy bluffs. When I thought of something, I just said it.

"…So what do you think about all this? I mean, about the way Konno is harassing Tama-chan and how everyone else is obviously avoiding her."

How did this awful situation look through Kikuchi-san's unclouded eyes? I wanted to know, pure and simple.

"I…"

Kikuchi-san parted her pale-pink lips and paused. I doubted there was much (if any) lipstick on them, and yet they glistened mysteriously, as if they were covered in a glossy, translucent veil.

After thinking for a moment, she continued.

"I feel really bad for Hanabi-chan. I think the situation is unfair. But…I can't blame Konno-san or the rest of the class."

I hadn't expected that answer. One thing in particular caught my attention.

"You can't blame them? What do you mean?" I asked directly.

Kikuchi-san gripped the fingers on her left hand with her right hand.

"Um…I think it's wrong to harass someone or avoid a certain person just because everyone else is doing it."

"Uh-huh…"

She shook her head. "But I think the reason they do that…is because they're weak."

"…Weak?"

That was unexpected.

Kikuchi-san nodded hesitantly. "I'm sure…that they have a kind of conflict inside them that they can't resolve themselves. They have to release that tension somehow…and they know it's not right, but they worry about what other people think. So they go along with it. That's what I think is going on…"

Her words were halting and unsure, but the sketch they created was certain, powerful, and deep. She went on transforming the scene she saw into words.

"I think Konno-san and everyone else is doing this to escape from something they can't resolve on their own… Of course, it's the wrong way to handle it."

"Escape…huh?"

In Konno's case, she must be running from the stress caused by Izumi and Nakamura getting together. For everyone else, there was the general feeling that people who brought everyone down should be held responsible. Instead of facing up to the sources of stress, they were taking the path of least resistance.

"Yes…although, I'm hardly one to speak since I've just been watching passively." She shook her head in chagrin.

"Th-that's not true. Sometimes, you can't get involved even if you want to…"

"Thank you," she said softly, smiling modestly, then went on talking. "If you think about Konno-san, our classmates, and Hanabi-chan, I think the strongest person of them all is really Hanabi-chan."

She lowered her long lashes as she spoke. I reflected quietly on her words, which rang out as beautifully as graceful ripples on the water's surface.

"…I think you might be right. Tama-chan is very strong."

Kikuchi-san pressed her lips together for a moment before responding.

"Yes. I think Konno-san and everyone else depends on her strength. It's easier than fighting their own internal confusion. Because no matter how much they lean on her, Hanabi-chan never collapses."

She rubbed her delicate collarbone, which was as white and beautiful as a snow-covered mountainside.

"…Leaning on her, huh?"

Her perspective was more than a little surprising to me. She carefully considered each player in the drama—truly a heaven's-eye view. But that didn't mean what she was saying was odd.

Konno wasn't just attacking Tama-chan. She was turning away from the stress she felt and compensating with harassment to make herself feel better, a strategy that depended on Tama-chan's strength. Meanwhile, the rest of the class wasn't merely avoiding Tama-chan; they were avoiding a battle with the mood and justifying their own behavior by labeling the invincible Tama-chan as "the culprit" and attacking her in the name of "justice."

And it was happening because Tama-chan was strong and they were weak, according to Kikuchi-san.

"But that doesn't mean they should be doing those things…and I think the problem has to be resolved. I'm thrilled you're giving me the chance to get involved. Thank you."

She looked straight at me as she spoke. Her skin was as smooth and clear as porcelain; I couldn't help staring. Her radiance was so powerful, it seemed to be its own source of light. But more than anything, the words this beautiful being was saying were so positive, so human.

"Yeah. Let's get to work on it, then."

Kikuchi-san's innocent, unguarded smile enveloped me like the arms of a goddess.

"Yes. Let's work on it…together," she said in a fluent, kind voice filled with gentle determination. I nodded and returned her smile, convinced that the overwhelming brilliance of her expression would remain etched in my retinas for eternity.

We were walking together toward the same goal. That was a first for me. I realized I was oddly tickled by the idea of fighting alongside this person who was so important to me.

As always, the time I spent with her felt natural, unhurried, gentle, and warm.

* * *

After I got a message from Mizusawa in our LINE group chat, Kikuchi-san and I headed to the classroom where he and Tama-chan were already waiting. They were looking out the window and talking; they didn't seem to have noticed us yet.

I hadn't had a chance to tell them who was going to help us. Neither of them had mentioned it after Mizusawa said he'd let me handle it. They really did seem to trust me on this one. That sort of acceptance was typical Mizusawa, and I wanted to live up to his expectations.

With Kikuchi-san trailing half a step behind me, I went into the classroom, somewhat nervous about how they would react to her.

"Um...hey," I called to them. They both looked at me, and then at Kikuchi-san. Both of them widened their eyes in surprise. Well, I could have predicted that. Mizusawa was the first to talk.

"Hey, Fumiya...and Kikuchi-san?"

Half-hidden behind me, she peered out at them.

"H-hello," she said, her voice a little high from nervousness. She was still using me for cover. Tama-chan must have noticed how nervous she was, because she changed her expression from surprise to a friendly smile and looked straight at her.

"Hi, Fuka-chan. Hi, Tomozaki."

Her direct, strong reply was pure Tama-chan. But I wondered why she called Kikuchi-san by her first name even though she didn't know her well. Were girls just less formal with each other from the start?

"H-hello," Kikuchi-san said again. This was her second hello of the day.

Mizusawa-san scratched his head softly, still looking surprised.

"Um, thanks for helping us out, Kikuchi-san. So this was the person you were thinking of, Fumiya?"

"Um, yeah."

"Huh."

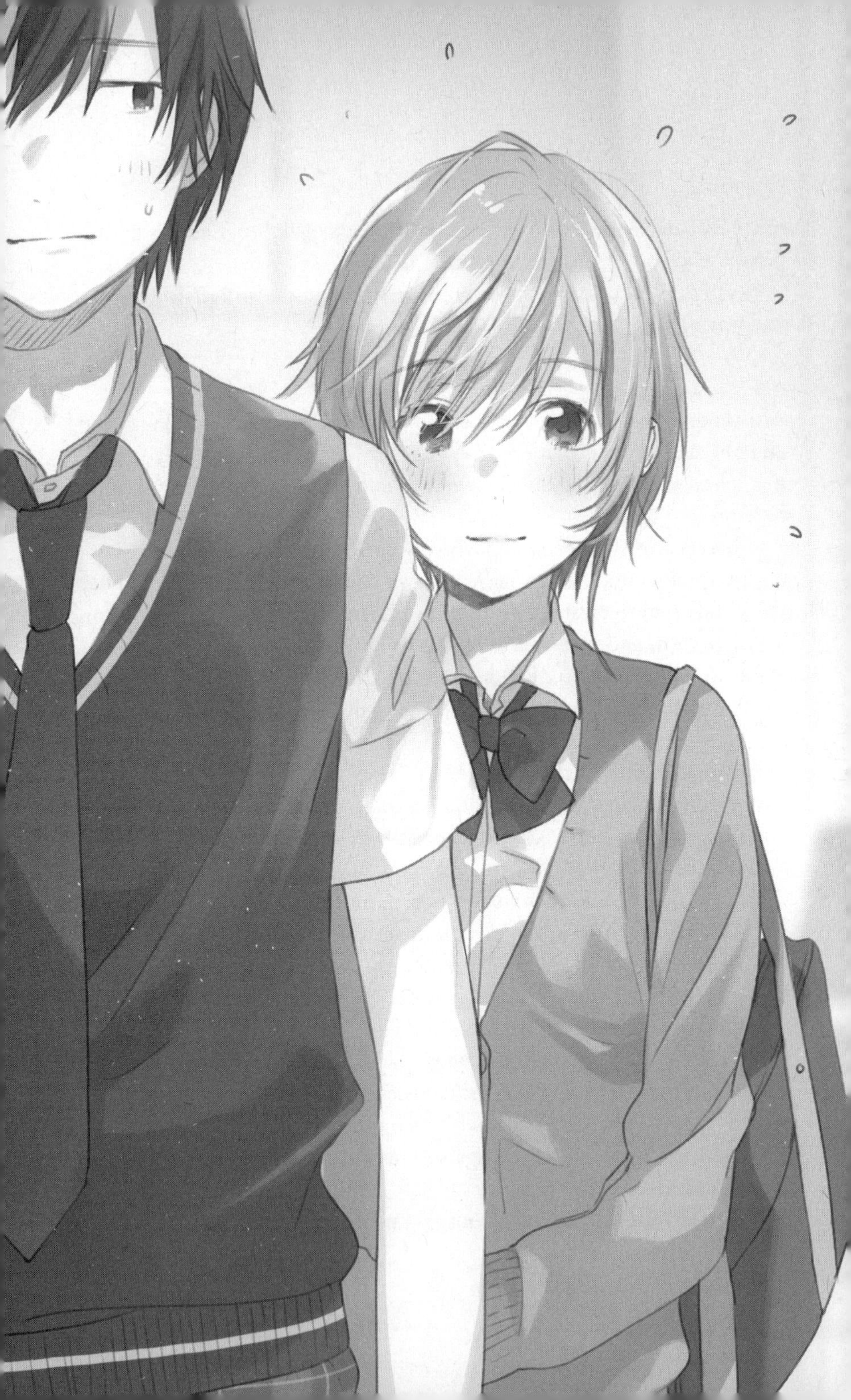

He looked at me intently. There it was again—that look he got when he was searching someone's soul. Right now, he was probing our relationship. I'd better watch out—Mizusawa could always see straight through me. Not that I had anything to hide, really.

Eventually, he shifted his gaze to Kikuchi-san and nodded. *Wh-what? What was that nod supposed to mean?*

"Well, she's neutral in this whole situation, doesn't have a big influence on the class, isn't connected to Konno, and isn't friends with Tama-chan… Just like we said."

"R-right?" I said, still flustered.

"Um, Kikuchi-san, has Fumiya explained everything to you?"

"…What do you mean, 'everything'?"

Kikuchi-san was slowly emerging from behind me as she talked to Mizusawa. Now she was maybe 70 percent out in the open. *Doing good, Kikuchi-san.*

"Well, did he tell you about our strategy to help Tama? And that today, we just want you to have a normal conversation with her?"

"Oh, um, yes. He did."

By now, she was about 80 percent out.

"Okay then!" Mizusawa said casually, then smirked. "By the way, why do you seem so anxious?"

"Oh, um, because I don't know you very well…"

"Hmm," Mizusawa said, not sounding convinced, but then next moment, he nodded. After his comment, Kikuchi-san shrank back to being 60 percent exposed. What a weird barometer.

"Okay, no big deal. Let's get started."

"O-okay."

That was how the conversation, which now included Kikuchi-san, began. Now that I thought about it, I'd never seen Kikuchi-san in a group setting. Aside from when I borrowed the tissue from Izumi and the time Hinami and I happened to go to the café where she worked, I hadn't really seen her talking to other people. I mean, there were times in class when we naturally had to speak with our classmates, but aside from that, I'd almost never seen her having a conversation.

"Well, should we get started?" Mizusawa called, like he was starting a lesson. Tama-chan nodded timidly.

"I guess so."

"Great. The two of us will watch."

He walked over to me and nudged Kikuchi-san toward Tama-chan with a smile.

"Oh, okay."

Maybe out of nervousness, she walked over to Tama-chan, a bit more squirrel-like than usual, and bowed politely. *Um, this isn't a martial arts match...*

I chuckled a little when Mizusawa whispered into my ear.

"Hey, Fumiya, I didn't know you guys were friends."

"Um, well, I guess we are," I mumbled incoherently.

Mizusawa hmmed. "There's more to you than meets the eye," he whispered, and grinned teasingly.

"Wh-what's that supposed to mean?" I said anxiously.

He nudged me with his elbow. "Nothing, it's just..."

"Wh-what?"

He glanced at her before continuing in a whisper.

"She doesn't stand out much, but she's supercute in a quiet sort of way."

My brain froze for a second. I stood there blinking, my head spinning as I tried unsuccessfully to figure out what I should be thinking. After a minute, I muttered some vague response.

"...What's the matter?" Mizusawa said, tilting his head at me. I had no idea.

It was just like, when I heard someone else say she was cute, my brain got all fuzzy, and even though that should have been a good thing because he was complimenting her, my heart jumped, and I didn't know what that meant. Yeah, I just had no idea.

"Nothing," I said. I wasn't so much talking as making an emotionless sound, but that was all I was capable of. Mizusawa was watching me with a grin. *Wh-what's that face for?*

* * *

Tama-chan and Kikuchi-san were facing each other. The classroom had practically become a magical forest, showcasing a meeting between a woodland creature and a fairy, but the first thing Tama-chan said kinda shattered that.

"Fuka-chan, I didn't know you and Tomozaki were friends!"

Plunging straight into that level of intimacy was a move reminiscent of a certain idiot, but she also had his vulnerability in her tone to make that brave first step feel less harsh. Huh. I think Tama-chan picked things up so fast because she was honest right down to her core.

Maybe out of surprise, Kikuchi-san burst out laughing. The tension drained from her face as she looked Tama-chan in the eye.

"Yes. I'm fortunate to call him a friend."

She smiled lovingly. Her stiffness had disappeared, and the orb of glowing light that usually surrounded her was back. Tama-chan smiled back at her.

"Tomozaki has gotten a lot happier lately, hasn't he?"

Kikuchi-san blinked, her eyes opening again, as round as acorns and as bright as pools of water reflecting the clouds and sun, and she answered after a pause.

"Yes, he has… I think it's wonderful when people make the effort to become the person they want to be."

Mizusawa looked surprised by the way her gentle, affirming words reverberated through the classroom like a majestic song. Eventually, he glanced at me jokingly.

"You heard the lady," he said, slapping my shoulder.

"Uh, yeah."

He was definitely teasing me because Kikuchi-san had called my recent changes wonderful. But I was sure those words weren't intended for only me.

"…You think so?" Tama-chan mumbled, sinking somewhere deep inside herself.

"Yes…I think it's just terrific."

"…Huh."

The two of them exchanged a look that suggested some sort of important thread had been tied between them. Finally, Kikuchi-san asked Tama-chan a question with some concern.

"Hanabi-chan...have you been doing all right lately?"

Tama-chan nodded firmly, and the gesture was honest.

"Yeah. Sometimes, I don't like what's going on, but I'm fine! Aoi and Minmi are there for me, and Tomozaki and Mizusawa are helping me, too. I've been able to work on some things!"

Kikuchi-san smiled, apparently relieved by Tama-chan's positivity and spirit.

"I'm happy to hear that."

"Thanks for worrying about me!"

"You're welcome. I'm jealous that you have so many friends you can count on."

"Yes, I really can rely on everyone aside from Tomozaki!"

"Hey!" I said, jumping into their conversation. Kikuchi-san giggled.

"...I think the reason everyone gathers around you despite the difficulty is because they all care about you so much."

She smiled a soft smile that seemed to wrap itself around Tama-chan. Yeah, Kikuchi-san's angel wings were definitely out.

"N-now you're making me shy!"

Maybe since this was the first time she was experiencing Kikuchi-san's holy aura, Tama-chan blushed and looked flustered.

"Hee-hee. I always knew you were a lovely, adorable person."

"No! ...It's just because I'm short!"

"...Short?"

Kikuchi-san tilted her head, puzzled, and Mizusawa and I burst out laughing.

"Oh, no, never mind! Forget I said that!"

Tama-chan blushed and looked even more flustered. *Glad we did this dry run.*

"Hey, Tama!" I called. "You don't have to run all the way over there just because you're embarrassed!"

"Come on! I'm just short! I didn't go anywhere; I'm just hard to see."

"Oh, really?"

"Really! It's just an optical illusion!"

"Hee-hee-hee. You're so cute."

"Come on!"

There was something refreshing about the sight of Kikuchi-san smothering Tama-chan with compliments and Tama-chan blushing and being completely at a loss on how to respond. Practice and all that aside, maybe it was really good that these two just got to talk.

* * *

The conversation between Tama-chan and Kikuchi-san had reached a natural ending point, and we were all walking down the hallway.

"Well…how was that?" Mizusawa gently asked Kikuchi-san, who was floating among us like a celestial nymph.

She gave him an elegant smile. "She was very easy to talk to."

Huh. So Kikuchi-san graces Mizusawa with that beautiful smile, too. As I reflected on this completely obvious fact, I continued listening to their conversation.

"Excellent. So the training was a success… Uh, Fumiya?"

"Huh? Oh right," I answered lifelessly, caught off guard.

"Why are you so out of it?"

"Um, no reason. It's nothing."

"What? You're acting weird today."

"I—I am? I don't think I am."

"…Hmm."

Mizusawa gave a knowing grin and finally looked away from me. Honestly, what was that about?

The four of us left the school building and headed toward the field, with me still an emotional wreck.

"Okay, so aside from this, the main question is whether Tama-chan has any interest in our other classmates, right?" Mizusawa said, readjusting the heel of the outside shoes he'd just changed into.

"…Yeah," Tama-chan mumbled without much confidence. After all, that wasn't a simple problem to solve.

"Fumiya, what was the spark that got you interested in other people?"

"Me? Well…"

I reflected, trying to remember what had changed my outlook.

"At first, I decided to try to find out a little bit more about other people. And once I knew one thing, I wanted to know the next, and it just bubbled up from there."

"You tried to find out more about them, huh…?"

Tama-chan's quiet voice drifted to me on the autumn breeze. Kikuchi-san was listening to our conversation silently, a serious expression on her face.

"If you're like me, then my guess is you're holding yourself back from taking that first step," I said to Tama-chan.

She looked at me anxiously. "Holding myself back?"

"Yeah. You tell yourself their world doesn't have anything to do with yours. That you can't be part of their group."

She glanced down. "…That might be true."

Yeah, we really were similar. I kept going, like I was talking to the old me.

"When you look at people talking and messing around in class, and you have those assumptions at the bottom of your heart, then they feel far away from you, like they're characters in a book. Farther than that, really. The whole world looks gray."

Mizusawa sighed quietly.

"A gray world, huh…?"

Gray. That was the word Kikuchi-san had said to me over summer vacation. Now she was walking along next to me, listening to our conversation, watching our hearts with those clear eyes of hers.

"But there's no real basis for that. If you decide to jump in and do it, the world starts to take on color, and gradually, you feel better about being there. Your life starts getting more fun, and the world draws you in more, too."

"…I can see that," Tama-chan said, like she was remembering something.

"It's not about forcing yourself to be interested. I think the first step is to believe that maybe, if you take that step, you might enjoy it. Then you try to learn a little bit about other people. That's what happened to me. I got myself involved, and the interest came from there."

"It just came from there…"

Tama-chan echoed my words to herself. I was fairly sure she hadn't taken that first step yet—she still lived in her own world. In my case, Hinami had pushed me forward so I could finally leap into the world at large. That leap had carried me over all kinds of stereotypes, fears, and beliefs that things could never change. Getting past all of it was tough, but on the other side was a colorful world I didn't even know existed.

"I bet you think you won't like people that much—but actually, there aren't many truly bad people out there."

I stopped there. That was as much as I could say about my motivation for moving forward as aggressively as I was.

When I did, Kikuchi-san finally spoke up. Her voice was quiet, but it drew everyone's attention.

"For example…"

"For example?" I echoed, glancing at her. She was looking intently at Tama-chan, almost like she was praying.

"For example, Konno-san hates to lose, and she hates feeling less than others. But she can also be very compassionate toward the people she decides are her friends," she began, full of emotion, like she was reading a book out loud.

"…Fuka-chan?"

"And Akiyama-san—well, I'm sure she doesn't have any self-confidence. To make up for that, she tries to be friends with confident people. In a sense, it's a beautiful way of taking the initiative to change the situation around her."

All three of us were mesmerized by Kikuchi-san's words.

"And another example…Izumi-san puts other people before herself, so she tends to be on the losing end a lot. But from another perspective, you can see her gentleness. She feels the pain of others like it's her own."

She sighed like she was shutting the book and suddenly looked in front of her.

"…I think each character in the story of our class has their own background and their own struggles and their own growth and false beliefs. Not one of them is going through life without thinking. Of course, the same goes for you and me and Mizusawa-kun and Tomozaki-kun as well."

She smiled at Tama-chan with a literary aura around her.

"I think if you take that perspective, you'll start to find you want to know more."

The tale she'd woven had completely absorbed me. When I glanced at Mizusawa, he was uncharacteristically flustered. When our eyes met, he nodded meaningfully and then turned away. Tama-chan was gazing at Kikuchi-san with surprise, but she also seemed encouraged. She bobbed her head slightly.

"…I think I understand a little better now. Thank you, Tomozaki and Fuka-chan."

"Uh-huh."

"You're welcome."

I was embarrassed by her direct thanks. No matter how much time passed, I never seemed to build up any defenses against that sort of thing. Meanwhile, Kikuchi-san accepted her gratitude gracefully.

"I was thinking," Mizusawa suddenly said.

"Huh?"

"Fumiya…and Kikuchi-san, too, maybe. You move forward slowly, but you're very careful about it."

"Uh, really?"

I didn't know how to take his abstract comment. He let out a quiet, little laugh, while Kikuchi-san looked at him with interest.

"Yeah. It's like you notice every grain of sand dropped on the ground… the total opposite of me."

He sounded kind of like he was putting himself down, but his gaze was fixed straight ahead.

"Which means…?" I asked.

He hurried on, like he was trying to cut me off before I could say anything else. "Anyway, I feel like we've chased some ghosts away. How about you, Tama?"

"Um…okay," I mumbled, while Tama-chan looked at him with a mixture of fear and determination.

"I'll do the best I can," she mumbled. She glanced down, as if to confirm to herself that she was still physically there. "I wonder if I can get along with everyone after all," she said with a sigh. She sounded very earnest. To me, her unspoken message showed her single-minded determination not to bring Mimimi any more grief.

"I'm sure you can," I said confidently, before anyone else could respond.

Tama-chan pressed her lips together and nodded like she was trying to encourage herself.

"Thanks... I'll do my best!"

This time, her voice was filled with the same directness as always, but it also had an outward brightness. A big smile shone on her face.

* * *

"So the ranks have grown again...and now it's Kikuchi-san?!"

"H-hi."

Mimimi was definitely surprised by the new addition to our group. Kikuchi-san gave a flustered, polite bow as she stood on the school field.

"Uh, um, hi!"

"Hi!"

Once again, Kikuchi-san did a double greeting, then walked backward a couple of steps and hid about 10 percent of herself behind me. Huh. So she was 90 percent out from the start this time. *Good progress, Kikuchi-san.*

"What is this group all about?!"

"Ha-ha-ha. Figures you'd be confused!" Mizusawa laughed, watching the bewildered Mimimi. Her teammates weren't paying much attention, maybe because they were used to us coming to meet her by now.

"Is Kikuchi-san part of the Tama-rescue team, too?"

"Uh, um...," Kikuchi-san said, still flustered.

"Yeah, kind of. More like a temporary assistant on Team Tomozaki," Mizusawa interjected, coming to Kikuchi-san's rescue. *Nice move. I better get on top of that.*

"Oh, huh..."

Mimimi still seemed totally lost, but she nevertheless nodded in a show of understanding. She could adapt quickly.

"Apparently, she and Tomozaki were friends, and she offered to help."

Mimimi froze with her eyes round and mouth gaping.

"...Huh? Tomozaki and her?" she said in a daze.

Mizusawa cackled. "Yup. Never would've guessed, huh?"

Mimimi nodded a few more times, eyes still wide, and looked back and forth between the two of us.

"Definitely. Huh..."

"...Wh-what?"

I didn't know how to react to the look she gave me with those bewildered, blinking eyes.

Kikuchi-san tilted her face down awkwardly and flashed a few glances up at Mimimi. What was with this mood?

"Hmm..."

Mimimi stared appraisingly at Kikuchi-san.

Probably nervous, Kikuchi-san was turning redder and redder as she struggled to keep eye contact with Mimimi. I bet she was trying not to be rude. Angel.

After this mysterious interlude, Mimimi finally mumbled, "...You're cute."

"Umm...?"

Her expression was utterly serious as she kept her gaze fixed on Kikuchi-san, who looked slightly frightened by the sudden compliment.

"Yes...you're adorable!!"

She turned toward Kikuchi-san, welcoming her with open arms.

"How could I have missed someone as adorable as you?! You're totally my type! You're almost as incredible as Tama!! Welcome to Nanami World!"

"Nanami...what?"

Her excitement suddenly exploded, leaving Kikuchi-san completely confused. I figured I'd better come to her rescue before Mizusawa did.

"Come on, Mimimi, tone it down!"

She gave me a sulky look, then suddenly brought both hands to her eyes and pretended to burst into tears.

"You're so mean...taking Kikuchi-san's side over mine..."

"That's not the issue!"

"You must have forgotten, Tomozaki...about our dazzling days of love..."

"What are you talking about?! That never happened!" I cried in a panic. She was crazy!

She brushed me off with a laugh. "You're getting better at your comebacks, Brain! All the more reason to make more jokes!"

I sighed at her total refusal to tone anything down.

"Fine, make your jokes; just don't start any rumors…"

"Ah-ha-ha! Good point!"

"Man…"

I let go of my tension and smiled, looking at Mimimi. She seemed pleased with herself. Apparently, she was satisfied now. Mizusawa shrugged and rolled his eyes.

"Would you two quit it with the comedy routine?"

"That's asking too much, Takahiro! Our husband-and-wife routine is pure improv!"

"I know that…," he sighed.

"Wh-what?!" I yelped.

"Minmi?" Tama chimed in. "No one thought you had a script to start with."

All this ruckus was going on near the track-team office. I happened to look over at Kikuchi-san and noticed she was staring at me in a daze. Her eyes were filled half with surprise, half with girlish interest. Suddenly, she giggled, covering her mouth daintily with her hand. If there's a smile that could be described as *gentle beaming*, this was it.

"…Kikuchi-san?" I said.

"This is so fun," she said softly, the words leaving her delicate lips with warm emotion.

"…Huh?"

Mimimi gave Kikuchi-san a blank look. Kikuchi-san smiled back at her, her warmth embracing even Mimimi's confusion.

"I feel like…I'm starting to understand why Tomozaki-kun changed," she said gently, as if she was putting away something very important for safekeeping. Her words seemed to glow with a certain inner warmth. Mimimi blinked at her.

"…Yeah, makes sense," I answered. I'm sure this would be enough for her to see. I glanced up and noticed Mizusawa was carefully observing the two of us, as usual.

He was nodding slowly over and over as he hmmed to himself. He was getting a kick out of something in the midst of all this.

"Wh-what?" I said accusingly.

"Oh, nothing," he answered with a wicked grin. Liar.

"Come on, what?"

"Hmm? You have a guess?"

"What are you talking about?!"

"What's the matter, Fumiya? I bet you wanted to say—"

That was enough to completely shatter my composure, and I interrupted him midsentence.

"Okay, I've had enough. I'm leaving!" I shouted. Everyone, including Kikuchi-san, broke out laughing.

* * *

I'd been tricked.

As I walked home on the dark streets, I cursed my own carelessness.

It had happened a couple minutes earlier. Mimimi had changed out of her track uniform, and we were all about to leave.

First, Mimimi said she had to use the bathroom and disappeared into the school with Tama-chan. That was normal enough. But then Mizusawa said they were taking forever to come back and went to look for them. That's when I should have realized what was up.

Why would Mizusawa go look for them in the girl's bathroom?

A few minutes later, I got a LINE message from him saying, [*We headed home! Good luck.*] The second I read it, everything became very clear.

I'm not sure if he was doing it as a joke or because he thought he was helping, but he'd cooked up a scheme to get Kikuchi-san and me alone.

So now Kikuchi-san and I were walking together down a dim, country road. *S-screw you, Mizusawa.* Now that I thought about it, the trap was totally obvious, but I didn't have the EXP to see it. Behold, the level gap.

Anyway, my only choice now was to roll with it.

If Kikuchi-san and I had already been out to eat and gone to the movies together, why did I feel so nervous about suddenly walking home from school with her, like it was some huge deal? Maybe it was because everyone was teasing me so much earlier.

"Um…," I ventured.

Kikuchi-san looked at me. It was well past six, but even in the dusky light, she was as pale and beautiful as an albino Yggdragon. The air sparkled with an attractiveness so powerful that I was sure some spell had been cast over it.

I took the hit from the magic head-on, even as I searched my heart for what I wanted to talk to Kikuchi-san about. This was what came out.

"How did you like talking with everyone?"

I didn't think she'd interacted much with the other kids in our class up to this point. Then today, she'd suddenly jumped into talking about all sorts of stuff in a big group. I wondered what she thought about the whole experience. As for me, the only thing I really remembered was the weird way my heart jumped every time Mizusawa teased me about her, but we'll leave that aside for now.

"Um…I was nervous."

"Really?!"

"There were so many people I hadn't talked to before…"

"Oh, that's what you meant. Yeah, makes sense."

"…?"

She tilted her head, puzzled. I'd been startled for a second because I was thinking about how my own heart kept pounding from being teased, but yeah, of course that's not what she meant. Putting on a calm front to hopefully hide that, I kept talking.

"It was a nice change of pace to see you speaking with everyone like that."

She looked a little embarrassed. "Yes…it was a nice change of pace for me, too." She brought her hand to her chest. "And it was nice to see you up close, having a good time with everyone."

"R-really?"

She nodded slowly and kindly. Her strangely alluring smile melted my heart like a chunk of chocolate in a warm hand.

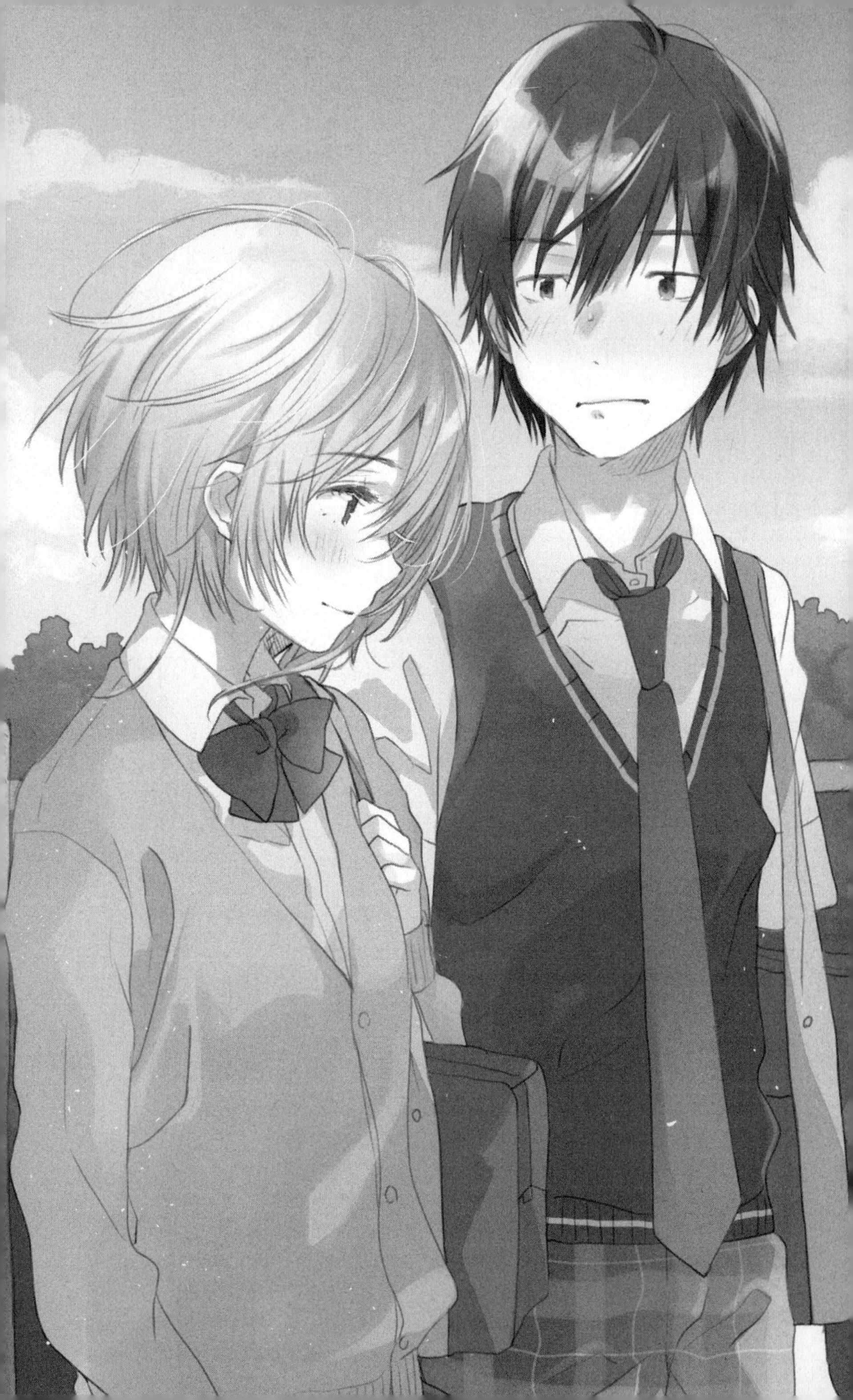

"Yes. I've seen you with other people in class, but this was the first time I got to watch up close... It was a great thing to see."

She smiled a warm, grown-up smile. Then she looked up at me, the autumn breeze ruffling her moonlit hair.

"You always show me things I've never seen before."

Her eyes each held a miniature universe inside of which were glittering stars that harbored all the mysteries of life. Perhaps I had already fallen into them.

"Oh, uh-huh..."

My brain was dangerously close to overheating. When I got home, I could hardly remember anything we talked about after that. All I knew was that a pleasant warmth lingered in my chest.

I was done for. Kikuchi-san truly was an enchantress.

* * *

The next day, it was finally time for Tama-chan to take the next step; she was going to go through with her plan to be more charming while interacting with other people.

The first part of the strategy was simple. With Mimimi's help, she would hang out with Mimimi's group of girls and try to join their conversation. Hinami would probably be there, too, which would make her more comfortable. Apparently, Mizusawa had talked it through with Mimimi the day before, while I was walking home with Kikuchi-san. Props to the guy who can do everything.

During break after first period, Tama-chan got right to work with Mimimi. I watched from the back of the classroom with Mizusawa.

"Wonder how this will go."

"Yeah, who knows...?"

Up till now, most of the kids in class had avoided her somewhat. But when she stopped fighting back against Konno, the mood improved a little. Then she'd done some training to stop putting up walls and defending herself so completely. Those two steps should have removed the surface-level obstacles keeping her from fitting in.

What she needed now was the courage to take the first step into the fray.

"Oh, hey, I forgot to tell you," Mizusawa said.

"Huh? What?"

"When I was walking home with Mimimi and Tama the other day, I took your advice to heart and asked Mimimi some stuff."

"...Like what?"

"I mean, you were talking about how important it is to take an interest in other people and accept them if you want to get along. Getting to know them a little is a key part of that, right?"

"Oh, uh-huh," I agreed.

"And Kikuchi-san pointed out some things, too, right? About everyone's personality."

"Yeah..."

Mizusawa looked at Mimimi and Tama-chan.

"So I got Mimimi to tell me some things, for Tama's sake. About what her friends are like."

"...Oh."

"I asked her what she liked most about different people. She had thoughts or a story about each one of them. Tama-chan seemed surprised."

"...Because she wouldn't have been able to do that?"

Mizusawa nodded. "It was like something hit her. I think she was surprised by the fact that Kikuchi-san and Mimimi both pay so much attention to our classmates...and just the simple fact that everyone has something likable about them."

I nodded slowly in return. "So she's starting to develop an interest?"

Mizusawa tilted his head to the side. "Maybe. My guess is that after she heard everything you and Kikuchi-san said, and after seeing it in practice with Mimimi, she probably felt motivated to give it a try."

"Huh...well, that's promising," I replied.

Mizusawa was looking at Tama-chan. "I've got a good feeling about this." He smiled gently and let out a relieved sigh.

"You could be right," I said admiringly.

Mizusawa's smile grew more teasing, then suddenly, he gave me a serious look. "Actually, I learned a lot myself," he said.

"What's that mean?"

He cackled and laid a hand on my shoulder. "Wouldn't expect any less from the Brain-slash-Leader."

"You and Mimimi just gave me those names randomly!"

"Ha-ha-ha. Well, Team Tomozaki has done all it could."

"So it's still named after me, huh…?"

The day passed like that, with the two of us watching from a distance as Tama-chan talked earnestly and cheerfully with our classmates. Even from afar, I could see that her expressions and gestures were winning people over. I could only hear fragments of her conversations, but it was obvious that the mood was cheerful and lively.

At first, everyone was a little unnerved by Tama-chan's presence, but by lunchtime, the tension was gone, and she seemed to have been accepted into the group. Mizusawa must have talked to Mimimi about the short joke, because she and Tama-chan did that routine a couple of times, too.

Still, that acceptance could very well be at only a surface-level. They'd been avoiding her until very recently, so maybe they secretly felt awkward. But time would probably take care of that.

If we continued on this path, the mood should soon be on our side.

* * *

"Cheers!"

Takei took the lead in making a toast at the bar—the drink bar, of course. School was out, and we were at a diner just off the road between school and the station. The group included Tama-chan, Mizusawa, Takei, and me. As soon as her extralong track practice ended, Mimimi was supposed to meet us here.

"How's the response so far, Tama?" Mizusawa asked. Tama-chan nodded, taking a sip of orange juice.

"Once I started trying to be more cheerful, the conversation gradually started to go better."

I couldn't help grinning. "Really? So you did it!"

"Yeah! Thanks, guys."

"Whoo-hoo! That's awesome!!"

As usual, Takei probably only understood half of what was going on, but he was twice as affected as anyone else. Mizusawa smiled wryly and took the helm.

"I think from here on out, you'll be fine if you just go with the flow. I'm betting Konno will stop harassing you pretty soon."

"Really?" Tama-chan tilted her head, looking puzzled.

Mizusawa nodded at her. "Yeah, although, it's just a guess. Once you've got the class on your side, they'll be upset if she harasses you, right?"

"Ah, makes sense," I said. It had to do with Konno's sense of balance, which Mizusawa had brought up before. "So once the mood shifts in our favor, Konno will realize she'll be making things awkward if she keeps up the harassment, right?"

Mizusawa smiled.

"Right. And she's a good politician—when that happens, I'm guessing she'll quit."

Mizusawa and I were on the same page, but Tama-chan was frowning and kept her head tilted to the side still.

"Are you sure?" she said.

"Ha-ha-ha. Don't worry about the details. All we're saying is that the problem should resolve itself soon."

"You think so? Then we can toast?"

"Ha-ha-ha. Yeah. Cheers!"

And so our party went on. *Are you watching, Hinami? While you were restricting yourself and trying to avoid changing Tama-chan, we tackled the problem head-on and used all the strategies available to us, and now we're in sight of our goal. Would you still say we made a mistake?*

And why did you insist on playing with a handicap for so long anyway?

"By the way, Fumiya, how'd things go the other day?"

"Huh? The other day?" I said, returning to the present and turning to Mizusawa.

"Don't play dumb, man. You and Kikuchi-san walked to the station together, right?"

"Oh yeah, that…"

The universe inside Kikuchi-san's eyes came back to me. The words she said that night were still echoing inside me, and yet all I could remember was my overheated brain.

"…Tomozaki? You're blushing," Tama-chan said.

"What?!" I cried, flustered. Mizusawa might lie just to mess with me, but not Tama-chan. I was definitely blushing.

"Hmm, I see… It's more serious than I thought," Mizusawa said, smiling sadistically.

"What's serious?" I said, looking away.

"Oh, you don't know? Should I give it to you straight, then?"

"Fine, I know! I know, so don't say anything! But you're also wrong!"

"Uh-oh! Farm Boy is growing up!!"

"No I'm not!"

Just as everyone was mercilessly teasing me, I spotted Mimimi walking into the restaurant. What timing.

"Hey! Having fun, huh? What's up? What are you talking about?!"

"We're not talking about anything!!" I shouted, wiping the cold sweat off my face.

4

Sometimes the victory flag and white flag are both just pieces of paper

But the next day, something felt off.

The mood was steadily shifting in Tama-chan's favor, and Konno's harassment seemed to be gradually easing up. She wasn't kicking Tama-chan's desk anymore or doing little things like breaking her pens and mechanical pencils. But Konno's group was still bad-mouthing her behind her back. And there was something else.

What they were saying about her was making me anxious.

Normally, they'd ridicule her inner strength and attack her personality; they'd say things like *"She's tone-deaf,"* or *"She's self-centered,"* or *"She's so violent."* Maybe they'd bring up the time she pushed Konno's hand away.

But that day, during lunch, they were saying something different.

"Who does she think she is, some kind of tragic heroine?"
"She's a real slut, conning those guys."

At first, I didn't understand what they meant. But after a second, it clicked. And if I was right…then we were in trouble.

I decided to bring it up with Mizusawa after school.

"Mizusawa."

"What? What's up?" he said, spinning a fat mechanical pencil around in his hand.

"Can I talk to you?"

I motioned for him to follow me. We couldn't exactly talk about it in class. He nodded, not looking especially suspicious, and followed me to the stair landing.

"What's wrong?"

"Well, actually..."

I lowered my voice and told him what I'd overheard at lunch. I told him how the gossip had changed, and what they were calling her: *"tragic heroine"* and *"slut."* He frowned and tapped the floor with the tip of his slipper.

"I guess we were...kind of stupid."

I nodded. My own worries matched up with what Mizusawa had just said. In other words...

"I'm guessing someone saw the four of us at the restaurant yesterday."

It probably happened before Mimimi got there, when it was just Tama-chan, Mizusawa, Takei, and me. Either Konno or one of her groupies had seen us.

Mizusawa nodded. "Probably. If you think about it, it would look like three guys were protecting her. Erika wouldn't be happy about that...and now here we are."

"Yeah..."

"No matter how you slice it, going to that place near school was risky. Kids from our class go there all the time... Damn it, we got too excited because our plan was working..."

Mizusawa bit his lip regretfully. He was right. Hinami had even warned Nakamura and Izumi to watch where they went together on the weekends. Obviously, a restaurant near school would be out of the question.

We were both silent for a while. Part of our strategy to help Tama-chan had backfired. Just when her situation was improving, we'd set off the source of all the problems, and now we were regressing. There was no point in getting depressed about it, though. Focusing on our next steps, I told Mizusawa what I was thinking.

"There's a chance Konno's harassment could escalate because of this, isn't there?"

He frowned.

"Definitely. Konno hates that stuff, and it's worse because Takei and I were there."

"Because you're part of a group that's friends with her?"

"Yeah," Mizusawa said, leaning against the wall. "…Well, at least Shuji wasn't there."

A shiver went down my back as I imagined that scenario.

"I can imagine how bad that would have been…"

Seeing the guy she liked helping out the girl she hated would have infuriated her. She probably would have taken all that rage out on Tama-chan, too. The backlash would be insane.

Mizusawa licked his lips, looking less calm and cool than usual.

"But the situation still sucks. From now on…we probably need to pay more attention to Erika's attacks than the class mood."

I nodded in agreement. "You're right… She's been careful not to leave any tracks, but now that we've pissed her off, she might start to do more dramatic things."

Mizusawa nodded.

"Let's try to keep someone with Tama-chan at all times. Mimimi and Hinami are already doing that, but we can help out, too."

"Got it. And when Mimimi and Hinami are with her, we'd better keep an eye on her stuff."

"True. We don't know what she might do."

"Okay."

Having agreed on a plan, we headed back toward the classroom. If the situation was deteriorating, we'd act fast and do everything we could. As usual, talking it over with someone else brought out ideas I wouldn't have had on my own. If we took one step at a time toward our goal, we should be able to achieve it eventually, just like we'd done for the class mood. I was mulling over this as we walked along.

But a few minutes later, the ominous cloud was back.

We were too late.

* * *

The second we walked into the classroom, I sensed something was wrong. It was strangely quiet, considering school was over. Mizusawa must have sensed it, too, because he stopped near the door and looked around. Finally, the two of us realized what was going on. All eyes were on a single point in the room.

Tama-chan was sitting between Hinami and Mimimi, shivering. Mizusawa and I looked at each other. We didn't know what had happened, but we knew it was serious. The near-invincible Tama-chan looked weak and broken. Something was terribly wrong.

While I was looking at Tama-chan, Mizusawa walked quietly over to Nakamura and Takei, probably to ask them what the damage was. I followed him.

"What's going on?" Mizusawa whispered to Nakamura.

"Not sure," Nakamura whispered back.

"You don't know?" Mizusawa asked. Nakamura frowned.

"Not really. Something about her charm?"

As soon as he said it, a bad feeling shot through me. Right away, my mind went to one possibility.

A charm.

Tama-chan with her head down.

Erika Konno, more pissed off than ever.

No way.

I rushed over to Tama-chan. Everyone stared at me because that wasn't exactly the acceptable thing to do. But I didn't care.

I walked right up to Tama-chan—and that's when I saw it. She was sitting there with Hinami and Mimimi trying to soothe her, gripping the striped character that looked like an ancient clay haniwa sculpture.

Its back was ripped open.

I stood there in a wordless daze.

"I'm so sorry… This was a gift from you, Minmi, and…," Tama-chan said in a quaking voice, still looking down.

Mimimi smiled reassuringly and rubbed her back.

"What are you talking about? You didn't do anything! We'll just buy another one, okay?"

"But…you gave one to all of us that time…"

"Don't worry about that! We'll all get matching ones again! Okay?"

Mimimi's cheerful words didn't seem to be reaching Tama-chan. She was tracing the roughly torn fabric over and over again with her finger, like she was imprinting it with her horrible regret. I was also sure that charm meant a lot to her. Behind her facade, Mimimi had to know what Tama-chan was trying to say. But there was nothing she could do about it, so all she could do was try to soothe her a little.

"I'm so sorry, Minmi…"

Tama-chan kept apologizing to Mimimi, even though she hadn't done anything wrong. But that one-of-a-kind gift she'd received from Mimimi had been damaged.

"I'm so sorry…"

That was the most honest thing she could say. After all, everything she'd been doing had been to protect Mimimi. I stared at the two of them, unable to speak. My gaze met Tama-chan's.

"Tomozaki…"

"Yeah?" I tried to answer as gently as possible. Her eyes were filled with tears.

"Konno and her friends were still in class when I found it."

She stared at the charm.

"They were?"

"Yeah. I almost exploded and yelled at them."

"…Uh-huh."

"But you, and Mizusawa, and Takei, and Fuka-chan—all of you were trying to help me, right?"

"…Yeah."

"I didn't want to undo all our work…so I didn't say anything."

"…You didn't? That must have been hard."

All I could do was listen. She bit her lip in frustration and let out a shuddery sigh.

"I held it in, though. It was really hard." Then, as if a dam had broken, her next words left her mouth like a wail. "But I just want to run away..."

I ground my teeth together. Tama-chan had been so strong. But now even she wanted to run.

Tama-chan stayed true to her core, no matter what, even when the class queen Erika Konno harassed her day in, day out and her classmates avoided her. She always stood on her own two feet, persevering and steadfast. But now that very same Tama-chan wanted to flee.

If she was the only one being affected, she would have been able to take it. But the one thing she couldn't handle was the attack on her friendship and the sadness her friend was going through because of it.

"...!"

I felt my head getting hot, and frustration and anger were turning my vision red. When I looked around the classroom, Konno was nowhere in sight, but one of her hangers-on was still there. I didn't know if she was the one responsible, or if she'd watched, or if she had just stood there. Whatever it was, she had probably been involved somehow. In which case—

I took a deep breath and prepared to take aim.

"Fumiya."

At the sound of the quiet, calm voice behind me, I came back to my senses.

"Is that really the best idea?"

When I turned around, Mizusawa was looking around the classroom, his brows furrowed.

"...Sorry. Thanks for stopping me."

"No problem. There's no proof, and our kingpin isn't here, so..."

"Yeah."

I caught my breath and looked at Tama-chan again.

As soon as I did, Hinami—who had been sitting next to her—suddenly rose to her feet with spine-chilling silence. My eyes were glued to her. She was fixated on something far away, her gaze sharper and colder than I'd ever seen before.

"She's not getting away with this."

Those six words were only just loud enough for Tama-chan, Mimimi, and me to hear, and the terrifying fury behind them could not have been further from her persona as the perfect heroine.

"…Aoi?" Mimimi said, obviously surprised by this new side of Hinami. Hinami ignored her.

"Forget it," she snapped.

"…What's wrong?" Tama-chan asked, looking at Hinami with a hint of fear in her eyes.

"I'm fine. I'll take care of it," she said flatly. That was all.

Gradually, Izumi, Takei, and Nakamura gathered around, and Hinami returned to her usual self. She and Mimimi explained what had happened. Mimimi had bought matching charms for everyone, so they were very important and represented how much they cared about one another. And then Tama-chan's had been destroyed. As they listened, they became more and more upset.

"That…is really bad," Mizusawa said, looking unusually angry.

"…Erika went too far." Izumi bit her lip and gripped the hem of her skirt in frustration.

"Tama…! I'm sorry I couldn't stop them…!" Takei said, stifling his voice and looking down like he believed it was all his fault.

"What the hell was she thinking…?" Nakamura frowned and glared at the classroom door.

"Thanks, guys… I'm sorry."

Tama-chan wiped her tears and tried to put on a more neutral expression; her attempt at a brave front only made us feel worse.

Izumi stared at the ripped charm. "Hey, you know what? I've been knitting lately. I can repair a little rip like this! I'll fix it!"

She made an *okay* sign with her fingers.

"…Okay, thanks. Would you, please?"

Tama-chan smiled, although tears still pooled in her eyes.

"Of course! Leave it to me!" Izumi chirped, sitting down next to Tama-chan and peering at the charm. Probably to fill up the silence, she started muttering about how exactly she was going to fix it.

Mizusawa watched and then gave her a teasing look in an attempt to lighten the mood a little. "You sure you can handle that? Aren't you kind of a klutz?"

"It's no problem! I even learned how to make a pocket tissue cover lately!" she answered in a loud, cheerful voice.

Mizusawa cackled. "Isn't that like baby's first knitting project?"

"Uh-oh…my secret's out!"

She glared at Mizusawa. Their back-and-forth was pretty shallow, but it still managed to loosen up the tension a little.

"For now…should we head home?" Hinami asked, resting her hand on Tama-chan's shoulder.

"Yeah, let's get going!" Mimimi said, smiling at Tama-chan.

"Okay…thanks. Yeah, let's go."

Tama-chan stood up slowly. Mizusawa watched, sighed, then slapped Hinami and Mimimi on the back.

"Okay, ladies, I'll leave it up to you two today."

"…Yeah," I chimed. It was probably best to leave Tama-chan with the two of them. Izumi nodded enthusiastically, and we all saw them off. After that, everyone else went to practice, and I headed home.

* * *

The next day, before class, Mizusawa and I gathered around Mimimi's desk to ask her how Tama-chan seemed after they left.

"…I think it was a huge shock for her. I've never seen her like that before," she said dejectedly. Mizusawa nodded.

"Doesn't surprise me. They really crossed a line." In place of his usual soft tone, anger shaded his words.

"Did she seem like she was feeling any better?" I asked.

Mimimi tilted her head. "When we were walking home, she was smiling and saying she was fine, but I felt like she was faking it…"

"Hmm…"

I looked down. Tama-chan was definitely putting on a strong front so she wouldn't hurt Mimimi anymore. She had that kind of strength and kindness.

"For now, let's all stick by her side. Given what happened yesterday, we don't know what they'll do," Mizusawa said, looking around the classroom. Konno and Tama-chan weren't there yet, but the air was more strained than usual.

Just then, I noticed Hinami talking to Akiyama, like she had been all last week. I didn't know what she was up to, but after what had happened the day before, it was unusual that she wasn't speaking with us.

The whole day, we protected Tama-chan, and aside from her decoy mechanical pencil leads, nothing of hers was damaged by the end of the day.

And then after school, it happened.

* * *

After our final homeroom of the day, everyone was chatting and enjoying their newfound freedom. Konno came back into the classroom from the bathroom or something with a couple of her friends, walked over to her desk, and went pale.

"What? What the hell?"

The outraged voice of the queen rang through the classroom, commanding everyone's attention.

"Who broke these?"

Her tone was extremely domineering. Those three, short words were so intense that they ripped right through the casual conversation.

Konno was gripping a case of mechanical pencil lead in her hands.

In other words, someone had broken her lead. I couldn't see the details, but judging from her voice, the evidence pointed to a deliberate attack rather than an accident.

But who had done it?

Konno glared around the classroom. Everyone was watching silently to see what would happen. Finally, her eyes landed on one person.

"Natsubayashi."

Tama-chan's eyes went round with surprise, and she paused for a moment as her mind worked. I know her training was to thank for the fact that she didn't immediately explode. She was probably searching for the words and tone that wouldn't escalate the situation. The air was thick enough to cut with a knife.

But it wasn't Tama-chan who broke the silence. It was someone in the middle of the room.

"Hanabi was with me until a second ago."

Another top-level girl. Not the queen, but the perfect heroine. Hinami. Konno turned slowly toward her, taking her in.

"...What? Why are you getting involved?"

Konno didn't try to hide her anger at all. Hinami was smiling softly, but her eyes said she could not care less.

"Because I can prove that it wasn't Hanabi who did it. That's all," she said in a leisurely tone.

"...Hmm."

The verbal rally alternated between cold on one side and warm but extremely confident on the other.

"I mean, are you sure someone did that on purpose? Maybe they just fell."

"If they could take themselves out of the case and fall, then you might be right."

Every time the fireworks exploded, the mood in the classroom grew tenser. With good reason. The two of them had essentially stayed out of each other's territory up to this point. They were the two most important figures in class, and they shared the top spot. Now they were suddenly facing off.

"Anyway, it wasn't Hanabi. Lots of other people saw her with me."

"...Is that so?"

Finally, Konno looked away, maybe because she'd given up, and sighed grumpily. Then she turned back toward the classroom, her gaze crawling over each student like a snake until finally, it stopped. This time, she was glaring at Akiyama.

"Then it must have been you."

"...What?" Akiyama sounded surprised and angry at the same time.

"Don't play dumb. I'm saying you did it."

"...No I didn't."

"Then who?"

"Why are you asking me? I have no idea."

"What's with your attitude?" Konno frowned.

"Because you're accusing me of something without any proof? ... Come on."

Akiyama sounded hesitant and scared, but also like she was trying to psyche herself up for a fight. Konno tapped the floor angrily and glared intimidatingly. Akiyama shrank in on herself a bit, but she didn't look away.

The showdown felt slightly unnatural to me. As far as I'd heard, Akiyama was picked on more than anyone else in Konno's group. She was the one who had to do the dirty jobs. Now for some reason, despite her fear, she was fighting back hard against Konno. Someone must be backing her up.

"Proof? What's that supposed to mean? Anyway, you've been acting weird since last week."

Akiyama raised her eyebrows in surprise. "What do you mean, 'weird'?"

"You haven't been getting along with us. You've been hanging out with other people, haven't you?"

I'm sure she meant Hinami. After all, the two of them were together all of last week. I suspected she was up to something, but I never managed to solve the puzzle. Then today, Akiyama was taking more of a stand than usual, almost like she had backup now. Plus, there was everything I'd learned about her position from Mizusawa. Hinami's plan was coming partly into focus.

"I have no idea what you're talking about." Akiyama was playing dumb now.

I wasn't sure how accurately Hinami predicted the current situation. But if anyone was supporting Akiyama, it was definitely her.

What I still didn't know was how, exactly, or why. I doubt she'd do something as childish as have Akiyama break Konno's pencil leads for revenge. Then what?

"I mean, I can do what I want, can't I?" Akiyama said, looking down and sounding slightly panicked. Perhaps seeing an opening, Konno laughed derisively.

"Oh, you can, huh? You can't handle getting teased, so you think you'll just move over to their group? And then you'll get your stupid little revenge? God, how dumb are you? Yeah, I can see exactly what you're up to, so watch yourself." She took the offensive, giving Akiyama a haughty, hate-filled smile.

Akiyama glared silently at Konno for a moment. I could see the hatred and anger in her eyes as she appeared to come to a decision. She smiled back derisively at Konno.

"You're the one who looks like a stupid middle schooler in that black off-shoulder thing you always wear."

The classroom went silent. I didn't think the tension could get any worse, but I was wrong. Izumi covered her mouth with both hands in complete shock.

Konno bore down on Akiyama like some switch had just been flipped inside her. "What did you just say?"

Her voice was filled with a different kind of anger than before. I could see it in her face, too—it was something like urgency. But even though Akiyama glanced away a couple of times, she didn't fold. Her next words were like a fan building up the weakening flames inside her.

"...I said, whenever you wear that off-shoulder thing, you look like a stupid middle schooler. And...you're bad at putting on lashes. Right now, they look super fake." Akiyama pointed at her own eyes.

"You'd better shut your mouth!" Konno hissed, taking another step toward Akiyama. And then she pounced.

"Ahhh!"

Akiyama lost her balance and hit the desk behind her with a *bang*. The pens and pencils sitting on top of it went flying. She pressed her hand to her right eye and crumpled forward at the waist. Konno must have shoved her finger right into her eye.

"Shit..."

Konno floundered for a second. Maybe because she guessed what had happened, she sputtered in panic. Based on her reaction, I didn't think she meant to hurt Akiyama that badly. She'd probably just reacted impulsively after everything Akiyama said.

"A-are you okay...?" one of Konno's followers asked, crouching next to Akiyama. "Erika, that was too far..."

She said it softly, but unmistakably.

That was the trigger for the mood to start shifting.

It was very simple. Up to this point, Konno had limited her actions to things no one could criticize her for. But she'd just crossed the line. I remembered something Izumi had told me about Konno.

Erika was super picky about her clothes and makeup, she'd said.

Akiyama had aimed her attack right where it hurt the most.

I realized something else. Nothing made the proud Konno angrier than if someone she viewed as beneath her mocked her for the things she was most sensitive about. It wasn't surprising at all that she'd lashed out.

The question was, why had someone as low-ranking as Akiyama been able to hit Erika's most vulnerable spot? It was unnatural—but totally possible if someone else had planned it all out for her.

Someone like Hinami, for example.

I thought back to her mysterious maneuvering. What had she and Akiyama been talking about? Maybe they'd been badmouthing Erika to set up the current situation. What if Hinami had manipulated the mood within their little group to help Akiyama criticize Konno's clothes and fake eyelashes? Before, Akiyama had been subject to the mood of Konno's group, so she'd accepted Konno's standards wholesale for what was cool and what wasn't. But now Hinami had given her an outside perspective, a new mood—a new standard for judging. That would explain why she was able to criticize Konno so harshly.

I thought about what was under Hinami's mask. About her malice, and the anxiety I'd had about her recently. If everything had come together in today's incident, then I was sure Hinami had orchestrated that moment.

She had lured Konno into going too far.

And the truth was, that one moment was now quietly lowering the class's opinion of Konno. A buzz was going around the class, and people were looking at her accusingly.

"Um, Mika…," Konno began hesitantly. Maybe she was planning to apologize; she was definitely at fault here. And if she had a good sense for keeping the mood favorable to herself, like Mizusawa said, then apologizing at this point was completely possible. Plus, she still had no proof Akiyama had even broken her pencil leads. This was still a case of infighting. She'd probably be wise to apologize humbly.

But just then, something happened.

Someone fired another shot, aimed right at her moment of vulnerability.

"You should apologize to her."

Hinami's words were perfectly neutral. No frills, completely fair. Just a simple, well-justified request.

But instantly, reflexively, Konno shouted back. "What?! Did you even hear what she said to me?!"

As soon as she said it, Konno gave a start, and her face crumpled slightly.

Still squatting, Akiyama scowled up at her. "…What the hell? You're unbelievable."

She couldn't have sounded more pissed off. Konno had only made a minor mistake, but anyone watching could tell. She'd left herself wide-open.

"No, it's just…"

Konno scrambled for an excuse. Her voice was shaky. She'd let her emotions get the better of her and made a strategic mistake.

Hinami watched the scene, cold and calculating. She took in the movements of Konno's eyes, the angle of her body, and her expression. Hinami's gaze was like a cold flame searching for the perfect opening to overcome and destroy her.

Most likely, Hinami had maliciously lured Konno into making a mistake. But our classmates would never suspect it, because they didn't know Hinami's true nature.

The mood of the class was gradually moving in a single direction.

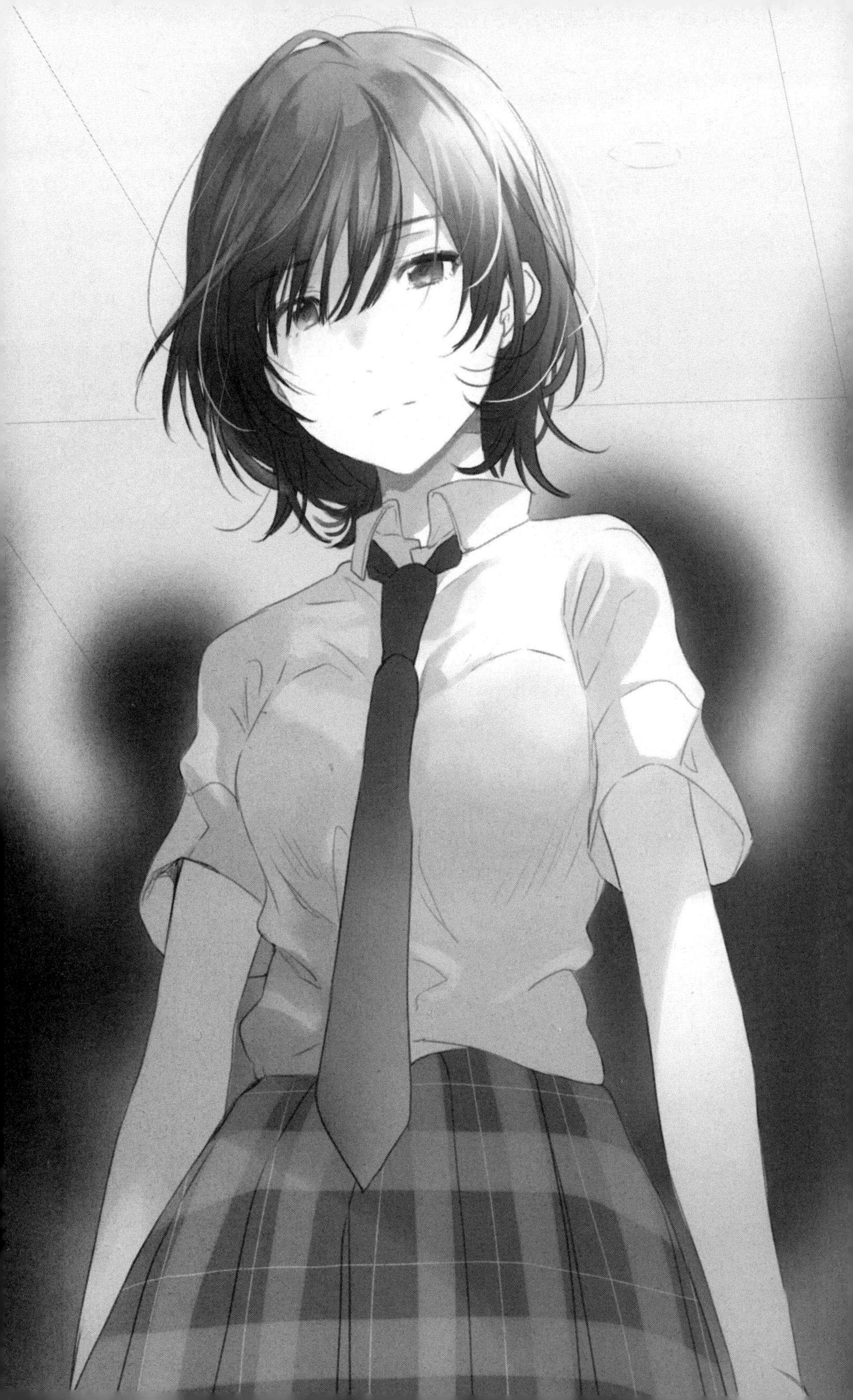

Konno must have realized it, because her gaze wavered slightly in panic. I didn't think any of us had seen her this weak before.

And then there was another short phrase, aimed straight at her newly exposed weakness.

"Erika, I can't believe you just said that."

It was Hinami, scolding her. Her words contained only the tiniest amount of censure, and they only lasted a second or two. They weren't very powerful in themselves, but they were more than enough to demonstrate that it was now acceptable to criticize Konno.

"I can see why you're upset, but why can't you even say you're sorry? That's not right."

Konno's lips trembled slightly. Hinami's scolding was clearly justified, an appeal to both logic and emotion that pushed the mood in the exact direction she wanted. But before Konno could find the perfect retort, the monster that was group solidarity delivered its verdict. The muddy stream swept over her.

"...Yeah, that was a shitty thing to do."

It was the girl from Konno's group who had been crouching beside Akiyama.

"I've gotta say, Erika was totally in the wrong this time," another member of her group said scathingly, staring straight at her.

"!"

Konno's lips trembled. As far as I knew, that was the first time either of them had openly opposed her. Most likely, Konno's harassment had caused so much discomfort that stress had started building up. Or maybe it was all the resentment created by the unfair balance Konno maintained that just barely prevented rebellion. Whatever it was, all of it exploded in that one moment.

"...I'm with you there."

Next was Tachibana from the basketball team, another actor stepping into the carefully orchestrated scenario. That was the spark for the icy air to slowly but certainly overtake Konno and carry her toward the bottom of the valley.

"Yeah, like...ugh."

"Can't she even say sorry?"

"Nope, not the queen."

The negative feelings spread like a disease, malice breeding malice, until greed and desire coated in the language of justice bore down on Konno. And at the root of it all was Hinami.

Her skill and hatred sent ice through my spine. I remembered that indecipherable look in her eyes all those times we had talked about Tama-chan. The class was like a puppet theater that she manipulated without moving a finger. Instead, she manipulated the marionette strings with her words. And now the puppet master was watching Konno with a hint of sorrow.

She was the final boss, the demon queen herself, wearing the skin of the heroine.

"Can I say something?" Tachibana asked the class in general. Everyone slowly looked toward him as he stood near the door at the back of the classroom. He leaned lazily against the wall and fiddled with his hair. "You shouldn't hit people, y'know?" he said, imitating Konno's cool-girl tone.

Every time Konno had argued with Tama-chan, she had used those very words as a surface-level excuse to imply Tama-chan was in the wrong. The irony was bitter.

About a third of the class laughed.

It wasn't a lot, but for Konno, who usually wasn't the subject of put-downs, it was shocking enough. She glared at Tachibana, although not with her usual ferocity.

"What? That was an accident. You think that actually counts as *hitting* her?"

Konno was taking an aggressive stand against the crushing mood. She had no chance of winning, but she probably didn't have any other choice. Or maybe she didn't know how to do anything else.

"I could say the same thing to her."

"So true."

"Doesn't that mean Natsubayashi didn't hit her, either?"

One after another, the knifelike words sliced into her. Hinami was definitely the one who brought forth the onslaught, but I don't think she gave them the knives.

I think she gave them permission to use their own.

The frustration had been building up from the start. But Konno had used her prerogative as a top-level member of the class hierarchy, her naturally intimidating aura, and her ability to manipulate people with her words and actions to suppress rebellion from the masses. She used her position to be unfair, but it was always within certain limits. Even if she obviously intended to hurt people, she never did anything she couldn't make up a believable excuse for. Therefore, she was never forced into a situation where she had to apologize. That's how she'd gotten away with harassing Hirabayashi-san and Tama-chan.

Essentially, she knew how to be unfair without crossing a line. Like Mizusawa said, that was probably why she'd been able to maintain her position as class queen for so long.

But that line had just been crossed.

The equilibrium she'd maintained for more than a year, ever since the start of high school, had crumbled. The only thing left to do was watch silently as the torrent overflowed its banks and washed her away. Or at least, that's what should've happened.

"I think an apology is called for, no?"

Hinami wasn't done talking. She directed her question at Nakamura, who was standing next to her.

There was something odd about the way she moved. She shifted her gaze very slightly and subtly changed her posture and the movement of her arms. If you hadn't been following her with your eyes, you would have missed the tiny change.

Given how clear and easy-to-understand her expressions and gestures normally were, it was a very restrained adjustment toward Nakamura. Apparently, she was giving her all in this act this time.

"Yeah. I mean, come on, Erika. All this crap lately has been your fault. Just apologize," Nakamura said. I could hear how irritated he was with Konno.

Konno gasped audibly. Her expression was close to anguish, like a fatal arrow had just pierced her chest. It was impossible to look away.

That's when I realized Hinami had set another trap.

"...What?" Konno said.

The harsh situation was starting to pull her under.

Konno was still looking at Akiyama, the first one to rebel. She'd glanced at Tachibana for a second when he made his ironic comment, but then she'd returned her focus to Akiyama. I'm guessing her first experience as the target of open antipathy was too much for her, so she naturally kept her eyes on an easier opponent to fight. As a bottom-tier character, I'd had similar experiences quite a few times. There's nothing scarier than people coming at you to kick you while you're down.

In which case, when Hinami said to Nakamura, *"I think an apology is called for, no?"* Konno could have very well thought she was talking to her. Because like I said, if you hadn't been watching Hinami very closely, her gestures would have been too subtle to pick up.

In other words, I wouldn't be surprised if Konno thought Nakamura had jumped in with his own comment, backing Hinami up *without any prompting from her.* And when Konno gasped in shock and stopped breathing, I assumed that was what was going through her mind.

This misunderstanding left Konno wide-open; if Hinami went in for the kill with another combo of words and body language, I would be convinced. Her determination was as twisted as it was immovable, and her strategy was as abnormal as it was clever. What in the world was Hinami thinking and feeling at that moment? I couldn't see anything except her perfect-heroine mask.

"Mika would still accept an apology, right?" she said, delivering the follow-up punch. It didn't escape me that this was the exact same strategy she'd used a minute ago. Just as she said the word *right*, she turned very subtly toward Izumi, who was standing to her right, indicating whom she was talking to through that tiny gesture.

…Yup.

Anyone who was watching Hinami would know whom she was talking to. But to Konno, it would sound like Hinami was scolding her directly. The sleight of hand took my breath away.

"She's right, Erika. Everyone knows you just lost your temper for a second. Why don't you both apologize, and we'll call it even?"

Konno gasped again. That's when I finally grasped the full picture of what Hinami was trying to do. Another chill ran down my spine as the extent of her hatred dawned on me.

Izumi's words had been warm and kind, rooted in consideration for Konno's situation and state of mind. Even though Konno was clearly at fault here, Izumi had gone out of her way to say they could both apologize. If her words had reached Konno untainted, Konno would probably have let Izumi's kindness move her, and the situation would have been resolved.

"…What is with you guys?"

But Izumi's words were poisoned by the demon queen's reflect spell.

Konno glared at Nakamura and Izumi in turn, looking not unlike a demon herself. Then she erupted in a barrage of her true, pitch-black feelings.

"You've both been so stuck-up ever since you started dating."

Nakamura stared at her, expressionless. Izumi widened her eyes in shock.

"E-Erika…?" she stuttered nervously.

I'd been doing my best to observe the whole class, and I was aware of Hinami's hatred. I knew exactly what was going on here.

Hinami had talked first to Nakamura and then to Izumi, getting them both to agree with her and suggest that Konno apologize. That was all. But to Konno, Hinami had directed a comment at her, Nakamura had jumped on the bandwagon on his own, and Izumi had piled on, too. Meaning her crush, Nakamura, had criticized her, and then Nakamura's girlfriend, Izumi, had stepped in to agree with him. From her perspective, they were attacking her as a couple.

Hinami's illusion was complete.

There was the guy she liked and the girl who had stolen him. Konno already felt inferior, and now they were banding together to tell her what to do. *Just be nice and apologize.* I'd never had a real relationship, and even I could guess the level of stress that setup would induce.

"Come on, everyone agrees it's the right thing to do," the demon queen said, underlining the misleading word *everyone.*

Konno scowled. She may be the "queen," but she was still just a high school girl, and Hinami was tugging at her romantic feelings until she could rip out her heart.

I shuddered with genuine fear at the cruelty of a truly pissed-off Aoi Hinami.

"Why don't you two get a room? This is disgusting."

Konno's tone was high-handed and harsh, but everyone was probably thinking about her sudden jealousy of Nakamura and Izumi. I bet that was exactly what Hinami wanted.

"What are you talking about? They didn't do anything wrong," Hinami said. An irritated look spread over Konno's face. She stood up from the desk she'd been sitting on and kicked the leg.

"...Seriously, you two are so pathetic. Just 'cause you're dating, you think it's cool to hold hands and gang up on people," she snapped in an attempt to get a rise out of them. Her tone hadn't changed, and neither had her attitude; she was being just as disparaging as she'd been through this whole exchange. On the surface, it was the same old Konno everyone was used to.

But the whole class was stunned by what they were seeing.

"God, what the hell? Just leave me alone!"

Tears were falling from Erika Konno's eyes.

"You can date whoever you want. I don't care. But don't go around rubbing it in everyone's faces. It's fucking gross!"

The dam of her emotions had burst wide-open; she thought they were scolding her spontaneously, as a couple. If she were right about that, her irritation would have made sense.

But from the perspective of anyone who had noticed Hinami's actions—which was most of the kids in class—Konno had gotten so emotional that she'd suddenly developed a victim complex. What else could they think? To them, her tears were shameful and ugly.

She was dancing in the palm of the demon queen.

"What are you, twelve?" she said.

Same tone, same attitude. Even as tears were pouring down her cheeks, she stubbornly clung to the same high-handed act. She just kept on attacking, like she had no idea she was crying, like she *couldn't* know. Like she wouldn't let anyone mention it. She was so strong, and so weak.

The whole class was at a loss for words as they stared at this strange picture: the same Konno they knew, in tears.

"...Umm..."

That was when Hinami stepped in again. Erika turned her damp eyes toward her.

"I understand how you must feel, but Yuzu and Shuji didn't do any-thing wrong. They just want you two to make up," she said slowly, her voice tinged with sadness. The perfect heroine, the lone, neutral figure trying to calm a rocky situation—she was both the firefighter and the arsonist, acting with meticulously calculated enmity. First, she had orchestrated Konno's misunderstanding, and now she was gently urging her to be reasonable.

Konno glared at Hinami, refusing to even acknowledge the tears fall-ing from her eyes, let alone wipe them away.

"I wasn't talking to you," she growled through a sob.

"Recently…I feel like you've been letting your crush get the better of you and losing perspective," Hinami parried, accenting the word *crush* just faintly enough to avoid sounding sarcastic.

"…!"

Konno blushed. Her tears, which had started to subside, flooded out again.

"I totally get it—I'm the same way sometimes. But try to calm down for a minute," Hinami said, like she was pacifying a child. She appeared as kind as Mother Mary, but there was no question in my mind. This was a spiteful public shaming. Konno hadn't started crying again out of anger or frustration. She was crying from embarrassment.

Hinami's cruel method made use of the soft spots in her victim's heart. Her knife was sharp and forged purely to inflict maximum harm. Even if she was mad at Konno for hurting Tama-chan, there was something awful about what she was choosing to do.

"But I don't…!"

Konno tried to argue back, but she trailed off midsentence. She just stood there, unable to do anything except look down and try not to wipe her tears away.

Honestly speaking, considering everything Konno herself had done up to this point, Hinami's verbal assault *might* have been justifiable until about midway. After all, Konno had jumped into the fight head-on, and that was her choice. She was responsible for her own wounds, up to a point.

But for Hinami to make such a show of her superior strength, to use her words to carve out her opponent's heart so viciously, to make her cry in front of everyone? That was clearly a TKO. Any more would be too much, right?

"Hinami."

I walked up to her from behind and subtly poked her in the back. Knowing her, this should be enough to get my point across. When she glanced back at me, I looked straight at her to make sure she got the hint. If she still didn't quit, I had another strategy. Lately, since going rogue, I felt like I'd used up all my move PP. Regardless, I could still use struggle and flail like an idiot if I had to. Like that one time I flew off the handle, the backlash would be severe, but I didn't have a choice right now.

Hinami let out a breath, relaxed her shoulders, and clapped her hands.

"Anyway, let's drop the subject for now. Sorry for saying all that. I don't think we can have a rational conversation right now. Let's talk about it again when everyone has calmed down."

Guess she took my advice without a struggle. She continued in a lighter tone than before, rebooting the mood a bit.

"Wipe your tears, okay? I think I have a tissue…," she said, searching her pockets. But she didn't seem to have one, so she glanced over at Nakamura.

"Sorry, Shuji, can I get a tissue from you?"

"Oh yeah, sure."

Abnormal merged back into normal. We were all still a little stunned, but Nakamura obeyed Hinami's request, stuck his hand in his pocket, and pulled something out.

Right then, I realized something.

The flames of Hinami's hatred weren't yet extinguished.

"Hey, wa—!"

But my realization came too late. Her pretense of wrapping this up was so natural; the conversation was perfectly smooth. Before I could stop it, Hinami's hatred slashed into Konno one more time.

Nakamura extended his hand not to Hinami, but directly to Konno. Then he looked down at it with a surprised expression. Since he'd simply gone along with her request, I guess he hadn't had time to think about what he was doing, or what exactly was in his hand.

He was holding out a packet of tissues *in a hand-knit cover.*

Anyone would know immediately he hadn't made it himself. So who had? The answer was obvious. And when Konno saw it, what would she think?

"...!"

For a few seconds, she froze, then her expression contorted with sorrow.

She swatted his hand away roughly.

The packet of tissues flew out onto the floor. Everyone in the classroom turned their gazes onto the tissues, lying on the floor like garbage.

"What?" "What just happened?" "Why'd she do that?"

An air of disgust and confusion was rising. Some people probably couldn't see the tissue cover or didn't realize what it meant. To them, it must look like Konno was sneering at Hinami and Nakamura's kindness.

"No, I just..."

Konno parted her lips slightly, searching for words. But a male voice interrupted her attempt to explain.

"This is ridiculous."

I'm sure she acted out of self-defense, in the best way she could. Maybe she wanted to get away from that symbol of their relationship as quickly as possible, or maybe it was hard for her to even look at the thing. But just like before, her defiance had been emotional and sudden—and nearly as unavoidable as an act of God.

But the antipathy of the class had already been ignited, and this was enough of an offense to send it boiling over.

"I always thought she was kind of a bitch."

"I know, right? It's like she thinks being queen bee means she can do whatever she wants."

"Does she think everything has to go her way or something?"

They weren't talking to each other like before—now it felt more like each student was attacking Konno directly.

The sharply honed words were like knives.

"So the guy she likes gets together with another girl, and she takes it out on someone else... Like geez, get over yourself."

"And now she's crying for sympathy points."

She'd been pretending she wasn't crying, but everyone could see it. Now it was becoming a part of their hatred. That was the nail in the coffin that labeled her a "loser" in the eyes of the sneering, snickering, superior students all around her.

"..."

Konno was shivering slightly. She had no words left. The monster of mood had given rise to a poisonous judgment: She was labeled a loser, an "uncool" human, a bad person. She had nowhere left to run. It was mob justice.

"Well, you deserve it, though."

That one came from Akiyama. She wasn't even trying to hide the blatant verbal attack. The new rules were now so firmly established that even a cruel act of aggression was deemed "good."

This mood, which was evident in how Konno was labeled as "bad," added ominous teeth to the get-out-of-jail-free card that Hinami had provided.

Yes, it was all very simple.

Konno had been banished.

Hinami had manipulated the monster of mood, led it in a certain direction, and then set it free. Its fangs were now sunk deep in Konno's neck.

"I'm gonna run to the bathroom," Akiyama said innocently. The smile on her lips was quietly cruel, but fresh and unrestrained. And then, as she walked toward the door, she kicked Konno's desk way harder than Konno ever kicked the desks of her victims.

Akiyama's kick was nothing like an accidental bump as she walked past. She did a windup and kicked as hard as she could. It was pure violence, with no need for clever cover-ups.

Konno's desk tilted dramatically to one side, and the pencil case and writing implements on top of it scattered onto the floor. The class watched and giggled. Not everyone did, but the group reaction was enough to crush any attempt at resistance on her part.

Konno glared at Akiyama, but she couldn't do anything else. Akiyama glared right back.

To me, this was a decisive moment. Akiyama's gaze was clearly more powerful than the class queen Konno's. But the fangs weren't done biting.

"Oh, I'm coming with you!" another former member of Konno's group said, kicking one of her mechanical pencils into the distance. I heard some people laugh. The pencil ricocheted off a couple of desks and came to a halt by the wall next to the door.

The group was out of control. And the flag they were running under was the "righteous cause" of punishing the class dictator Erika Konno. As long as they had their get-out-of-jail-free cards, "good" was defined as attacking Konno, and no one could stop them—

—or so I, and probably Hinami, thought.

All of us, except one.

"Hey! Quit ganging up on her!"

The whole class paused in surprise at that bright, honest, righteous, and purely *confident* voice.

As for me, I was in total shock. That voice absorbed every drop of my consciousness. It was so strong, standing up for what she thought was right. Just like always.

Tama-chan was standing still as a statue in the center of the class, looking around at our classmates as they attacked Konno. She was reprimanding them in the cheerful tone she'd practiced so hard.

"If you do the same thing back just because she was doing it, you're as bad as her!"

It was an incredible thing to do.

For the past few weeks, she'd been on the receiving end of Konno's worst harassment. She'd even had a symbol of her closest friendships destroyed. All the same, when the crime boss turned into the victim, she looked to her own standards of right and wrong, and she didn't hesitate to call out the whole class because of it.

That was Tama-chan's strength.

Everyone stared at her in surprise. I mean, this was basically unthinkable. Even kids who hadn't ever been Konno's targets found her offensive in some way. But Tama-chan, who'd had her desk kicked, her things broken, her special charm ripped open—who'd suffered daily—she was the one who spoke out against the class's persecution and protected Konno.

The class went quiet for a moment, and then it erupted with chatter.

Maybe all these people who believed in a made-up definition of "good" wouldn't understand Tama-chan's extreme strength. Maybe they'd brush her off as a girl who failed to read the mood, like they did until recently.

But her words came from her core, the part that didn't change even when she created vulnerabilities or altered the way she talked. The part that was more righteous and honest than anyone else.

No matter what anyone said to her or how they treated her, I made up my mind to stand behind her. With that decision in my heart, I watched the scene unfold. Which was when it happened.

"After all, *tama*rrow is another day! So let's just start fresh!"

She smiled naively, like she had a playful plot up her sleeve.

"Y'know, so *tama*rrow will be better!"

She thrust her pointer finger into the air so dramatically that it seemed kinda silly. She was leaving herself completely vulnerable.

There was a moment of silence.

"...Pfft, ha!"

From one corner of the classroom, I heard a feminine laugh. When I turned around, I saw it was a girl in Hinami's group, whom Tama-chan had become friends with through Mimimi. Her hand was pressed over her mouth like she was in shock or overwhelmed.

"...Hanabi-chan really is incredible, isn't she?"

Her words, a mixture of respect and surprise, spread outward in quiet ripples. These ripples gradually expanded as if they were taking over the water's surface.

"...Ah-ha-ha. She really is. I wasn't ready for that. But she might be right."

That was another girl Tama-chan had befriended after her charm-school sessions. She gave a bewildered laugh, like someone had just woken her up by throwing cold water on her.

And that wasn't all.

"Well, if the main victim is saying we should stop...I guess we better stop," a guy in the jock group said with a wry smile.

The comments, honest and fair, were spreading through the class like waves from Tama-chan's heart.

It was a sight to see.

The core of what Tama-chan was saying hadn't changed since before Konno started harassing her. She didn't waver an inch. Her essence was exactly as it always had been.

But until very recently, her message hadn't reached anyone. Now it was reverberating through the whole class with so much strength and directness that it was hard to believe.

It gave me chills.

She'd made herself more vulnerable, learned to talk more cheerfully, and gotten some charm. She'd made an effort to be more accepting of other people, take an interest in them, and break down the walls she'd built. She'd challenged herself to work on her weaknesses and genuinely tried to change herself even though she believed she didn't have to.

All of that bore fruit in this one moment.

*   *   *

The one thing she never changed was that all-important core at the center of her heart. But by adjusting the way she communicated it, her attitude toward others, and the influence that attitude had on her relationships, she could now relay that part of herself.

I'd never have been able to help her achieve that goal on my own. We'd reached this incredible moment by talking together, thinking together, and staying strong together.

I think that for Tama-chan, for the class, for me, and I'm pretty sure for Konno, too, this was the end point—all-embracing, all-forgiving, all-accepting.

I started to hear astonished giggles spreading through the class, like the thread of tension had just broken. When I looked around, everyone was relaxed and full of affection for the terribly vulnerable Tama-chan.

My eyes met hers. I smiled slightly, sending her a silent congratulations as her mentor. She returned my smile with a peace sign and a huge grin that lit up her face like the sun. Where did all this charm come from? Once again, she'd pulled far ahead of me.

The mood in class was becoming more peaceful and less poisonous.

And Konno tore it open.

Snatching up her bag, which had fallen onto the floor, she stomped out of the room without picking up any of the pencils and erasers that had scattered around and without making eye contact with anyone.

"Erika!"

Izumi chased after Konno, who had turned virtually the whole class against her. All the other members of her group just watched without moving. There was a very brief silence after the commotion. Then everything gradually relaxed again.

"...You guys are incredible," Mizusawa said, looking vaguely overwhelmed. He was glancing back and forth between Hinami and Tama-chan.

"Thank you, Aoi!" Akiyama ran to Hinami, grabbed her hands, and pumped them up and down.

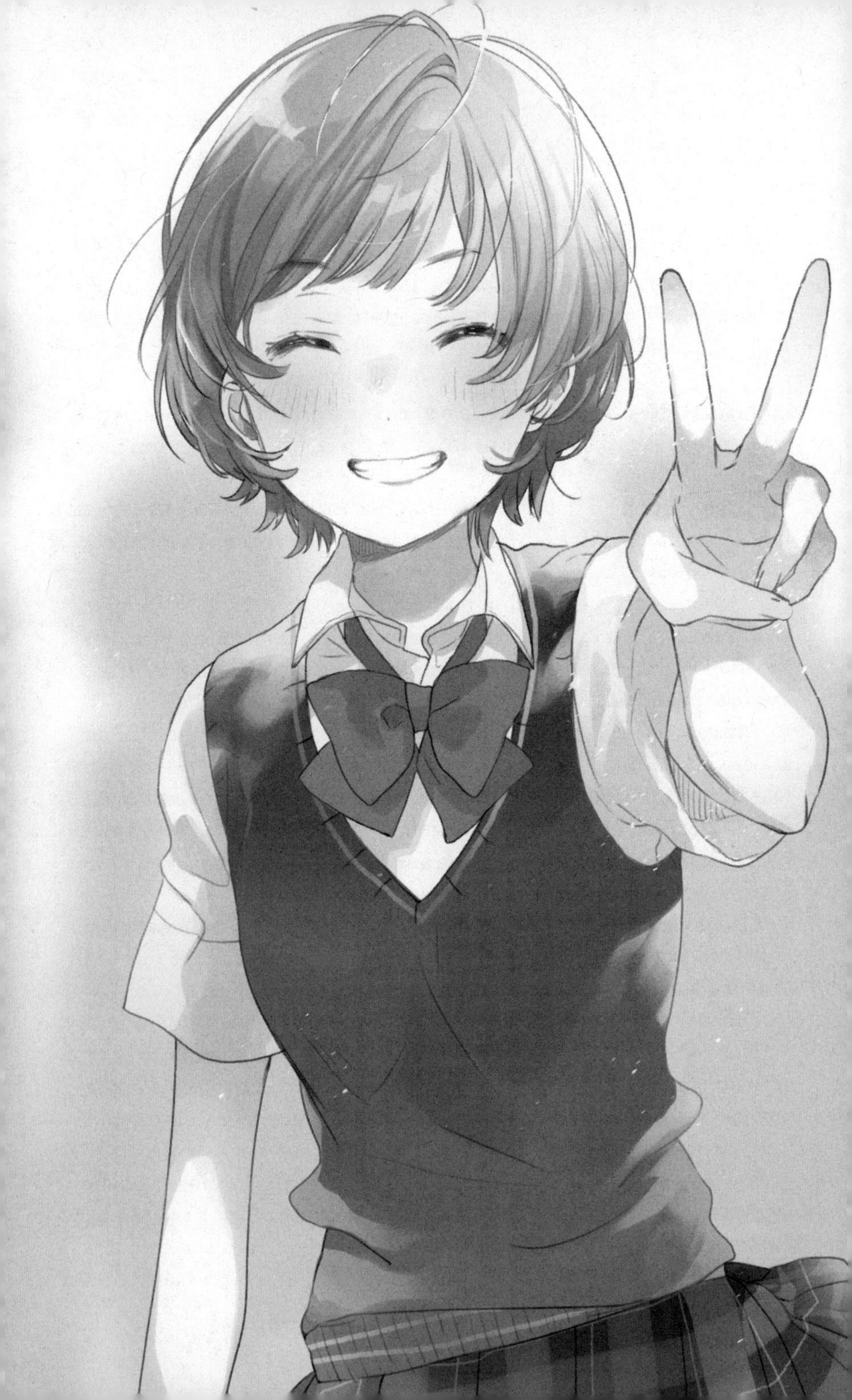

"No worries. Is your eye okay?"

"I think so. She just poked me a little," she said, blinking and looking up, down, left, and right to check before giving an Izumi-style "okay!" Eventually, she looked awkwardly at Tama-chan.

"...I'm sorry, Natsubayashi."

She met Tama-chan's gaze fleetingly, like she was battling guilt. The other members of Konno's group followed suit by gathering around and apologizing. This was the cease-fire agreement at the end of the war.

"..."

Tama-chan didn't brush it off with a casual *don't worry about it*, but she didn't punish them, either. She just looked at Akiyama with clear but solemn eyes and said, "Okay."

That one word and the firm nod she made were filled with meaning and warmth. With that, the tension unspooled even more; everyone was either apologizing to Tama-chan, praising her, or stammering in dazed surprise. I noticed Hinami slowly walking up to her.

"Hanabi, thank you... I don't think I could have dealt with that on my own."

It was so frighteningly superficial. It was another illusion of the demon queen, lamenting her failure against the violent explosion she herself had ignited. But her words were so earnest that no one would ever have guessed the truth.

Hinami smiled kindly at Tama-chan. I'd been planning to join them, but as I listened to their conversation, the urge evaporated. I couldn't pretend I didn't know about Hinami's dark side—and I didn't want to.

"Thank you, too, Aoi... Thank you for fighting for me."

Tama-chan looked back at Hinami's face, as direct as she was with everything, and Hinami returned her gaze tenderly. Hinami smiled gently again and tilted her head slowly to one side.

"It was nothing. You were doing all the fighting."

"...Thanks," Tama-chan mumbled, and her smile grew sad, no doubt thinking about all the harassment she'd put up with. Then she looked down and sighed. Unusually for her, she was quiet when she continued, and she was staring at the floor.

*   *   *

"I didn't want to see you do that, Aoi."

She looked up and stared Hinami straight in the face. I'd never seen that expression from her before, filled with both anxiety and determination. I couldn't tear my eyes away.

She didn't want to see her do that.

Hinami was still probably burning with black flames inside, and Tama-chan must have sensed her hatred. Hinami looked back at her blankly and paused for a natural interval, like she was trying to remember.

"Do anything like what?"

There was no sign of hesitation; Hinami was feigning perfect ignorance as she looked into Tama-chan's eyes. The kids sitting near them shared a glance, confused by this mysterious, halting conversation. After a few seconds, Tama-chan looked away, glancing at the classroom door.

"I really didn't," she said quietly and left it at that. Then she added, with all the charm she'd practiced so hard, "Welp, I better get going!" With that, she slipped past Hinami and left the room.

I was stunned. What did that conversation mean? Had Tama-chan sensed Hinami's hatred or not? Where was Tama-chan going right now by herself? There was too much to think about. I didn't know what I should do.

I noticed someone standing next to me and felt a hand pounding my shoulder.

"You're slow on the uptake today, Leader. Knowing you, I thought you'd follow her. And the sooner the better, right?"

It was Mizusawa, giving me a sidelong glance as he raised one eyebrow and gave me his trademark smirk. Why was he so damn handsome? Anyway, his comment cleared my mind.

"Oh right. Might surprise you, but I operate on instinct."

"I know you do."

We turned away from Hinami's group and headed out of the classroom. I heard Mimimi calling to us.

"Wait a second! We'll come with you!"

Mizusawa and I looked at each other, then back at the classroom. Mizusawa gave a cool wave and answered casually.

"Sorry, Mimimi. This is Team Tomozaki business. You guys wait here."

He said good-bye, and we started toward the shoe cupboard by the school entrance. I felt like I should say something before we left, too. Flustered, I called out the first thing that popped into my head.

"Um, leave this one to us!"

I tried to sound confident but ended up saying *us* instead of *me*. Although, I feel like being able to say *us* was a big step forward for me.

* * *

We caught up with Tama-chan while she was getting ready to change shoes.

"...Oh, hey, Tomozaki. Hey, Mizusawa." Tama-chan smiled awkwardly when she recognized us.

"Hey, Tama-chan...," I said softly.

She shook her head regretfully, then answered in a shaky voice.

"I—I made Aoi do something awful."

At that moment, I knew whatever I was going to say wouldn't have been right. A few minutes earlier, she'd said, *"I didn't want to see you do that, Aoi,"* and then *"I really didn't."* I thought that meant Tama-chan had seen through to part of Hinami's true nature, that she'd been disappointed. Given Tama-chan's unbiased sincerity, I wouldn't have been surprised if she guessed everything from that incident.

That's what I thought. But I was wrong.

"I'm sure Aoi didn't want to do that, but..."

"Tama-chan..."

She wasn't disappointed. Most likely, she'd seen Hinami's plotting against Konno and her sly, malicious attack during their showdown in class. She probably also realized just how cruel those actions were, and how warped Hinami's determination was. Her honest heart and sense of justice were like a light breaking into Hinami's darkness.

But more than that—more important than the awful darkness she'd seen—was the trust in Hinami that glowed powerfully within her.

"So you noticed it, too, huh, Tama? ...That it was on purpose?" Mizusawa said, sighing and scratching his neck.

"Yeah, I think it all was on purpose. Aoi was genuinely mad."

"…Yeah," I said.

"She's a mystery," Mizusawa said, frowning.

Tama-chan nodded silently, while Mizusawa glanced at me. Huh?

"Anyway, Tama, you better go back to class for now. Everyone is worried about you."

"…Okay. Sorry, guys. I know I made you worry, too."

"Forget about it. Just say you were a little upset or something. And you probably shouldn't mention anything about Hinami doing that on purpose."

"Yeah, I won't."

"Okay, see you later," Mizusawa said.

Tama-chan looked up at him questioningly. "What about you two?"

"I've gotta stop by the bathroom. You're coming with me, right, Fumiya?" he said casually, throwing me another quick glance.

"Yeah, sure," I said in a natural tone. He must want to talk about something.

"Oh, okay. See you later, then," Tama-chan said and headed briskly toward the classroom. When we couldn't hear her steps anymore, Mizusawa turned to me.

"My bet is that Tama's half-right." He wasn't being very clear, but I got his point.

"…You mean about Hinami?"

"Yeah," Mizusawa said, nodding like he always did. "…As I see it…"

"Yeah…?"

He gave me an unusually serious look.

"…I feel like I can see the parts of herself that she hides better than most people. The fake stuff, too," he said, resting his hand on the shoe cabinet. "But you know even more about what she's hiding than I do, don't you?"

His gaze was so direct that I might even call it challenging.

"…Uh…"

I remembered something. Mizusawa was sharp. He always knew exactly what I was thinking, so he probably saw through Hinami's secrets, too. Should I look away? Or would that be more suspicious? I had no idea what to do.

But before he could sniff out the truth, he shifted that searching gaze away from me and sighed.

"...Don't worry about it. Even if you do know more than me, it just means she told you something she didn't tell me. It wouldn't be fair to ask you about it."

"Mizusawa..."

He crossed his arms and glanced down for a second.

"You know I like her, right?" he said, looking me in the eye again. Even though he was the one laying his soul bare, his eyes were so intense, I felt like I might have to turn away.

"Yeah, I remember what you said on the trip."

His look somehow became even more penetrating. It reminded me of Tama-chan's.

"I've learned something from hanging out with you and Tama-chan lately. About how to say what I'm really thinking."

"...Yeah?"

"So I'm going to say what I want to say right now. No BS."

I nodded silently, returned his gaze steadily, and waited. When he continued, his expression was less cool than usual, and his voice was more emotional.

"I have feelings for Aoi. But what do you think of her?"

His words reached all the way to my core—to the outlines of emotions I had never experienced before, that didn't even have a clear shape in my own mind.

What did Fumiya Tomozaki think of Aoi Hinami? How did he feel about her?

I dived inside myself, searching my own heart to express in concrete terms what I found there.

Mizusawa watched me silently. He wasn't trying to read me. He was just waiting to hear what I would say. That's why I decided to tell him what I was feeling in its rawest form.

"I..."

* * *

Mizusawa and I walked side by side toward the classroom, not saying a word. The sound of our shoes hitting the floor echoed coldly down the long, narrow hallway. Outside the windows, the leafless trees stood in a wintry line.

I was considering what Hinami had done that afternoon—how her actions made me feel, and the question Mizusawa had asked me so directly.

Hinami had been furious. But even in her rage, she put each piece in place with utter calm. Not everything could be nailed down without some ad-libbing, so I wasn't sure how well it matched up with the scenario she'd constructed in her mind. But Hinami had nurtured Nakamura's distaste for Konno by asking him not to see Izumi too often, and with that piece in play, she would have been able to respond flexibly to a range of conditions.

Which meant the cruel method she ended up using was probably something she had both hoped for and calculated in advance.

Perhaps, her strategy had been a little milder before Tama-chan's haniwa charm was destroyed. But after that, she'd been resolved to wound Konno and use the class mood to tear her apart and send her to hell.

And if that was the case—I honestly couldn't comprehend her.

If she planned all this out—if the heat of the moment wasn't to blame—then there was a dark, deep chasm between us that I would never understand.

But maybe because I'd heard Tama-chan talk about her with such trust...
Or maybe because I trusted her myself as her faithful student...
Or maybe because we had a connection and an instinctive bond as nanashi and NO NAME...

Or maybe…because what I felt for her transcended all of it…
Even after seeing how cruel and heartless she could be…

…part of me believed the real Hinami wasn't like that.

For the past few weeks, she'd been acting weird. I couldn't help thinking her cruel actions were connected in some way to whatever was behind that weirdness.

Was it trust, or a bond, or instinct, or a guess? Speculation? Wishful thinking? Something else? I was so confused, I had no idea what the answer was. But I still wanted to figure out what wasn't adding up and truly understand this person who had brought color to the game of life for me. And once I did, I wanted to keep moving forward. Those were my genuine feelings. And I guess all of that was my answer to Mizusawa's question.

"What do I think of Hinami?"

"I think I want to see who she really is."

5

If you keep upgrading your initial equipment, they'll usually become your most powerful weapon

Several days passed. Thanks to Tama-chan's scolding, the negative feelings toward Konno gradually faded, and while she didn't return to her former top position, she did regain some of her standing in the cool-girl group. Of course, the incident with Hinami meant she couldn't flaunt her control anymore, but she was still accepted. Gradually, she pulled herself back up to a powerful position in the class hierarchy.

Her own political savvy and sense of balance were partly to thank, but I think Izumi's support played an even bigger role. Right after the incident, people didn't exactly victimize her, but they did treat her kind of distantly. Izumi was the only one who consistently stayed by her side.

Of course, the harassment stopped. Not just toward Tama-chan, but the others, too, including Konno. And as for Tama-chan herself…

"Tama-chan, want to come do karaoke with us?"

"Well, okay, if everyone's going!"

"What's that supposed to mean? Feel the love!"

"Shut up! I said I'm going!"

"Ah-ha-ha. You guys are playing around again!"

"Hey, wait! That wasn't playing around!"

"At it again, huh?"

To put it simply, she had way more friends. Ever since the charm-school strategy, people had started to accept her, and then when she scolded the whole class, that cemented her status. She'd gained a stable position as a really good, really solid person.

In other words, the class came to define her character as the essence of her personality. When we had talked about people getting used to her character, I think this was it.

It went without saying that her charm, developed through training and some help from all of us, played a big role in all that.

And me? I was at a restaurant on the way home from school with some people. The group included Mizusawa, Nakamura, Takei, Hinami, Mimimi, Izumi, and Tama-chan.

"Shut up, Nakamura! I'd never do that!"

"Shit, you really are stubborn…"

Believe it or not, Nakamura and Tama-chan were joking around. The charm-school strategy wasn't enough to make the two of them friends, but after she defended Konno, the tension softened. According to Mizusawa, *"he probably just needed a reason to forgive her."*

If Nakamura gave in when Tama-chan didn't, he would have felt like he'd lost. Given his position at the top of the hierarchy, that wasn't acceptable. So he needed some kind of "story" that would convince the rest of the class that it was okay for him to give in. The Konno incident was more than enough to serve that role. It's a real pain to have a higher position than everyone else.

"Okay! Everyone, listen up!" Mimimi said, clapping her hands. Once the whole group was looking at her, she coughed. "We've gathered here today for one reason…"

After that overly formal introduction, she pulled a paper bag from her school bag.

"Reinforcements!!!"

This mysterious military reference was followed by her dumping the contents of the bag onto the table. Colorful items rolled out, covering the whole surface. There were enough striped haniwa charms for everyone at the table to have one.

"Oh wow…," Tama-chan said in surprise.

Everyone else grinned. We were all in on this one.

"Hee-hee-hee. Tama, look at this."

Mimimi flipped each of the charms over so that their back sides showed. When she was done, she smiled wide.

"Now there won't be any more problems!" she said, giving a thumbs-up. Tama-chan looked at the charms with an astonished smile. Of course she did. I'd probably react the same way.

"...So was Tomozaki the one who came up with this idea?"

"How'd you know?"

My heart skipped a beat; she saw right through me. I did come up with this plan.

The eight haniwa charms on the table in front of us each had a red line of stitches down its back. I got the idea when Konno destroyed Tama's charm. If the rip on that charm made it not special anymore, why not rip all the others and sew their backs up, too? Then they'd all be the same again.

"You're an idiot, Tomozaki...but thanks."

Tama-chan smiled happily, looking just a little more grown-up than usual. In addition to the charms that Mimimi, Hinami, and I already had, we'd bought new ones for Mizusawa, Nakamura, Takei, and Izumi, too. We tore them, then sewed them back up. Yeah, I'll admit it was a little silly.

"I worked hard to sew those!" Izumi said proudly. Eight of them must have been a slog; no wonder she felt like boasting.

"Mine's coming unraveled already!" Nakamura said teasingly.

"You're lying!" Izumi anxiously inspected the spot he was pointing at. Glad to see they're getting along.

"Yeah, I was."

"What?! ...Hey!"

That was when Hinami smoothly jumped in. "Okay, okay, enough flirting."

"We're not flirting."

"Y-yeah!"

Nakamura's denial was resolute, Izumi's less so.

"Man, which one should I choose?!" Takei butted in, looking excitedly at the pile of bright charms.

"Calm down, everyone! I'll flip them over again, and everyone can choose the Haniwa-chan they like!"

Mizusawa rolled his eyes and smiled. "All their faces are the same, but anyway..."

"Stop being so picky! They all look different to me!" Mimimi said, flipping them all faceup and arranging them in a circle. "See? They're all different!"

"Really, now? Your eyesight must be great, Mimimi."

"You're asking for a fight, buddy."

The two of them glared at each other playfully. Mizusawa's got a good touch with Mimimi.

Suddenly, Hinami mumbled something. "Huh...when you line them up like that, they really are beautiful."

Her hushed words brought everyone's eyes to the table. True enough, the striped charms lined up in a circle, each its own color, made a vivid picture.

"...You're right. They are," I said softly.

Mimimi nodded with emotion. "Yeah! They're so round and colorful, like fireworks!" Then she realized what she'd just said—Tama-chan's real name meant *fireworks*. "Just like you!"

Tama-chan pointed at her with a smirk on her face. "The fireworks might be gone for the summer, but I'll still be here...*tama*rrow!"

"Nooo, don't take my joke!"

"Come on, guys, can we choose already?" Takei interrupted impatiently. Why was he so motivated when it came to these charms?

"Wait a second! Those of you who had a Haniwa-chan to start with, please pick it up!" Mimimi said, making her hands into a megaphone. What was she imagining now, a sound truck or something?

"Damn!! I liked that one, but I guess it's Tomozaki's!!"

"Sorry, man."

Honestly, I couldn't care less what color I had. But Takei always did have strong preferences.

"All right, now the remaining individuals may choose which one they want! And no pushing!"

Mizusawa, Nakamura, Takei, and Izumi followed her instructions and chose their charms. Incidentally, I think Mimimi was envisioning herself as a lifeguard, not a sound-truck driver.

The four of them stared at their new charms, as bewildered as the rest of us had been. Who'd have guessed we'd end up in this situation again? Mizusawa broke the silence.

"This thing is...," he mumbled. Nakamura, Izumi, and Takei nodded.

"Yeah."

"Uh-huh, I thought so."

"You're right!"

Here it was again—the test of normie-ness. When I got my charm, I was the only one who had said the wrong thing, which made me feel horribly isolated. But since then, I'd been gradually developing my social sensibilities, and my feelings toward these charms had slowly changed as well!

"Yeah," I chimed in, hoping to make up for last time. A second later, Mizusawa, Nakamura, Takei, Izumi, and I all spoke at once.

""""So ugly!"""""

"""Cute!"""

Mizusawa, Nakamura, and Izumi weighed in for *ugly*, while Takei and I were on the *cute* side. Mizusawa burst out laughing.

"Ha-ha-ha! Fumiya and Takei are two of a kind!"

I had nothing to say. All I could do was suffer through my humiliation. Okay, maybe we're a little similar, but something about that comparison just doesn't feel right!

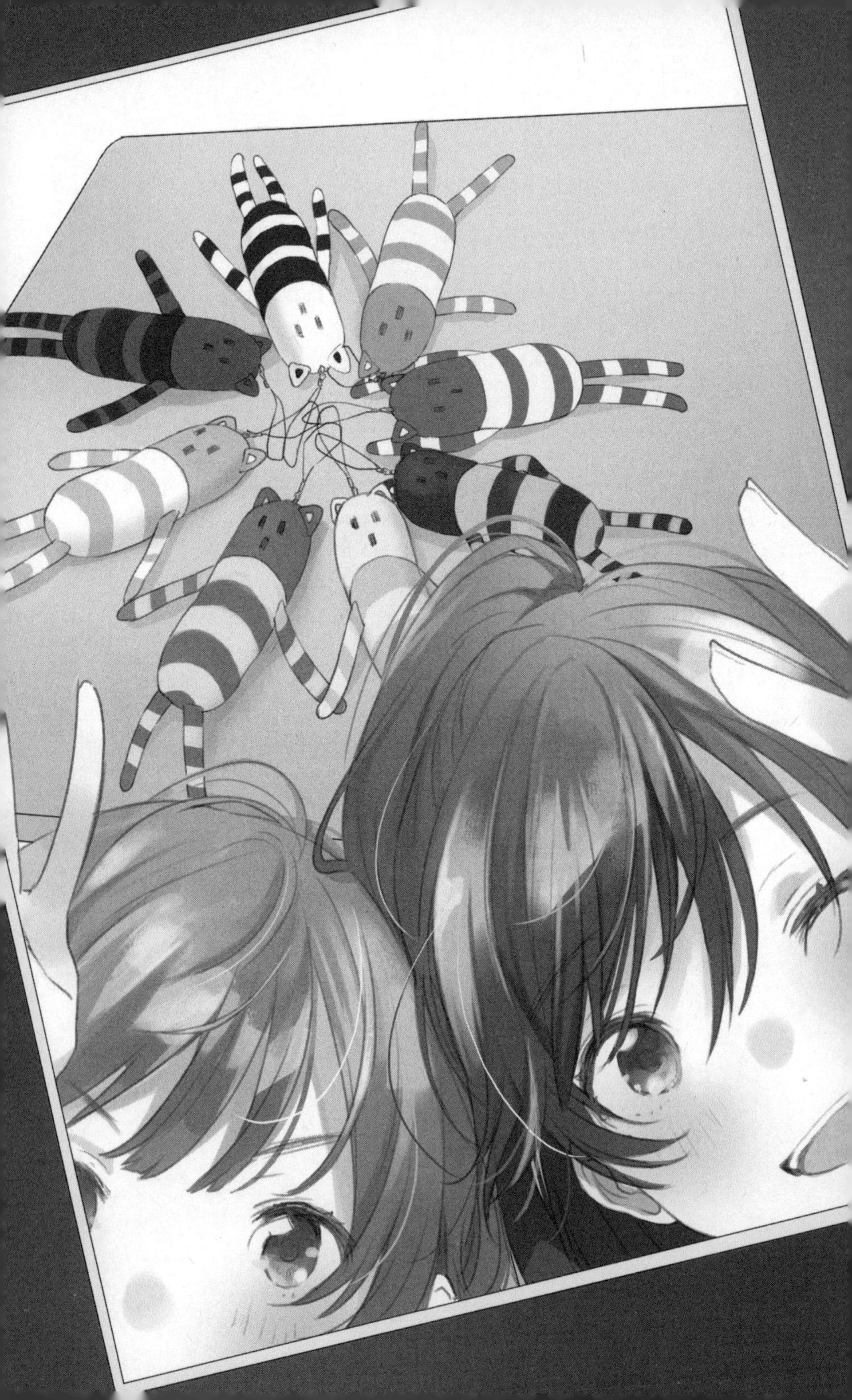

Afterword

Hello again, readers. Yuki Yaku here.

With this book, the *Bottom-Tier Character Tomozaki* series reaches its fifth installment. Life has been hectic since the first volume came out last May, and I'm constantly surprised by how quickly light novels are published. But as I look around, I see heaps of authors writing books at an even faster pace than me. This world is indeed a scary place.

Now for an announcement. I mentioned before that this series was going to be turned into a manga. Well, the manga artist has been selected. Eito Chida-sensei, author of the original *Girls Go Around* series and the manga adaptation of the TV anime *Hanasaku Iroha*, will be in charge of the series. I've already had a chance to look at the character design and names for the first volume, and while it's true to the important elements of the original, it's also full of uniquely manga-style expressions and compositions that I'd never have thought of myself. I'm very excited as it promises to develop into a fresh and interesting manga. But while it's original, it's also unmistakably in the spirit of *Bottom-Tier Character Tomozaki*, so I feel quite reassured as I wait for its release. The manga will be serialized in *Gangan Joker*, published by Square Enix, starting with the January issue (release date 12/22/2017), so I hope you'll pick up a copy.

This series started from zero a year and a half ago, and now it's been adapted as a manga. That's definitely thanks to the support I've received from my readers as well as from everyone who's worked on the project. In addition to my gratitude, however, there's something else I feel I need to share with you: the differences in the school uniform as worn by the three guys depicted in the color illustrations of this volume. Some of you may scold me for using my gratitude as a mere lead-in to my real topic, but what can I say? I wanted to ensure you received my message, so I didn't have a choice.

If you look at the picture, you'll see that while Tomozaki, Mizusawa, and Takei are all wearing the same uniform, each of them sports it in a completely different way. That difference speaks to more than their clothing preferences—in my opinion, it's clearly a reflection of their personalities.

Takei's got the top and bottom buttons on his shirt undone, showing he's here for a good time. Plus, the T-shirt he has on underneath is pink, and his chest is puffed out more than it needs to be. All these elements suggest he's full of himself.

On the other hand, Mizusawa looks very fashionable and put-together in his blazer. But if you zero in on his chest, you'll see his necktie is loose and his top button is undone. Wouldn't you agree that reflects Mizusawa's cool but casual attitude?

As for Tomozaki, he's made the somewhat bizarre fashion choice of wearing his necktie over his vest. Interpreting this depiction is challenging, but what I'm picking up is a touching, trial-and-error attempt on his part to look casual like a normie, even though he's not one.

In other words, these little nonverbal cues communicate the background of each character. The viewer senses that although the illustrator randomly chose to depict this one moment in time, the characters were alive before that moment and will go on with their lives afterward. That's what I admire so much about these illustrations.

Now on to the acknowledgments.

Fly-san, thank you for once again providing fresh, cute illustrations. I'm a fan of you and your quietly crazy appearances on the Gagaga Channel.

To my editor, Iwaasa-san, this one really was a close call, huh? Thanks for all the all-nighters.

To my readers, I'm motivated by each and every reply, fan letter, and review. Thank you for everything.

I'd like to mention this afterword is followed by a special section titled "A Secret Between Two Friends" that was included as a bonus for readers who bought the previous volume at a brick-and-mortar store. Since it was tough to find a copy outside the Kanto region, we're providing it here for your reading pleasure.

I hope you'll join me again for the next volume!

Yuki Yaku

Bottom-Tier CHARACTER TOMOZAKI SPECIAL SECTION

A Secret Between Two Friends

Mimimi and Tama go downtown to hang out. But when Tama leaves for a moment, another classmate shows up… Read on for a peek into the daily lives of these two characters!

Yes, it's true; I, Minami Nanami, am sitting in a café in Omiya right now on a date. A coffee date, of course, with someone I can always count on—Tama. I don't have a boyfriend, so I always go out with a supercute girl like Tama or Aoi. And that's enough for me. Aoi is so pretty, I could watch her all day, and tiny Tama puts her all into everything, which is so adorable. Just talking to her cheers me up. Hee-hee-hee, bet you're jealous!

"Hey, Minmi, are you listening?"

Sitting across from me at the table, Tama starts talking to me. She just bought that bracelet, and she's already put it on. So cute. But uh…what was I supposed to be listening to? I was off in my own world and missed everything. When I look up, I notice she's a little mad and pouty. Uh-oh. They look so soft, I want to squish them.

"Huh?"

I give in to temptation and try an experimental poke. Still springy, even when she's mad. I'm a bit surprised by something else, though. They look so soft, but when they're all puffed out, the skin is stretched tight, so they're actually less soft than usual. Interesting! Some facts about cheeks you'll never know until you touch them. Minami Nanami just got a little smarter!

"Oh, come on! …Sheesh, never mind. I'm going to the bathroom."

"What? You're leaving me alone? Don't go!"

"Stop being so selfish!"

My pleas are in vain, and she abandons me for the bathroom. Ah, 'tis the fate of young maidens to suffer when our plans are foiled. Also, Tama looks so tiny from behind, it's adorable.

I sit alone waiting for Tama and the food we ordered. As I do, someone approaches.

"Hey, it's Mimimi!"

"What? …Oh, hey, Kana!"

She's a friend from class. Behind her, I see a few more of our friends at the register. They wave in my direction as they pay. I wave back. Hi, hi!

"Are you guys just hanging out?" I ask.

"Yeah, we're on our way to the karaoke place. How about you?"

"Tama and I came here to eat. She's in the bathroom right now!"

"Really? Why don't you guys come with us when you're done eating?"

"Sounds good—," I start to say, then hesitate. I love to cut loose at karaoke, but not Tama. She's not a fan of that kind of thing. Technically speaking, she hates it.

"—but actually, we already have plans to go somewhere else. Sorry, next time!"

"Okay!" Kana says and heads back to the register. That's when Tama comes back.

"Hey, you took forever! Did you go number two or something?!"

"Don't talk about that; it's rude! …Oh, everyone's here?"

"Yup! I just talked to Kana! They're done eating, and now they're going to the karaoke place."

"Really? I've only tried it once, but I didn't like it."

See? Tama and I have a spiritual connection. Secretly, I'm pretty proud of myself, but out loud, I say, "Thought so!" I don't tell her I turned down their invitation. After all, I didn't even ask her. This is Minami Nanami's philosophy of kindness!

As we're chatting, our food arrives. Tama's having the mushroom risotto, and I got the pasta with crab cream sauce. I'm licking my lips. It's super creamy, and it looks amazing. This is gonna be sooo many calories. I take a bite and lose my mind.

"Wow! This is so good!"

"Really?"

Tama smiles like she's looking at a little kid. Must be because I'm so worked up.

"Yeah, it's incredible! I think I'll get this again the next time I come here!"

Now Tama's smiling and shaking her head at me. Can't imagine why. I stare at her, and she says, "Mine is good, too." Is that an invitation?

"Gimme a bite!" I say, invading her plate with my fork and helping myself.

"Hey! I'm eating that!"

"Oh yeah, yours is delicious, too! Lemme have some more!"

"Normal people only take one bite!"

Enjoying Tama's scolding, I help myself to some more of her risotto. Yum! Yeah, hanging out in a big group is fun, but this is nice, too.

When our highly entertaining lunch comes to an end, I leave the café with Tama, rubbing my belly.

"Where to next, Minmi?"

"Hmm…"

I'm not sure, but I have some thoughts. Today, I turned down the invitation for karaoke, but one day, I hope Tama will be able to come with us and go crazy. Meaning she'll need some practice for that day…

"How about the two of us go to the karaoke place?! Just to try it out!"

"What?!"

She looks at me, a little surprised. But for some reason, when I smile back at her, she seems convinced.

"Okay…just for a little while."

"I knew you'd be up for it! Let's go!"

We walk toward the karaoke place. Hope this gets her a little more used to it.

So goes another day in the life of Minami Nanami, the bridge between Tama and the world!

Bottom-Tier
CHARACTER TOMOZAKI

SPECIAL SECTION
A Secret Between Two Friends / Tama's Perspective

"And that's why even my mom calls me Tama now— Hey, Minmi, are you listening?"

I'm at a café in Omiya. Minmi is sitting across from me, but when I say her name, she just looks up at me in a daze and freezes for a minute. She definitely wasn't listening. Not that it really matters, because I wasn't saying anything important, but she's so spacey. Wonder how she'll try to cover up this time. I can imagine her being her usual silly self: *Sorry, Tama! Tell me again!* Sheesh. Of course, I'm used to it by now. Plus, I can never stay mad.

As I'm thinking about all this, out of nowhere, something touches my cheek. At the same time, I hear her say "Huh?" When I glance up, Minmi is rubbing her fingers on me with an extremely solemn expression. She really is hopeless.

"Oh, come on! ...Sheesh, never mind. I'm going to the bathroom," I say, standing up. I'm not mad, I just have to go to the bathroom. Plus, the timing is perfect because we ordered a minute ago, and the food should be here by the time I get back.

"What? You're leaving me alone? Don't go!"

"Stop being so selfish!"

I dodge Minmi's hand as she tries to grab onto the bottom of my shirt, and I walk toward the bathroom. I hear her calling my name and look over my shoulder with a little smile. As I head down the hallway toward the bathroom, I glance at the pictures on the menu tacked to the wall. There's a big picture with the words *New Menu Items!* written over it. The pasta with crab cream sauce that Minmi just ordered is featured front and center.

"Uh-oh…"

That's when I realize: The sauce doesn't just have crab in it—it's got shrimp, too. Minmi hates shrimp. She must have gotten excited and ordered it without really looking at the picture.

"...So hopeless."

Minmi really is impossible. I walk over to a waiter standing nearby.

"The girl sitting at that table ordered the pasta with crab cream sauce, and I'm wondering if it's too late to get it without the shrimp."

"Wait a second; I'll go check for you."

The waiter disappears into the kitchen and returns after a minute or two.

"They said they could!"

He's so cheerful about it that it puts me in a better mood, too. I bow slightly.

"Great, then could you ask them to take it out? Thanks so much!"

I continue on to the bathroom and then go back to our table. Minmi greets me with her usual laugh.

"Hey, you took forever! Did you go number two or something?!"

"Don't talk about that; it's rude!"

I was expecting her to say something ridiculous when I got back, but not *that* ridiculous. She caught me off guard, but I'm not about to tell her that I took some extra time because I was talking to the waiter about her shrimp. After all, I didn't ask her permission.

Just then, I notice some vaguely familiar faces by the register.

"...Oh, everyone's here?"

"Yup! I just talked to Kana! They're done eating, and now they're going to the karaoke place."

"Really? I've only tried it once, but I didn't like it," I say, thinking back to that experience. I remember I couldn't get comfortable. It was too crazy, too much energy. Plus, I wasn't really friends with everyone in that group. After that, I've always turned down karaoke invitations.

A few minutes later, the waiter brings our food over. I'm having the mushroom risotto and Minmi got the pasta with crab cream sauce—no shrimp. As soon as the waiter sets it down, Minmi takes a bite.

"Wow! This is so good!"

"Really?"

She's greedily devouring her pasta. The sight is funny to me for some reason, and I can't help giggling. Glad it didn't have shrimp!

"Yeah, it's incredible! I think I'll get this again the next time I come here!"

Hmm, guess I'll have to secretly ask the waiter to leave out the shrimp next time, too. I smile and shake my head. Then to cover it up, I look down at my risotto.

"Mine is good, too," I say.

As soon as I do, Minmi says, "Gimme a bite!" The next instant, she's got a forkful of my risotto in her mouth. So hopeless! She ends up eating about a quarter of it, but I get the same back in pasta before the meal is over. We leave the restaurant and breathe in some fresh air.

"Where to next, Minmi?"

She crosses her arms like she's not sure. Then after a minute, she looks at me. Apparently, she thought of something.

"How about the two of us go to the karaoke place?! Just to try it out!"

I'm surprised, but I guess maybe she wanted to go to the karaoke place with the others. Plus, last time, I didn't have fun, but maybe it will be different with Minmi...

"Okay...just for a little while," I say.

"I knew you'd be up for it! Let's go!"

She looks genuinely happy, which makes me happy, too. And since we're going anyway, I might as well try to enjoy myself!

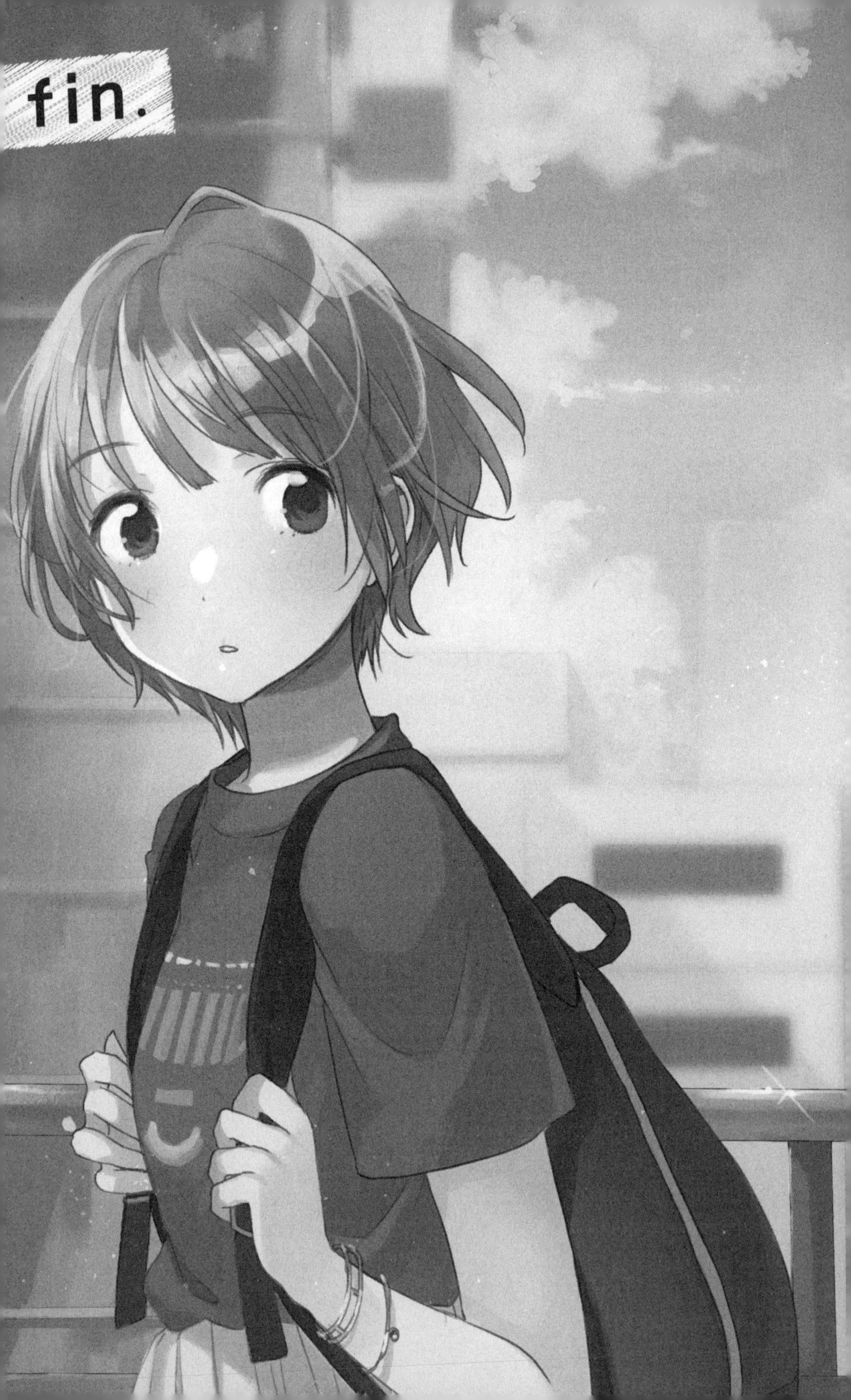
fin.

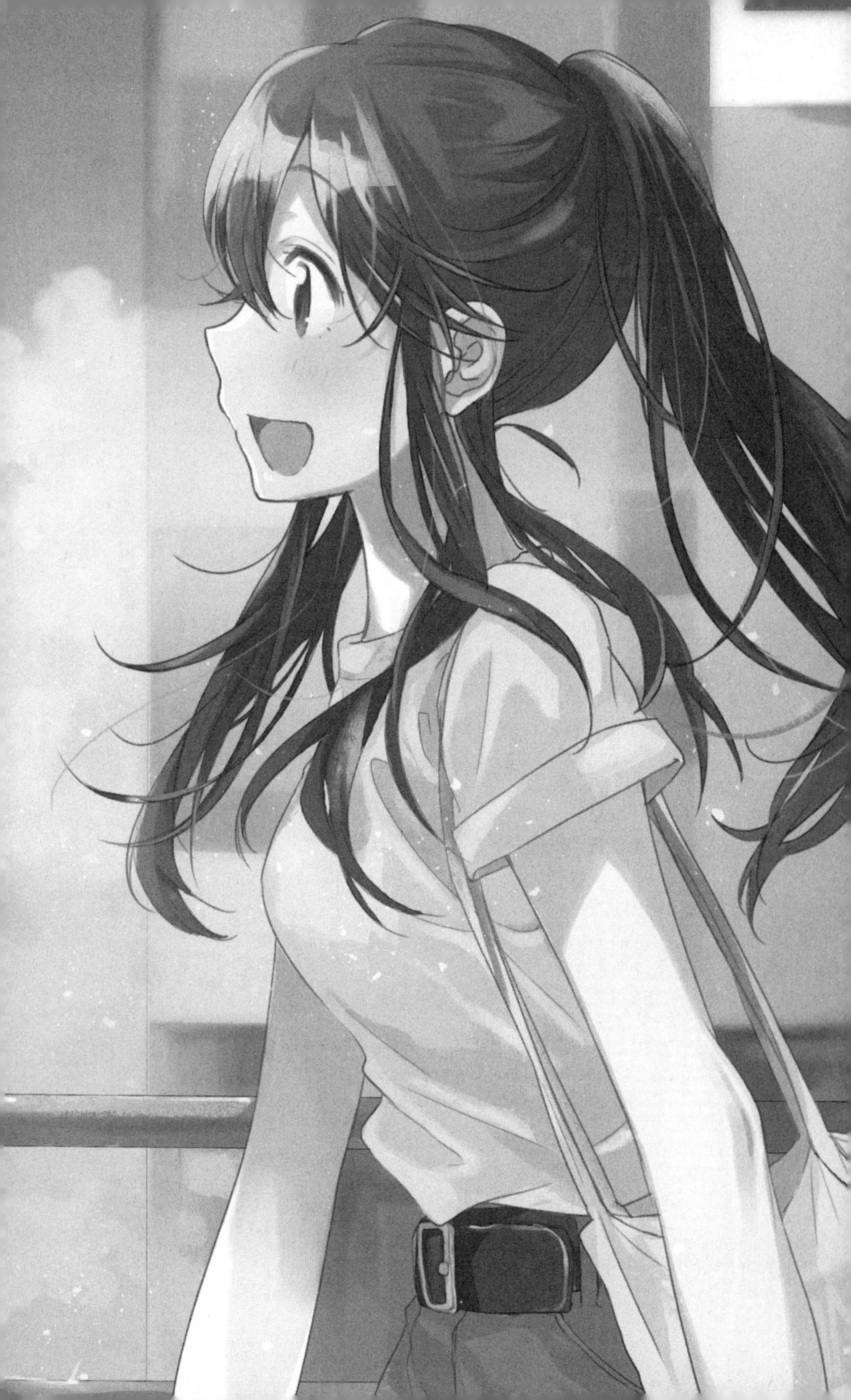

A Loner's Worst Nightmare: Human Interaction!

MY YOUTH R♥MANTIC COMEDY iS WRØNG, AS I EXPECTED

Wataru Watari
Illustration Ponkan⑧

1

Volumes 1–10 on sale now!

MY YOUTH R♥MANTIC COMEDY iS WRØNG, AS I EXPECTED

Hachiman Hikigaya is a cynic. He believes "youth" is a crock—a sucker's game, an illusion woven from failure and hypocrisy. But when he turns in an essay for a school assignment espousing this view, he's sentenced to work in the Service Club, an organization dedicated to helping students with problems! Worse, the only other member of the club is the haughty Yukino Yukinoshita, a girl with beauty, brains, and the personality of a garbage fire. How will Hachiman the Cynic cope with a job that requires—*gasp!*—social skills?

Check out the manga too!

Light Novel © 2011 Wataru WATARI / SHOGAKUKAN, Illustrations by PONKAN⑧
Manga ©2013 Wataru WATARI, Naomichi IO, Ponkan⑧/SHOGAKUKAN